LEGACY OF HOPE

THE STRATTON LEGACY ~ BOOK 3

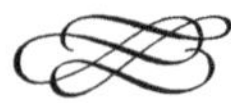

RENAE BRUMBAUGH GREEN

Cover design by: Carpe Librum Book Design

ISBN-13:

To my daddy, James Lyndel Smith (1941-2012), who was a beautiful example of what a father's love should look like.

To my husband Rick, who loves me, protects me, and supports me as Christ loves the church.

And to my Heavenly Father, who gives me hope.

May the God of hope fill you with all joy and peace as you trust in him, so that you may overflow with hope by the power of the Holy Spirit.

— ROMANS 15:13

ACKNOWLEDGMENTS

Almost anyone can write a book. But for me, it takes a village to write a book I'm *proud* of. Thank you to the following for helping me stretch my abilities and do my best work:

My amazing husband, Rick M. Green, who offers just the right balance of critique and encouragement.

My gifted editor, Denise Weimer, who frustrated me beyond measure because she was so *right* about the things I needed to improve, and who helped me take this book to my personal best with her suggestions.

My Wild Heart publisher, Misty M. Beller, who has shown immense grace with my slow writing pace.

To Chip Ricks, who blessed me with the idea for this series.

And to my Lord and Savior Jesus Christ, who died so I could live, and who never gives up on me, even when I give up on myself. He is my hope.

CHAPTER 1

May, 1898

Jackson Stratton looked over his shoulder, ignoring the knots in his gut. When he was confident no one followed him, he clicked to Fury, his spotted gray Appaloosa. She was a great horse, chosen for speed and stamina, and the perfect companion for a getaway. Jackson had studied *Poor Albert's Almanac* and chosen this night for the clear weather and full moon. He'd memorized the route between Lampasas and San Antonio. At the bottom of his knapsack was a folded-up advertisement from Theodore Roosevelt himself, looking for able-bodied men to join the ranks of the Rough Riders.

Most would question his need to get away from his life of wealth and luxury, but few could understand the veiled prison bars that came with being a Stratton. Or more accurately, that came with being Colt Stratton's son. His entire life could be summed up as endless stretches of subtle yet harsh judgment, interrupted by moments of intense anger and abuse, with an occasional, pleasant fishing trip thrown in for good measure. Each day was a crap shoot of who his father would be.

Not only that. It was an endless, upstream swim, trying to convince his friends, his acquaintances, everyone who knew him, that he wasn't his father. That they didn't need to fear Jackson or hold him at arm's length or walk on eggshells to avoid offending him. And he was exhausted, trying to distance himself from his father's reputation for being mean. Ruthless. Bigoted. Cruel.

As long as he stayed here, he had little chance of becoming his own person, apart from his father's name.

His entire life, he'd been an endless ball of nerves, and he'd thought that was normal until recently. The last couple of summers he'd spent working for Uncle Riley and Aunt Emma, giving riding lessons and putting on riding shows for the guests at their inn. Time with them had made him realize that everyone didn't live like his family did. Some people—like his aunt and uncle—felt relaxed and peaceful in their own homes. They were kind, whether or not kindness was deserved. They were generous without being fake.

They had *love.* And it was real, even behind closed doors. Not the toxic, made-for-show smiles that existed with Jackson and his parents.

He'd dreamed of making a clean cut for a while now. Then came the fight he had with his father just two days ago. Jackson didn't know what was worse—the blow Dad had given him in the gut, doubling him over, or the cruelty in his words, in his eyes. It was the worst he'd seen his father, and Jackson had seen some pretty bad stuff in his life—mostly behind the stately doors of his own home.

If it weren't for his aunt and uncle, he wouldn't have had the courage to leave. But the peace he felt in their house and the way they treated their children—Jackson's cousins Cordell and Anita, and Skye too, before she left home—with kindness and encouragement and laughter and that elusive thing called joy —that was what he wanted for himself.

Problem was, he was Colt Stratton's only child. The Stratton Cattle Company—Dad's empire—fell to Jackson.

Jackson hated cows. Stupid, smelly cows. He loved horses. Particularly, *riding* horses. The most freedom he'd felt in his life was astride the back of a horse, wind in his face. As a boy, he saw Buffalo Bill's Western Riding Show come to town. As a teen, he'd spent hours teaching himself those same tricks and developing a few of his own.

That's what he wanted to do.

Dad thought it was a stupid waste of time. As of today, Jackson no longer cared what his father thought.

For as long as he could remember, he'd jumped at Dad's command. And for just as long, he'd wondered what life would be like with no one to command him. Today, he'd find out.

Some might say he took the coward's way, sneaking out in the middle of the night. But Colt Stratton would stop at nothing to maintain control. As soon as the sun kissed the morning sky, Dad would wonder where he was. Look for him. Come after him, with a set of hunting dogs, if needed. Best be as far from Lampasas, Texas, as possible before then.

With any luck, this time next week, Jack would be on a ship to Cuba to fight in the Spanish-American War. It was a worthy cause. First, because the Spanish had taken over Cuba and the Philippines, and natives to those places were left with few rights. Then, a few weeks ago, a U.S. battleship, the *U.S.S. Maine*, exploded—bombed in Havana Harbor. Spain started this war, but the Americans would finish it. Hopefully, Jackson would come back a hero. Or at least alive. And with any luck, he'd return mentally and physically strong enough to stand up to his father.

Or avoid him for the rest of his life. He'd live on his army stipend while he started his own horse show. Who knew what that would look like, but he'd figure it out as he went.

Something crunched in the woods to his left, and he stiffened. Grabbed hold of the pistol in his holster. Silence settled back around him, and he loosened his grip. Probably a squirrel or coon. Still, as much as he hated to see morning come, he would welcome the increased visibility.

Two days, maybe three, and he'd be in San Antonio with a new life and a new name. At that point, he'd be *Jack*. Just Jack.

He just had to stay hidden until then.

~

Two Days Later

Ivelisse Garcia jumped when a horse nickered behind her. She squinted against the sun's morning glow and used her hand as a shield. Still, all she saw was the silhouette of a horse and rider. The man leaned forward, talking in a low voice to the animal. A tall, lean rider. Friend or foe, she couldn't tell. Why did she insist on coming to the San Antonio River alone?

Because she enjoyed the solitude, that's why. Growing up in a busy orphanage made her cherish time alone. And because the patients at the small mission hospital where she worked as a nurse enjoyed the flowers she picked. But she needed to be more careful.

"Can I help you?" she asked, her voice more confident than her heart.

"I'm looking for the Menger Hotel. I'm here to volunteer for Roosevelt's Rough Riders."

Ivelisse took in the deep, pleasant timbre of the man's voice. The Rough Riders were indeed a rough bunch. She avoided them when she could. But something about this man's voice seemed safe. At least, she didn't feel afraid, but it didn't keep her from gripping the stick she carried a little tighter. "The main square is about a mile ahead on this trail. Once you get there, there's a huge sign that says *Menger Hotel.* You can't miss it."

Instead of moving on, the man slid to the ground and led his horse to the water. "I appreciate it, ma'am."

Wavy blond hair stuck out from beneath his cowboy hat. His jaw was stubbled, but not the stubble of a full-grown man. Soft, golden whiskers lined his jaw, glistening in the sun. He was around her age, twenty-two at most. Thick brown lashes framed piercing green eyes, and when he smiled, deep dimples winked at her. He remained five or six yards away and kept his horse, a gorgeous spotted mare, between them. In a different circumstance, she would have asked to examine the horse more closely.

The man didn't seem to have ill intentions, so she relaxed. A little. "I'm happy to help. I wish you well in your endeavors." She turned to go, but something in her wanted to stay, to learn his name, to find out more about this handsome stranger and his beautiful mare. But stranger he was, and it would be foolish to engage him in conversation.

"Wait!" He removed his hat, and his hair lay sweaty and flat against his head. "I...don't know anyone here. Would you mind sharing your name? Mine's Jack."

He looked so hopeful and unsure and adorable. How could she deny his request? "It's Ivelisse."

"Eva... leese?"

"Yes! You're one of the few who's gotten it right on the first try. But you may call me Lisa. Most people do. It's nice to meet you." She stood there another few seconds, but he said nothing more, so she turned once again.

"Where might I find you, Miss Lisa?"

She smiled, and a warm flush fought its way up her neck

and into her cheeks. "I'll be at La Villita Church on Sunday, worshipping God." She said it with a bit of sass that she hoped told him she wasn't *that* kind of girl. Now that she'd said it, it sounded stupid and self-righteous. Oh, well. She'd probably never see him again, anyway.

"It just so happens I'm a church-goin' fella, myself. Maybe I'll see you on Sunday."

"Maybe so. Good day to you, Jack." With one final grin over her shoulder, she followed the trail in the opposite direction, back toward home.

Today was Friday. She could hardly wait for Sunday.

~

Jack didn't need to ask anyone else for directions. Lisa was right—once he hit the main road, the Menger Hotel was on the right. But as eager as he was to reach his destination, he'd had a hard time getting the pretty woman's face from his mind the rest of the way into town. *Lisa.* Her faint Spanish accent sounded like a song, and he wanted to hear more verses. The expressive, subtle way her eyes moved, and the way her dark, curly hair draped over one shoulder... it was all he could do to keep his mind on the reason he came here in the first place.

Lively music floated onto the street where men came and went from swinging saloon doors to one side of the main entrance. The words *Menger Bar* were painted on the exterior wall above the doors.

This was the place.

He found a free hitching post and secured Fury's reins, then offered her a couple of sugar cubes from his pocket. "I'll be right back. I hope."

Inside, it took a few seconds for his eyes to adjust to the dimly lit bar. The bar itself, as well as the walls, railings, cabinets, and furnishings, were carved from solid cherrywood. Even the ceiling was paneled cherry. The floor was red tile, and mirrors lined the walls, reflecting bare, Edison-style lights that gave the room a cozy feel. Long tables lined the room, where men wearing suits sat next to dusty wranglers as if they were all on the same social tier.

Yep. This was where he wanted to be.

Most of the customers paid him no mind. A few sized him up, then went back to their drinks. Jack approached the bar and slid onto one of the stools.

"What can I do for you?" the bartender asked, wiping down a clear glass with a white towel.

Jack pulled out the crinkled newspaper ad and showed it to the man. "I'm here about this."

The bartender nodded toward a small table in the corner where a middle-aged man with a mustache hunched over some papers, pen in hand. It was *him*—Lieutenant Colonel Theodore Roosevelt! He looked exactly like his picture.

Jack nodded his thanks, gripped the paper tightly, and approached his idol. "Uhm, excuse me. Mr. Roosevelt, sir?"

Roosevelt looked up, his eyes tired, a worried line creasing his brow. Even so, he didn't look threatening. "What can I do for you?"

Jack placed the ad on the table. "I'm here about your advertisement. I'd like to be a part of the Rough Riders."

"I wish they'd stop calling us that! Blasted journalists. We're a trained cavalry. At least we will be, by the time I'm done." He surveyed Jack, squinting his eyes. "How old are you?"

"I'm twenty-one."

"You know anything about horses?"

"I know a lot about them." He lifted his chin. "I was raised on a ranch."

"Can you shoot a gun?"

"Since I was knee-high to a bullfrog, sir."

Roosevelt guffawed, slapped his knee, and gestured to the chair across from him. "Have a seat, then. I'm sure we can find a place for you."

Within the half hour, Jack was a member of the 1st U.S. Volunteer Cavalry, with instructions to find his way to Camp Riverside, three miles east, and report to Colonel Leonard Wood to fill out paperwork. Training would be short. They were set to leave in four days' time.

Jack unhooked Fury from the post and led her through the town, taking in the smell of fresh bread from the bakery. To his left, a group of boys and one girl played a game of marbles. Behind them, a scruffy black dog gnawed on a stick, tail wagging as though it had a fresh T-bone. He passed a small church. An inset brick was carved with the words, *La Villita Church.* Would he be able to make good on his promise to see Lisa there on Sunday, or would training prevent him?

Across the street sat a post office. It was as good a time as any to send a letter. By the time it reached home, Jackson would be on a ship to Cuba. He paused, dug through his saddlebag, and found some paper and a pencil. Using Fury's saddle as a standing desk, he scrawled a note. He didn't tarry over what to say. Best to just state what needed to be said. He was a grown man. He didn't owe them an explanation.

Mom and Dad,

I've joined the Rough Riders. I think it will be a good experience for me. I'll be careful, I promise. I'll see you after the war.

I love you.

Jackson

Inside the small building, he paid the postage and deposited the letter. For the first time in his life, he was calling the shots. Still, for all his soldier-boy bravado, something inside felt cowardly.

CHAPTER 2

Lisa arranged her bouquet of wisteria, phlox, and lantana in a vase and placed it on the table at the end of the long hospital dormitory, then adjusted her apron and cap. As quietly as possible, she moved between beds refilling water glasses and fixing pillows and blankets, speaking soft, encouraging words to those who were awake. What would they think if they knew the smile lifting her lips was driven by memories of a handsome young man who might attend church on Sunday?

Jack.

She was being silly, of course. What had gotten into her? She'd seen plenty of fine, masculine faces in her time. But none had ever captivated her thoughts like this one. Was it the crooked smile or the deep dimples? The way his hair sparkled in the sun, like wheat ready for harvest? The way his eyes pierced into hers, flecks of green and gold all willy-nilly so she couldn't tell which color was more prominent? An audible sigh escaped without her permission.

Nonsense.

She pushed the young man from her mind and straightened the bedside table in front of her.

The ward door creaked open, and when Nurse Jacobs's steady footsteps approached, Lisa turned. Gray tinged the tall, slender woman's perfectly coifed red hair. A hint of kindness and grace peeked from behind her stern exterior, softening her sharp features.

"One of our patients has cholera, and Phyllis was exposed," Nurse Jacobs said. "Both have been quarantined, but that leaves us a nurse short. Can I count on you?"

"Of course, ma'am."

"I've spoken to Dr. Williamson about hiring more staff, but for right now, this is a profound loss. It's just you and me and our one volunteer. I know you prefer to attend church on Sunday mornings, but I'll need you here."

Lisa's heart seemed to drop several inches, and she fought to hide her disappointment. "I understand."

The woman nodded. "Thank you, Miss Garcia. Carry on."

Lisa continued with her duties, but her shoulders felt heavier than they had moments before. She'd looked forward to telling Phyllis about her encounter with Jack, but her friend had something much more serious to deal with.

And now, any hope of seeing Jack again was dashed. The soldiers planned to head out sometime next week.

~

Jack guided Fury toward the tent in the far eastern corner of the camp. To his left, men in plain clothes lined up, some on horses, some on foot, while another man in a blue uniform yelled orders. A few moved with confidence, as if they'd done this before. Others stood, stiff and anxious, darting glances. A couple muttered foul words as they tried to fall in line. He locked eyes with one about his own age, whose wide eyes betrayed his fear.

Maybe Jack should feel terrified. Instead, he felt excited. He felt *free.*

For the first time in his life, he was doing what *he* wanted, without having to look over his shoulder. And there wasn't a thing Dad could do about it.

Fury whinnied, her muscles tense. Maybe he should have taken her for an easy trick ride before bringing her here. She seemed to enjoy the stunts as much as he did. But he couldn't very well stand up in the saddle in the middle of an army camp. He didn't want to be labeled a showoff before he even began.

Guns fired, and Fury sidestepped. "Easy, girl. You'll be fine." He slid out of the saddle and guided her away from the gunfire —not that he could get very far from it. He looked around for clues as to his destination. Far eastern corner... There were several tents that direction.

In that general area, he stopped a man who might be a little older than himself. "Pardon me. I'm looking for Colonel Wood. Colonel Roosevelt sent me here to fill out enlistment paperwork."

"He's making the rounds, checking the different training groups. He'll be back in an hour or so. Why don't you tether your horse and come with me? You can get a little training in while you wait."

There were several open hitching posts, so Jack tied Fury to the one nearest the water trough. "Take a little break, girl. I'll be back." He pulled out his last two sugar cubes and gave them to her, rubbed her neck, and followed the man.

"This way. I'm Captain Smith." He didn't ask Jack's name, just pointed to the same group of men Jack had passed earlier. "Grab a rifle and join them. Try not to shoot anybody." With that, he was gone.

Jack approached the barrel of carbine rifles. Ammunition was in a box next to the guns. Was he supposed to load it? He looked around, grabbed a handful of bullets, and slid them into the magazine. Then he made his way to the line, next to the fellow he'd locked eyes with earlier. A line of targets sat about twenty yards in front of them. Off to the side, a man's voice boomed, "Ready! Aim! Fire!"

His ears nearly exploded with the noise. He wasn't ready for that shot, but he would be for the next. The commander wasted little time before repeating the orders, and this time, Jack aimed for the target. Did he hit it, or was someone else using the same target? He couldn't be sure.

They continued that way for a good twenty minutes more before the commander called for a water break. The men around Jack were covered in sweat and dust. Many of them made conversation with each other. The fellow next to him held out his hand. "My name's—"

"Hey! Somebody got an Appaloosa up by the colonel's quarters?" An out-of-breath soldier jogged up. When Jack held up his hand, the man added, "She's rearing up. You better go see to her."

Oh, no. The last thing Jack needed was a reprimand before he'd even fully registered. He emptied the rifle of ammunition and returned it to the barrel, then took off running. When he reached Fury, several men gathered around, trying to calm her. She whinnied and stomped, eyes wide, muscles taut.

Jack slowed his breathing and moved toward her, hands up. "It's okay, girl. I'm here."

Fury seemed too distracted to listen. He spoke to the men around him. "Anybody got any sugar? Or an apple?"

Somebody mentioned the mess tent, but Jack didn't take his eyes off Fury. "Calm down, girl. It's just noise. It's okay."

She reared again, pawing her front hooves, and Jack—along with the other men—moved back.

"I hope you weren't planning to take her to Cuba."

"I was..."

"I'm sure you can get a decent price for her." The soldier to his left removed his hat and wiped his brow as he spoke.

Jack bristled at the suggestion. Right now, all he could think about was calming Fury before she hurt herself—or someone else.

After a time, he caught and held her gaze. Whispered soft words, moving closer until he could grab hold of her reins.

She snuffed.

Someone placed an apple in his free hand, and he offered it to her. Fury calmed visibly, shifting her focus to the sweet treat. But something else in the air shifted as the men around him stood at attention.

"What is the meaning of this?" A middle-aged man in officer's gear approached, his voice quiet but forceful.

"I believe the situation is under control, Colonel Wood." Jack couldn't tell who spoke. Colonel Wood? Great. There went any hope of a good first impression.

"I'm sorry, sir." Jack straightened his posture and stepped back from Fury. Did he salute? He wasn't sure of the proper form. He lifted his hand to his forehead, copying the others around him. "I was on my way to enlist, and my horse got spooked by the gunfire."

"I see." He looked Jack up and down, taking his measure. "You're free to enlist. Your horse isn't. Get her out of here, and come back when you're a solo act. We'll issue you a horse better suited for battle."

Jack might lose what little lunch he'd eaten. How could he leave Fury behind? "Yes, sir." He should have thought this through more. Fury was a great horse but had always been spirited. Dad had an entire collection of expensive horses, and either of the two Arabians would have been more appropriate for war. Even Daphne, the Shire horse, would have suited. But those were Dad's horses. The last thing Jack needed was to add to Dad's ire by stealing one of his horses. Dad was better to those horses than he was to his own family. Especially Jackson.

But Fury—Fury was *Jack's.* They could read each others' moods, almost like each knew what the other was thinking. When Dad was at his worst, Fury was Jack's solace. He could no more sell her than he could sell his own foot. She was a part of him.

Maybe he could board her...

He'd met only one person before coming here—besides Colonel Roosevelt. Lisa. She'd been on foot. Maybe she needed a horse. On loan.

The men scattered, and Colonel Wood entered his tent accompanied by a couple other officers. At this point, the gunfire had ceased. Only a few minutes had passed. Maybe they were still having their water break.

Jack rubbed his hand along Fury's crest, down to her shoulder. Placed one foot in the stirrup and swung into the saddle. Clicked, guided the reins, and began the slow trot of shame back through camp.

This time, he guided her behind the tents, away from the exercises. Still, he could hear the commander yelling orders to line up.

He dug his heels into Fury's flank in an effort to get her to speed up. They needed to clear out before the gunfire started again. Too soon, he heard the now-familiar, "Ready.... Aim... Fire!"

Fury reared and twisted her head. Screamed.

Jack registered her bulging eyes just before she went down, just before searing pain shot through Jack's head and back.

He couldn't—couldn't breathe...

Fury was on top of him. And his head...throbbing. Pounding.

Voices.

Shouting.

Hands on him. Pulling. Tugging.

A buzzard flew a lazy circle against the blue sky above him just before everything went black.

CHAPTER 3

Lisa peered through the small window in the door of Phyllis's quarantine room. Her friend looked ready for a straightjacket. She paced the room, wringing her hands. What she *didn't* look was sick. But she'd have to stay here, locked away, for at least three more days.

Lisa tapped softly on the window, and Phyllis immediately crossed to the other side of the door.

"I'm so sorry," Phyllis said. "I guess you're having to pick up my shifts as well as your own."

"It's okay. I'm just concerned about you." Lisa kept her voice low so as not to disturb anyone, but the sound echoed in the sterile hallway.

"I'm fine. This is ridiculous. I barely touched the man."

"Still...better to be safe. I brought you some reading material to pass the time." Lisa slid the latest copies of *The Delineator* and *Ladies' Home Journal* through the narrow slot in the door.

"You're an angel. I'm going out of my mind in this place."

"Try to rest. You know symptoms may not appear for a couple of days."

"I'm *fine.*"

Nurse Jacobs's familiar, clipped footsteps rang in the adjacent hall. "I'd better go. I'll check on you later. Rest!" She waved through the window and made her way to the men's ward.

A quick glance at the chart showed a new patient. *Identity unknown.* Oh, dear. She hated when that happened. Somewhere out there, his family would be worried. She glanced through the notes. Bruised torso. Possible broken ribs. Possible internal injuries. Sprained wrist. Concussion. She sighed and pushed her way through the door.

The sleeping newcomer was propped up in the closest bed. His chest and head were wrapped in gauze. She checked him over as a nurse observes any patient, trying to see if she could make him more comfortable. After determining he was in the best position possible, she studied his face. There was something familiar...

Those golden locks of hair, partially shaved on one side...

Oh. No.

She sucked in a breath. Tenderly stroked his hair. *"Jack."* It came out as barely a whisper, almost a prayer. This couldn't be about the man she'd flirted with. But right now, she couldn't think about that. Right now, he was her patient and she, his nurse. She turned, pushed back through the door, then cast him one more long look before searching out Nurse Jacobs.

She found her in the women's ward, updating a patient's chart. "I know who the anonymous patient is. Sort of."

"You know the young man?" Nurse Jacobs continued scrawling on the page.

"I met him briefly. Once. His name is Jack."

The woman paused her writing. "Jack. Do you know his last name?"

"No, ma'am." Lisa stood straight and still, waiting to answer more questions.

The older nurse scribbled something else. "Where is he from?"

"I don't know that either."

Nurse Jacobs replaced the chart at the end of the patient's bed and led Lisa into the hallway. "His accident occurred at Camp Riverside. His horse spooked and reared before going down on top of the patient. The young man—Jack—hit his head on a rock. No one knows who he is. Colonel Roosevelt wasn't available, but he's supposed to stop by this morning. We're hoping he has more information."

Lisa waited, said nothing. She had nothing more to add.

"Add his name to his file and carry on."

She'd been dismissed. On the outside, Lisa remained calm, but her hummingbird heart pounded out a lament. *Possible internal injuries.* Would he recover? If he did, would he be the same?

She'd felt drawn to him—could barely get him out of her mind since their brief meeting. And now, here he was. *God, please let him be all right. Show me how to help him.*

For now, the best help she could offer was prayer. And though she knew that was the most—not the least—she could do, somehow it didn't seem like enough.

~

Two Days Later

Something warm touched Jack's forehead. Feather-soft, and then it was gone, and he wanted it back. His eyelids drooped as if loaded with lead, and he couldn't move his head. He wanted to call out, but the only sound he could make was a groan.

The touch returned. "There you are. Welcome back to the world, Jack."

That voice. Where had he heard it before? The slightest hint of a Spanish accent lilted like a lullaby. He tried to place it, but it made his head hurt. Tried again to open his eyes. This time, he was able to part his lids enough to see a blurry, feminine image. Was he dead? Was she an angel?

No. Angels were men. Warriors. He remembered that from Sunday school.

Why could he remember a Sunday school lesson from when he was a child, but he had no idea where he was or who was touching him?

"I have some broth here. Would you like some?"

Something touched his lips, and he parted them. The warm liquid tasted salty, felt good going down. He opened his mouth again, and she spooned more.

"That's good. This will help build your strength."

After a few more spoonfuls, he was as weary as if he'd walked a thousand miles in the desert. He heard a soft, deep moan, only to realize it came from his own mouth.

"Here. Drink a little water, and then you can sleep." Something touched his lips—not a spoon. A straw. He tried to suck in, but a sudden pain in his chest prevented him. Another moan escaped. Why couldn't he form words?

"It's okay. Here." The metal of a spoon touched his mouth again, and cool water dribbled down his chin, then that gentle touch, wiping him clean like a baby. Once more—and this time the water found its way into his mouth. It felt good, but it didn't compensate for the throbbing pain in his ribs and head. As if that wasn't enough, those gentle hands lifted his arm. He flinched as something bit him right in the bend of his elbow. A burning sensation melted through his veins, and that soft voice said, "There. That should help you sleep."

Lisa pulled her chair closer to Jack's bed. Her heart ached for the pain he was in. But the fact that he stirred was a good sign. Drinking broth and keeping it down was even better. It didn't take long for the sedative to take effect, and soon his breathing was steady, though shallow. The broken rib prevented deep breaths.

She was as weary as she could remember being.

Phyllis wasn't fine—she'd developed nausea on day two of her quarantine, followed by two days of severe vomiting. She couldn't hold anything down, even water. Now she was sleeping, connected to an intravenous drip to help her dehydration. She still threw up several times a day, but not as much as before.

A newer nursing student, Teresa, had also succumbed. Nurse Jacobs insisted on attending them, which left only Lisa and Doris, a matronly volunteer widow, to carry on the remainder of the duties. Nurse Jacobs set up three cots in her office, and they took turns napping.

Father Hidalgo—Papa—was the priest at the orphanage where Lisa was raised. He had recommended Lisa for this job with the small mission hospital a year ago. She'd always thought she'd just stay at the orphanage and help with the children, but Papa wanted more for her.

She'd started immediately with the hospital's pilot nurse's training program for The University of Texas Medical Branch. To think she—an orphan—had the opportunity for an education and a career with which she could support herself was beyond imagination.

Until the events of the last few days, she hadn't had a problem separating her feelings from her professional duties. She felt compassion and empathy for her patients, of course, but there was always another job to perform, another patient to attend, for her to grow too attached to any one of them. She simply followed Nurse Jacobs's instructions to be kind and quietly efficient, but not too personal.

But Jack... How could this not be personal? Aside from Colonel Roosevelt, it appeared she was the only one who knew anything about the young man. And Colonel Roosevelt hadn't been much help. He had no paperwork on Jack—said he'd sent him to camp to complete that. He couldn't recall where Jack was from or even his last name. Or his first name, even. Lisa knew more about him than anyone, and that wasn't much.

He stirred, and she adjusted his pillow. "Rest, Jack. Get your strength back. You're going to need it."

Now, sitting here, watching him sleep, she felt a strange kinship with her patient. They were the same. No one knew where *she* was from. No one knew who her parents were. She'd been found as infant in a basket on the steps of La Villita Church with a note that gave her name and birth date, asking whoever found her to care for her.

The church was Methodist, not Catholic. But Pastor James Smith, the man who found her, was an elderly widow and could not care for her on his own. He had tried for a few weeks, but he finally realized the futility of such a task. He and Father Hidalgo—the priest Lisa now called *Papa*—were friends, and Papa had offered more than once to take Lisa at St. Joseph's Orphanage. Pastor Smith finally agreed, and he visited her weekly at the orphanage until his death when she was just two years old. He left her his meager inheritance, which included a small house just off the main square. Three rooms—a kitchen, a small parlor with a fireplace, and a bedroom—for which she was ever so grateful.

Yet she often wondered what it would be like to have a real home...a family...a history. Most of the orphans in the home came and went. Some were dropped off by parents who fell on hard times, only to be picked up later when circumstances changed. Others—mostly the boys—were adopted in hopes they'd grow tall and strong and help with cattle or crops. Sometimes the girls went to live with families with babies, to act as nannies.

But Papa always found a reason for Lisa to be busy or away when potential families visited. At the time, she thought she'd done something wrong, or that something about her was undesirable. Now she could see that, in his own way, Papa loved her. As a priest, he wasn't allowed to adopt her, but he was the closest thing to a father she'd ever know here on earth. He'd even had her call him by the familiar name—Papa—instead of Father Hidalgo like the other orphans.

It wasn't a bad way to grow up. She was safe and loved, fussed over by the nuns who came and went and by Martha, who was their cook and enduring mother figure. But when Lisa's mind was still, when all was quiet, she imagined secret stories of what it must be like to have a real family.

Jack was the same, it seemed. At least that's what she told herself. It felt nice to have someone who understood...even if it was all a figment of her own creative musings.

But she'd sat here long enough. Too long. Her skirts whispered as she moved from the chair and made the rounds, checking on the other patients, doing all the things she'd done a thousand times before. But right now, it all felt different with Jack in the room.

The door scraped open, and she turned, expecting to see Nurse Jacobs. Instead she saw Father Hidalgo. She covered the floor between them in three long strides and threw her arms around his neck. "Papa. It's so good to see you."

"Long week, yes?"

"So long." She took her mentor by the hand and led him to Jack's bedside. "This is Jack. That's all we know of him."

"Yes. I've heard all about the mysterious patient. I've also heard you've taken a special interest in him."

"No! I mean—not any more than I take in all my patients," she lied.

"It's all right. It makes you human. But be careful. I don't want to see your heart break if he doesn't survive. Or if he does and turns out not to be who you'd like him to be."

"He will survive. He'll recover, and he'll leave. Just like the rest of them. And I'll keep doing what I've been doing."

He eyed her suspiciously but said nothing more. How did he always know her thoughts so well?

Another patient coughed, and she let go of Papa's hand, straightened her back, and went about her duties while he went about his. Later, if she ever got a break, she'd slip away to the livery down the street where she'd spent so many childhood hours and check on Jack's horse.

~

How long had Jack been trapped in this state? How long would it last? He was aware of everything going on around him. Aware of the blackest black he'd ever been in, only broken by brief moments of light followed by headaches each time he tried to force his eyes open.

His mind was clear, but he had no strength. He could hear the door open and close, could hear footsteps moving closer, then farther away. He felt that same warm hand on his forehead, brushing his hair away from his face or adjusting the covers and caring for his needs.

He'd never felt so humiliated. That it was a woman, he knew. Two different women, from what he could tell. He was helpless to care for himself, and that made him both angry and grateful for their skilled touch. He'd even grown to look forward to that pinch in his arm, that burning sensation that led to a deep sleep.

How did he get here?

During the long hours or minutes of consciousness—he wasn't sure which—he tried to figure that out. But he couldn't. He thought his name was Jack. The younger-sounding nurse called him that, and it seemed right. But he couldn't recall anything about his life or where he was before he was here. That he didn't want to be here was a comfort—it told him that somewhere in his past, he had another life, a different life than this one. He just couldn't remember it.

He wanted to move. Wanted to get up from this bed and walk out of here—to where, he didn't know. But thinking about it, trying to figure it out, gave him a headache every time. And every time, when the headache came like a blast of Arctic wind, piercing, cutting like a knife, he heard that voice. Not the women. This was a voice that came from inside him.

Don't be afraid. I will help you.

He wanted to say the voice was God. And that caused him to question his sanity.

Don't be afraid. Even the darkness is light to me.

He lay there, identifying sounds around him. A bird, somewhere in the distance. A chair scraping against a wood floor. Or was it linoleum?

Today something new happened. He heard a man's voice, felt a man's touch. The man prayed over him in another language—Spanish, he thought. As he prayed, Jack felt a new surge of strength. Determination. He wanted to see who was praying. Wanted out of this dark prison that had claimed him.

It took every bit of strength he had, but he opened his eyes, then squinted against the brightness. He was afraid to close them again—afraid no one would see him—no one would know he was in here, that he was aware of what was happening. He breathed in deep, ignoring the pain in his chest, and forced his head to turn toward the voice.

The man was a Catholic priest. How he knew that, he wasn't

sure. The priest's eyes met his. He smiled, and the skin around his eyes broke into deep crevices. "You're awake."

Another set of footsteps hurried across the room, and a beautiful girl—woman?—stepped into his line of vision.

"Jack!" Her voice broke, strong with emotion.

Did he know her? He didn't think so. Then again, he didn't know his last name or where he was from.

The girl nurse held one hand to her chest, the other over her mouth, and he wanted her to move it so he could see her better.

"I'll get Nurse Jacobs," she said, and she was gone.

CHAPTER 4

Lisa's heart thrummed in her ears as they hurried down the hallway moments after Jack awakened, and she struggled to keep a steady breath. Nurse Jacobs was just entering her office, shutting the door behind her.

Lisa turned the handle, but it was locked. "Nurse Jacobs? Jack is awake."

She was met with a long silence. Then, "Send for Dr. Williamson."

Odd. "Are you all right, ma'am?"

"Stay away. Wash your hands since you touched the doorknob. I think I have cholera."

"Oh, no."

"It will be okay. Send for the doctor. He'll know what to do."

Lisa's stomach churned—with anxiety, not cholera. But this was no time for nerves.

Think, Lisa. She found the nearest basin and washed her hands thoroughly. Retraced her steps to the men's ward. "Papa, Nurse Jacobs has come down with the cholera. I'm going for the doctor. Can you stay?"

"*Sí.* I'll be here when you return."

She stopped by the women's ward and found Doris, who looked as anxious as Lisa felt. "What will we do?" the woman asked.

"Let's see what Dr. Williamson suggests."

Doris nodded, and Lisa walked to the exit door, then ran the two blocks to the doctor's residence. He spent most of his time making house calls, stopping by the hospital each morning to monitor the patients there. It was nearing five in the evening—he should be getting home soon. *Please, God. Let him be home already.*

She turned the corner in time to see him climb from his wagon with his black doctor's bag. "Jack is awake!" She blurted out the news. His face broke into a smile before she caught her breath and continued. "And Nurse Jacobs has cholera."

His smile went flat. "Get in." He assisted her aboard the buggy before climbing in after her. The horse seemed to know where to go with very little lead. "Catch your breath, then tell me all you can."

By the time they arrived back at the hospital, Lisa was ready to get to work. But the doctor stopped her before she exited. "Take my buggy. Go to St. Joseph's Cathedral and tell whatever priest is there that we need any nuns with nursing experience. Then go next door to Joske and Sons and find the owner—Mr. Joske—and tell him I sent you. Ask him to be on standby for a large purchase of fresh linens. We'll need to burn the current ones. This could turn into a much bigger outbreak if we don't keep things in hand. And since most of our patients can't pay for care, I'm not sure anyone else will take them."

Lisa's experience driving a horse and buggy was limited. She mostly walked. But she had driven for supplies a few times at the orphanage. And she rode horses at the livery for exercise, using the small paddock behind the stables.

She could do this. With a nod, she watched Dr. Williamson disappear through the hospital door, flicked the reins, and prayed the horse was as tame as she seemed to be.

~

A priest walked through the room—a hospital ward filled with beds. How had Jack gotten here, again? The older man stopped and spoke to a couple of patients. Poured a glass of water and held the straw for one of them to drink.

Jack's head ached. Everything ached. He battled against the urge to close his eyes again. Now that they were open, he was afraid to shut them.

The priest made his way back up the ward to the chair next to Jack's bed and lowered himself into it. "Do you wish to talk?"

Jack licked his dry lips, and the man held a glass of water so he could drink. After a moment, he tested his voice, not sure if words would come. "Yes."

"That is good. Tell me about yourself."

"I...I was hoping you could tell me. I can't seem to remember much."

The man's forehead creased into a dozen deep lines. He leaned back. "I'm afraid I can't help you."

"How..." Jack stopped, took a breath. Speaking hurt. But he didn't want to stop. "How do you...know my name?"

"Ivelisse—Nurse Garcia—recognized you. Apparently, you asked her for directions the day of your accident."

"Directions..." Jack's eyelids got heavier. "To where?"

"You can ask her when she returns. Why don't you get some rest?"

"No. I..."

The priest placed a gentle, age-spotted hand on Jack's arm. "It's okay. It is not your time to go. You can sleep, and you will wake up again."

Jack succumbed to his drowsiness. This time, he wasn't sure if that distant voice belonged to the priest or to God. *In peace I will lie down and sleep, for you alone, Lord, make me dwell in safety.*

~

Lisa delivered the message to the priest in charge at St. Joseph's Cathedral, then went next door to the large department store. She'd only been inside a few times. It wasn't considered a place for orphans. Where would she find the owner? Where did she even begin?

A well-dressed, middle-aged woman approached from behind a display of fine china. "May I help you?" Her tone was cool and polite, but her body language said she wanted to help Lisa to the door.

"I'm looking for Mr. Joske."

"Which one?"

She hadn't expected that. "How many are there?"

"I'm sorry, miss, but the Joskes are very busy men. Unless you have an appointment—"

"Dr. Williamson sent me. It's important."

The woman pinched her lips together, then dragged her gaze from Lisa's worn shoes to her nurse's cap, which was probably crooked after her long run. "Wait here."

Lisa waited. After several minutes, she decided to distract herself by walking around, admiring the merchandise. What must it be like to own such beautiful things? And how were there enough people with that kind of money that a store of this size could stay in business?

She tentatively ran a finger along the edge of a china platter, white with tiny blue flowers around the rim, edged with the finest line of silver. It was the prettiest thing Lisa had ever seen. There were plates and cups and bowls to match. She gently lifted the tag attached to the platter.

It cost more than she made in a month!

She dropped the paper tag and walked to the ladies' wear to admire the gorgeous, readymade dresses. So many colors and styles. She'd never owned a store-bought dress. But she was pretty good with a sewing machine. She was just about to examine one of the dresses, to see if she could copy it, when the woman approached again.

"Unless you're planning to buy something, please don't touch the merchandise. Someone will see you soon."

Lisa stood still as a rabbit while the woman went about fluffing and moving and touching everything she saw. Lisa resisted the urge to ask if *she* planned on buying all those things. The insolent thought brought a hint of a smile before she remembered the gravity of the situation and why she was there.

After a time, a, middle-aged man approached from a side hallway. He wore glasses and a suit that probably cost more than a horse and buggy. "Are you the one sent by Dr. Williamson?" He spoke in a heavy German accent, but she didn't have trouble understanding him. "I am Alexander Joske. My father owns the store, but I am acting as manager at the moment."

"Yes, sir. We've had several new cases of cholera at the hospital, and the doctor feels we need to burn the linens. He'd like you to prepare some new ones for purchase. Probably twenty to thirty sets."

"Certainly, Miss..."

"Garcia."

"I will prepare the order, Miss Garcia. But please tell Dr. Williamson there will be no charge."

"Thank you, sir. That's very kind of you."

The man nodded and returned the way he came. The clerk eyed Lisa from a distance, as though she thought Lisa might steal something. Lisa smiled, held eye contact, and reached to stroke a silk shawl. “Good day, ma’am. Thank you for your help.”

The woman huffed but said nothing. Papa always said her cheekiness would land her in trouble one day. He was probably right. But in this case, her insolence felt so satisfying.

CHAPTER 5

Lisa stood in the hallway with Doris, Papa, and one of the nuns from St. Joseph's, waiting for Dr. Williamson to provide some directives. The doctor ran tense fingers through his hair and looked as lost as Lisa felt.

"I think we should remove the non-cholera patients to another location."

Papa spoke up. "We have extra beds at the orphanage. We can move the children to one wing and use the other one for patients."

The nun lifted her hand. "We have rooms and cots specifically designed to care for the sick. Several of our nuns have nursing experience."

"Excellent," Dr. Williamson replied. "I'll send most of the patients to St. Joseph's. Father Hidalgo, I'd like the amnesia patient to go with you. I think he'll do better in that environment. Do you have a private room for him?"

"Sí. That can be arranged."

The doctor shifted his attention to Lisa and Doris. "Nurse Garcia, you go to the orphanage with Father Hidalgo, since you're already familiar with the children there. I'd like you to stay with the amnesia patient as you're the only one who met him before his accident. I've never had an amnesia patient before, and I'd like to give him special attention, so keep excellent notes on his progress. I'll also give you some memory exercises to do with him. Doris, could you help the nuns at St. Joseph's? I'll send the remaining patients there, since there's more room and more help, as well."

"Certainly."

The doctor nodded. "Excellent. Father, can you round up some volunteers and wagons for transport?"

"Sí."

Dr. Williamson looked from Doris to Lisa. "I'll rely on each of you to keep notes about what happens at your locations and report to me. I'll try to stop by each day, but my time will be limited since I have the cholera patients here, as well. Are you comfortable with that plan?"

"Of course," Doris replied. "But what about you, doctor? Aren't you worried about getting cholera?"

"Fortunately, I was in Spain earlier this year and received a cholera vaccine while I was there. The vaccine hasn't become available here, but I'm protected."

Three more nuns, dressed in traditional black-and-white habits, entered the building. Lisa left Dr. Williamson to converse with them while she checked on patients. She peered through Phyllis's window on her way past, but her friend was sleeping. *God, let them be okay. Stop this spread. Don't let anyone else get it.*

She pushed open the door to the men's ward to find Jack looking at her, the sunlight from the window intensifying the green in his eyes and causing her heart to bounce.

So unprofessional.

"How are you feeling, Mr... Jack?"

"I've been better. I think." His voice was gravelly, and she offered him some water.

After a long drink, he said, "You're Nurse Garcia, right?"

"That's correct." *Lisa. We met before. You don't remember my name...*

"The priest that was here...he said you might be able to help me understand how I ended up here. I can't remember much. Or anything, really."

Lisa sat down. Crossed her ankles. "Dr. Williamson will be in soon. He might have some medical explanation about your memory, but basically, you got a bad bump on the head." He didn't say anything, so she continued. "We met briefly on Friday of last week, when you asked me for directions to the Menger Hotel. You wanted to join Colonel Roosevelt's Rough Riders. Does that sound familiar?"

"Unfortunately, no."

"You were on horseback. When they brought you here later that day, they said your horse took a fright after some gunfire. He threw you off and fell on top of you. You hit your head when you went down. You have injuries to your left arm, ribs, and skull. Those are the injuries we can see."

"No wonder I feel like he—uh...sorry. No wonder I hurt all over."

"Does any of that information stir your memory?"

He didn't answer right away. Strain etched his face, as though it hurt to think. Finally, he said, "You might as well be telling a story about someone else's life. None of it sounds familiar."

"I'm not a doctor. Dr. Williamson can tell you more about your injuries, and his information will be more reliable than mine. But I believe most people with...your types of injuries... do recover with time."

"That's good to know."

Lisa uncrossed her ankles. Even with a bandaged head, Jack was the most handsome man she'd ever seen. The knowledge that her thoughts were inappropriate and unprofessional stirred feelings of guilt...but not so much that she could push the thoughts aside. She'd have to be blind not to be affected by him.

"I'd best see to the other patients. If you need anything more, let me know."

"I'd say I need a good, stout whiskey, but I doubt you'd give it to me."

Lisa smiled. "You didn't strike me as a drinking man when we met on Friday."

"I'll bet my head wasn't pounding like it is now."

"Probably not. But too much whiskey will make that worse. I'll talk to the doctor about giving you something to help you sleep."

"No! I feel like Rip Van Winkle. I'd rather put up with the headache."

"You remember who Rip Van Winkle is, yet you can't remember your name. I'd say that's a good sign that your memories are in there somewhere. They'll make their way to the surface in time."

"I hope so." Jack's eyelids fluttered. Maybe he wouldn't need a sleep aid, after all.

"We'll pray so. Try to rest." Her shoes clicked softly on the floor as she moved from his bed and checked on the others in the room. She felt his eyes on her but refused to look at him again. The last thing she needed was for a patient to get the idea she was flirting.

CHAPTER 6

Lampasas, Texas

Riley Stratton stood on his brother Colt's porch—their childhood home—and knocked on the door. The stately porch, the European-imported door, everything about this place brought back memories of childhood—some happy. Most not.

The door opened, and when his sister-in-law, Allison, appeared, he took a quick step back. Normally, she had a servant answer the door. Her eyes were red and swollen, and her face was splotched. She clutched a wrinkled page in her left hand.

"Allison! What's happened? Are you all right?" Riley didn't wait to be invited in. He stepped over the threshold and placed a hand on Allison's shoulder.

"This came yesterday." She held up the page. "Colt is beside himself—as am I. I've given the staff the afternoon off. You know how Colt is. He was yelling at them and was about to fire the butler. I felt it best if we cleared everyone out."

Riley took the letter and scanned its contents. "Jackson has joined the Rough Riders? Why, I read this morning they're already en route to Cuba."

Allison's sudden sob told Riley he should've kept his response to himself.

"I'm sorry, Riley." She dabbed at her eyes with a handkerchief, drew up to her full height, and continued. "I didn't even ask why you're here. Is there something I can do for you? You might want to avoid Colt right now."

"I can imagine. I...uh..." Under the circumstances, maybe he shouldn't state his intended purpose. But he couldn't think of anything but the truth. "I was here to ask Jackson if he wanted to help out at the The Big Skye Inn this summer. The guests loved him as a riding instructor last year, and I thought if he didn't have any plans... I'd even thought he might put on a trick show. I guess that's out of the question now."

Allison dropped into the chair beside the ornate entry table, one hand to her chest, the other clenching the fabric of her skirt as though she was clinging for life. "I knew he was feeling restless. He and Colt haven't seen eye to eye lately, but I never ima—" Her statement cut off with a sob.

Riley searched for the right words. "Jackson's a smart, capable young man, Allison. And he's chosen an honorable cause. As much as we wish he hadn't done this, the Rough Riders are fortunate to have him."

"That's kind of you to say." Allison sniffed, wiped her tears with a trembling hand. "But he's so young. And he's led such a sheltered life here. What if..." Her voice broke again.

"Let's not borrow trouble." If only he could find words to comfort his sister-in-law. If only his wife, Emma, were here. She'd know what to say. "God's got His hand on Jackson, and he will have our prayers."

Allison nodded, smoothed her skirt, and stood. "Thank you, Riley."

"Keep us posted. Can I share this, or do you want to keep it private?"

"You'll tell no one." Colt's voice echoed from the dark hallway. "Honorable cause? That boy took the coward's way, sneaking off without even telling his mother goodbye. Letting us know in a letter."

Riley could just make out Colt's silhouette at the end of the hallway. "As you wish. Still, let us know if you hear anything." He didn't wait for a response. Just placed his hat back on his head and left, shutting the door behind him. He'd planned to go to town after this, but he decided to head back to the inn to share the news with the best pray-er he knew—his wife.

~

Jack lay in his new bed at the orphanage and tried to ignore the two pairs of eyes peeping at him through the crack in the door. Under better circumstances, he'd play some kind of trick to entertain the youngsters, but the ten-minute trip in the carriage—plus the half hour it took to get him loaded in and out—had taken everything he had. His body ached. He wanted to sleep, but his brain felt as though he'd been the loser in a schoolyard fight.

Funny about his name. Jack. It felt right and wrong at the same time. But Lisa didn't have any reason to lie to him. If he'd told her his name was Jack, it must be.

He closed his eyes and tried to remember, but the more he tried, the more his head pounded.

Whispers from the door turned Jack's head to the right. He opened his eyes and asked, "Can I help you with something?"

Silence. Then slowly, the door creaked open to reveal a little girl of about seven—twice. Was he seeing double? Maybe his injuries were worse than he thought.

But no. One of them moved toward him, while the other

stayed in the hallway. The bolder one reached back, grabbed her twin, and pulled her along. Both girls wore their orange-red hair in two braids down their backs. Their navy-blue dresses were covered with white aprons...or were they called pinafores?

"We're your nurses," the bold one said.

That turned one corner of his mouth up in a smile, despite his aching head. "I thought Miss Garcia was my nurse."

"She is. We're her assistants. I'm Lucy. This is Lydia."

"Nice to meet you. I'm not sure I'll remember which of you is which, though."

Lucy rolled her eyes. "Everyone says that. But it's easy. I'm the one who likes to talk. Lydia's the quiet one."

Jack shifted his gaze to Lydia. "Is that true?"

Lydia blushed, and her freckles blended with her cheeks. She looked at her shoes and nodded.

"Do you need anything?" Lucy crossed her arms in an authoritative stance. "We're not old enough to cook, but we can get you water. And I can read to you from my schoolbook."

"Water sounds nice."

He expected Lucy to complete the task, but she stayed put while Lydia stepped behind her to his bedside table and lifted the glass to his mouth. A little dribbled on his chin, but he pretended not to notice.

A tall, shapely figure appeared in the doorway. "I think that's enough, girls. Why don't we let our patient get some rest?" Lisa's voice held a blend of kindness and starch.

Lucy stamped her foot. "But I was gonna read to him."

"Later. You're missing class. Scoot!"

Lucy huffed but headed toward the door. Lydia gave him a quick wave and a smile before following her sister.

Lisa watched them move down the hallway. When she seemed satisfied of their destination, she faced him. "I'm sorry about that. I hope they weren't a bother."

"Not at all. I thought my mind was playing tricks on me at first."

She laughed. "It won't take you long to tell them apart. They're as different as bullfrogs and butterflies."

"I can see that."

She moved toward his bed, gave a cursory glance at him, head to toe, then leaned in to straighten his pillow. She smelled familiar, like a mixture of vanilla and lavender, and when she moved away he wanted her to come back.

Why could he remember that smell?

"I see I have a private room this time. What did I do to deserve that?"

Lisa smiled and glanced out the window to his right. "Dr. Williamson wants to start some memory work with you tomorrow, and he felt a private room would work best."

"Memory work, huh? I've already tried to recall anything from my past. So far, nothing significant has shown up—other than a headache."

"Patience. It will come in time."

Jack turned his face away from her. He could make out some trees through the gauzy curtain. Beyond that, he heard wagons, horses, voices. What would happen to him if he couldn't remember? How did a man without a past move forward? "I hope you're right."

Her voice lowered, and she whispered, "Try to rest." That was the last thing he heard before he dropped off to sleep.

CHAPTER 7

The next week passed in a haze of nursing duties and keeping the children occupied. They were so excited to have Lisa back with them, she found it difficult to get anything done. She constantly had a shadow... most often a set of twin shadows, who were full of questions.

"Why did you become a nurse?"

"Why didn't you become a teacher instead? You could be our teacher."

"How does taking someone's temp-a-ter help them?"

"How do you know you won't get what they have?"

"Can I help feed the patient?"

Fortunately, Papa did his best to keep the youngsters corralled and out of the way. One day, when she delivered lunch to Jack just as he'd finished a session with Dr. Williamson, she found him propped up with a pillow behind his back, rubbing his head. His blue hospital gown held deep wrinkles, and she reminded herself to bring him a fresh one.

"Are you in pain?" she asked.

"Yes. My head feels as though someone's beating on the inside my of skull with a pickaxe."

"Ouch. That can't be pleasant. Other than that, how is the therapy coming? Do you recall anything?"

"Nothing. Well, mostly nothing. I've had a couple of dreams that seem real, but every time I wake up, the details remain just out of reach. I don't know if they mean anything or not."

"I'm sorry. I know you must be frustrated."

Jack sighed, then looked at her, his expression pinched. "Can you join me?" His voice was low, husky.

The invitation thrilled her, and she reminded herself for the fortieth time that he was a patient. "For a few minutes." She sat in the chair.

"Tell me about your past. Maybe it will trigger something in mine."

Lisa chuckled. "I doubt that. I had a unique upbringing. What would you like to know?"

"Tell me about your parents. Where did you grow up?"

"I don't know anything about my parents. I was abandoned as an infant. This is my home. I was raised by Father Hidalgo and the nuns." She kept her voice at a whisper so as not to aggravate his headache further.

His jaw slacked for a moment before he closed his mouth. "Wow. I didn't know. I...I'm sorry."

"Why are you sorry? You didn't cause it." She smiled at him. She had become accustomed to people's pity and had worked hard to learn how to put others at ease. She didn't need pity. She wanted respect. "I had a good life here. It's all I knew...and I was loved."

"I'm surprised you weren't adopted."

Recollections of overheard conversations between Papa and Martha haunted her—news of orphans who didn't fare so well in their new homes. "Yes, well, adoption can be a dream or a nightmare, depending on who adopts you. My family isn't a traditional one, but I was well cared for."

"Didn't you ever long for a...a real family?"

Lisa tensed, and she shifted on her chair. His questions felt intrusive, but she didn't cut him off. If something she said could trigger his own memories, she was willing to share. "I was educated here, with others who were in the same plight. I viewed the other children as my brothers and sisters, and I mourned when they left because of adoption or because they became of age. Again, this is all I knew. I think I would have been sad to leave my home."

His brow wrinkled. "But you don't live here now, do you?"

"I live alone, in my own home. It's a small house a short distance from here."

They remained quiet for a few long moments, the air somehow thick and intimate. She should leave...

Jack scooted lower in the bed. "Tell me a happy memory from your childhood. Please. Then I'll go to sleep. I want to drift off to something pleasant."

She shifted her legs to the other side of the chair. "All right. Once, when I was about eight years old, a cardinal flew in my open window and lighted on my iron headboard. It was a female—I know because it was more brown than red. I talked to her, and she looked me right in the eye and cocked her head, as though she understood me."

His mouth turned up at the corners. "What did you say?"

Lisa looked through the paned glass, at the trees outside, remembering. "I asked if she was lost."

"Did she give you an answer?"

"I don't know. She sang and chirped some. Flew around the room, then landed in the same place. It felt like an answer, but I didn't speak her language."

"That's a shame." His voice fell off at the end, as though he were about to drift into sleep.

She turned her head to look at him, and his eyes were half shut. He was smiling at her. His lashes fluttered before closing, and his breathing slowed.

She gazed at her sleeping patient. "I've never told anyone that story," she whispered. "I always pretended it was my mother, telling me she loved me. Telling me she left me in the best possible place she could find. It made me feel less...abandoned." A single tear rolled down her cheek, and she wiped it with the back of her hand.

She stayed a few minutes longer, feeling an almost holy, reverent spirit in the room. She wouldn't tell Jack this had been *her* room. That seemed too familiar, too intimate. But deep down, she was glad he ended up here. After whispering a prayer for his recovery, she drew herself up and moved toward the door. Just as her hand rested on the knob, Jack spoke.

"Thank you for sharing that with me. I feel honored."

She paused but didn't turn around. Just nodded and shut the door quietly behind her.

~

Jack thrashed, trying to come awake, trying to escape from the disturbing scene. He was asleep—he knew he was—but something heavy and dark kept him chained here. He tried to cry out, but he couldn't form words.

He was a young teenager—maybe fourteen or fifteen. A towering figure loomed over him. He couldn't make out a face. "Hit me!" The deep, harsh voice seethed with anger.

"No, Pa. I don't want to hit you."

"I said, hit me, boy! That'll feel better than having you say you don't want to be a rancher. Like it or not, this is your destiny. I haven't worked my whole life just to have you say you don't want the ranch." The figure grabbed Jack's arm and forced his hand up, to hit the man's face. Then the man—his father?—slammed Jack's cheek with a right hook. "Hit me again!"

"No!" Jack's cheek throbbed. Salty tears burned his eyes.

The man grabbed Jack's arm and repeated the sequence again. And again and again until Jack lost count. Somewhere in the background, a woman cried, calling for them to stop. That this man was out of his mind was clear, though Jack sensed it was from anger, from a need for control, than out of a true loss of faculties.

"Dad! Stop!"

"Don't tell me to stop, boy! You'll do as I tell you."

Jack jolted awake, his hair drenched, his body shaking. It was just a dream. A nightmare. Yet somehow, Jack could sense there was truth there. Deep in his spirit, he knew the event was real... If only he could remember a face. Or a name.

But with memories like that, why would he want to remember?

As best he could, he used the sheet to wipe the sweat slicking his forehead, sliding down his cheeks and neck. Sunlight shone in the window. What time was it? What kind of person had nightmares in the daytime?

If he lay in this bed one more minute, he'd lose his mind. He'd already lost his memories, and he couldn't afford to part with anything else. But something told him if he asked for assistance, he'd be told to stay put.

It took every ounce of strength—both mental and physical—to heft himself to a sitting position. Using his good arm, he nudged one leg, then the other over the side of the bed. Pain shot through his rib cage. Dizziness, then nausea pulsed through him. He steadied himself on the mattress, breathed deeply. After a time, the nausea calmed.

He was just getting ready to push to his feet with the goal of moving to the chair when someone knocked. The door opened a crack. It was Lisa.

"Whoa! What are you doing?" Her voice, even in alarm, was soft, gentle, fully controlled. In a blink, she was by his side.

"If I stay in this bed another second, I'm going to scream."

"All right. But there's no use in prolonging your recovery by falling and causing more injury. Your head injury, as well as the length of time you've spent in bed, could lead to dizziness. Let me help you." She hovered over him, arms in midair, as if to prevent him from moving on his own.

He'd expected a rebuttal. A command to get back under the covers. Not an offer of help.

"I can assist you to this chair. Or I can fetch a wheelchair, and we can take you over by the window. Maybe even outside."

Relief flooded his senses. "Really?"

"I'll have to check with Dr. Williamson, but he's right down the hall, talking to Father Hidalgo." She straightened, dropped her arms to the side. "I can't speak for the doctor, but I think he'll say your desire to get out of bed is a good sign."

"And if he doesn't?"

"Then we'll wait until he leaves and do what we want." Her dark eyes sparked with humor.

"You'd risk losing your job for me?"

"You forget. I grew up here. I'm in my family home. I can do as I please."

Jack's eyebrows lifted. Was she serious?

"Okay, I'd probably lose my job. So I probably won't help you sneak out. But let's not put the cart before the horse."

Horse... "All right. We'll wait for the doctor. But speaking of horses, what became of mine? The one I was riding when—"

The door opened behind Lisa, and Dr. Williamson entered. "What have we here?"

"I...uh..." Jack couldn't find words.

Lisa took on a professional tone and stance. "The patient has requested some fresh air. Shall I bring a wheelchair, Doctor?"

Dr. Williamson shifted a stack of books he carried and referred to his clipboard, then looked at Jack. "That's not a bad idea."

Lisa nodded, then turned a rascally smile to Jack. "I'll be right back."

The doctor sat in the chair and placed both hands under Jack's chin. "Look up. Now down. To your left. Your right."

Jack followed the man's instructions.

He scribbled something in his notes, then looked at Jack. "Any progress with your memories?"

Jack didn't feel like reliving his nightmare, or even retelling it. "I still can't remember my last name or where I'm from, if that's what you're asking."

"I see. Can you read?"

"I think so..."

"Read this." He held up a book and pointed to the title.

"'Tom Sawyer'?"

"Have you read it?"

"Maybe. I can't remember." Jack laughed. "Is that a trick question?"

Dr. Williamson smiled. "Maybe. It's a popular book, and many people your age have read it. I'll leave it here. Perhaps it will stir something for you. But if your head starts hurting, stop."

His head was already hurting. But he didn't dare say that for fear the doctor would force him back into bed. "Thank you."

The physician placed some other books in the stack, along with a couple of magazines and a newspaper. "Here are a couple of novels, a farmer's almanac, and some other things that might help pass the hours. Next time I visit, we'll discuss what you've read."

Giggles sounded outside the door, followed by short taps.

"Come in," the doctor called.

The door swung open, and Lisa pushed a wheelchair into the room. The twins followed.

"Girls, wait in the hall until we get Mr. Jack settled in the chair," Lisa said. "We'll be out shortly."

The girls obeyed and shut the door behind them.

"Are you sure you're ready for this?" Dr. Williamson asked.

"I've never felt more ready for anything in my life, sir."

With the doctor on his left and Lisa on his right, they managed to get him up, turned, and seated in the wheelchair.

Lisa lifted one of his feet, then the other onto the foot shelf. Her hands were soft, tender, sending a strange, pleasant sensation through his body. He felt her touch long after she removed her hands. She spoke in that low, gentle voice, telling him to hold onto the armrests, warning that the movement may be jarring, but he barely registered her words. All he could think was that he wished the pretty nurse weren't pushing the chair, because that left her out of his view. And right now, she was a much more pleasant distraction than his own thoughts.

~

The last thing Lisa had expected when she entered Jack's room was to find him trying to get out of bed. She'd hoped for this day but didn't think it would come so soon. His restlessness was a good sign, wasn't it?

She pushed the wheelchair slowly, carefully, not wanting to cause him any physical pain. Lucy and Lydia ran ahead, holding doors and pointing out rooms and features like small tour guides. Jack seemed relaxed, as though he was enjoying the experience.

Dr. Williamson leaned closer and spoke in a low voice. "I need to get back to the hospital and check on our cholera patients."

"How are they?" Lisa thought about her colleagues every day. "Especially the nurses."

"Better. But recovery will be slow. It could be a few weeks before any of them is ready to return to work—maybe longer."

"As long as they recover, that's the important thing."

Dr. Williamson nodded. His eyes looked weary, and frustration etched his features. "I've had to turn new patients away. I've sent some to St. Joseph's, as they agreed to take a small number of charity cases. But they're understaffed, as well."

"You can count on me to help any way I can."

"I know I can, Miss Garcia. Thank you for that. For now, keep doing what you're doing. Today, please make note of anything Jack sees that stirs his memory."

"Yes, sir."

When they reached the outer door, Dr. Williamson took his leave. Lisa carefully turned Jack's wheelchair around before backing it over the threshold and onto the wide front porch of the red brick building. She didn't feel they should navigate the stairs just yet. She pushed him to a shady spot on the southeast corner, next to a small table beneath some hanging ferns. The neighborhood was a soothing combination of small businesses and private residences. The street was lined with elm and live oak trees, and alive with birdsong. "There. The change of scenery should do you good."

The twins fussed and fretted over "their" patient for a short time but asked to be excused when they heard their classmates laughing on the playground behind the orphanage.

Lisa sat in the chair opposite Jack. They shared a comfortable silence, watching horses and buggies move up and down the street, as well as pedestrians hurrying by with packages or to-do lists.

Jack's eyes followed one particular horse until it was out of view. "I had a horse."

"You did."

"I tried to ask earlier—what happened to it?"

"She's currently being cared for at the livery a couple of blocks from here. Colonel Roosevelt and Colonel Wood took care of the bill before they left." She'd stopped by several times to check on the animal, but instead of sharing that, she waited for his response.

His eyebrows lifted, and his eyes focused on some faraway place. After a long moment, he looked at Lisa. "I'd like to see her."

"I'm sure that can be arranged. We'll have to clear it with Dr. Williamson, but we could bring her here to see you. As soon as you're ready to travel, we can take you there. It's not a far walk. It will all depend on what the doctor feels is best."

"Tell me more about the day we met."

Lisa smiled. It had only been a few weeks, but in some ways, it seemed like a lifetime ago. She'd have to frame her words carefully. She certainly couldn't tell him how they'd flirted, or how she'd hoped they might become better acquainted.

"I was in the woods near the San Antonio River, at a spot where the most beautiful flowers grow. I like to go there to relax. I often pick flowers to share with the patients at the hospital. I was off in my own world, humming a hymn, when all of a sudden, I heard you approaching. I was afraid at first, but it didn't take long to figure out you were harmless."

He chuckled.

"You asked for directions to the Menger Hotel. You wanted to join the Rough Riders, and I pointed you in the right direction."

"I must have given my name at some point."

Blood rushed to Lisa's cheeks, and she shifted her head the other way in the guise that she was watching the children who'd moved to the side yard. "You did, and you asked mine."

"I hope I wasn't...rude."

"Not at all." She kept her face turned away.

"Then I'm not sure why your ears are the color of a ripe tomato."

Drat! She faced him, willing her heart to stop pounding.

Their eyes met, and he looked genuinely concerned. "I have no memory of our meeting, but I hope I was a gentleman. I apologize if I wasn't."

"The fact that you'd apologize, even without recalling the incident, shows you *are* a gentleman. But truly, you did nothing untoward. You simply..." How did she say it? He really needed some evidence of who he was before the accident. "You asked my name and where you might see me again."

He studied her intently, as if trying to solve a puzzle. Then slowly, like a summer sunrise, understanding lit his face. He grinned, and it was his turn to blush. "Oh."

They didn't say anything more for a few minutes, just let the town's noises soak in along with the afternoon's warmth.

Jack cleared his throat. "Did you...uh...tell me? Where I might...see you again?"

As much as she tried, she couldn't keep the smile from stretching her cheeks. "I told you I'd be at church on Sunday morning. You said you were a churchgoing fellow and that you might see me there."

His eyebrows lifted. "A churchgoer, huh? That explains a lot."

"Really? How?"

"I've been hearing a voice in my head. I think it's God. Or maybe Scripture."

"So you may have memorized Scripture at some point in your life." Lisa smiled at him. "That's a pretty good clue as to who you are, don't you think?"

"Maybe. But I still don't know my last name or where I'm from." He exhaled, and his shoulders drooped. "It seems as though if I'm a man of faith, God would give me a little help."

"Patience is a virtue, Jack. What are some of the words you're hearing, if you don't mind me asking?"

He shifted. Was he getting tired? He watched as another

buggy moved down the road. "Don't be afraid. I'm with you. Stuff like that."

"Well it seems to me, He is helping you. He's reminding you that you're not alone. It's a good place to start."

~

Lampasas, Texas

Emma Stratton paced from one end of her bedroom to the other. "I can't believe he'd do this, Riley. Well, I can. But I hate it. What do the papers say about the war? Any news?"

Riley leaned back in the overstuffed chair and stretched his legs onto the ottoman. "Only that the San Antonio unit arrived in Cuba on June nineteenth. All we can do is pray for his safe return."

Emma paused, looked at her husband. Even after twenty years of marriage, he was still the most handsome man she'd ever seen. "You're right. Thank you for the reminder." She plopped down in the rocking chair. Twisted and untwisted a loose curl from her chignon. "I just can't help picturing him as that baby I took care of, all those years ago. He and Skye were the one bright spot from that time in my life." Just after her mother's death, she'd been forced to take a job as the Strattons' maid, and Allison had been a most unrelenting boss. Not to mention, the senior Mr. Stratton. What a horrid—no. She wouldn't allow herself to think such thoughts about a man long in the grave.

That difficult time was what brought Skye into their lives. When Riley and Colt's older brother, Donovan, died, his daughter—half Coushatta Indian—was left orphaned. When Emma and Riley married, they adopted her. So really, the hardship had led to blessings.

Riley let out a *hmph.* "I thought I was your bright spot."

A smile softened the worry that undoubtedly lined her face. Riley always knew how to calm her spirit. "You are always my bright spot."

His grin filled with mischief. "Does that mean I don't have to paint the parlor as you asked me to?"

"It means nothing of the sort." Emma swatted him on the leg. "You'll do as you're told, Mr. Stratton."

"As you say, dear."

"I'm glad you know your place." Emma scooped up the dress she'd made for their daughter, Anita, and headed for the door. "Anita needs to try this on one more time before I make final adjustments." She looked at the small watch pinned to her bodice. "Goodness, it's later than I thought."

"I'll be here. Going over the bank statements. And praying."

Emma nodded. Until she learned her nephew was home, safe and sound, she'd pray nonstop.

CHAPTER 8

Three more days passed, and Jack felt a little stronger each day. Improvement was slower than he wanted, but progress was progress. At least physically. He'd even walked from the bed to the window yesterday. Twice.

His memory? That was another matter. He went through cycles of trying to remember until he ended up with a headache, to the opposite extreme—trying to forget he couldn't remember, hoping relaxation would aid in the memory process. Still, nothing, other than that horrible nightmare. Maybe that's all it was. He *hoped* that's all it was.

What if he spent the rest of his life as a man with no past?

He might not know who he was, but he knew who he wanted to be. Or at least *what* he wanted to be. And he didn't want to be a person who laid around in bed all day, letting others take care of him.

Today, Lisa and Dr. Williamson would accompany him to the livery to see his horse. Surely, she had a name? Maybe seeing her would trigger something. But after that, he planned to talk to Dr. Williamson about getting some kind of job. Even part time. Even an hour a day. Just something to be useful. At this point, he felt as though he'd go stir crazy.

"Good morning, Jack." Lisa's voice floated in from the hallway, through the cracked door. "Do you need any help?"

Yesterday, he'd gotten himself dressed for the first time since the accident. It felt nice to be wearing something other than the striped hospital gown. Today, he'd done the same. "I'm dressed. You can come in."

She pushed open the door just enough to poke her head through. "Your progress is remarkable."

He sat taller in his chair. "Putting a shirt and pants on is nothing to write home about. That is, if I knew where to write home to."

She entered the room, and her smile brightened the space far more than the filtered light from the window. "All ready for your excursion, I see."

"Ready to play detective. Hoping to find clues that may wake up this sleeping brain of mine."

She stood with hands on hips. "In that case, let's get started. You've had your breakfast, I presume?"

"Yes. The twins picked up my tray a half hour ago. Those two will make good nurses someday."

"That does seem to be their current goal. But don't be surprised if that changes. The week before you came, they wanted to be zookeepers."

"I'm sure the jobs have similarities." Jack made monkey noises, hoping to hear her laugh.

Lisa tried to look horrified, but when he continued, laughter spilled out, lighting up the room even more. "You're crazy. And not just because of your injuries, either."

"How do you know?"

"The fact that you can perfectly imitate an ape either means you once lived in a jungle or you were quite a handful as a boy. Something tells me it's the latter."

"I don't know. Wait, it's all coming back to me now. My mother used to sing me a lullaby. It went like this..." He started with the monkey sounds again, and she hooted. The harder she laughed, the more animated he became until—

The door opened, and Lisa stood at attention. "Hello, Dr. Williamson."

As the middle-aged physician stepped into the room, Jack changed his expression to one of serious dignity. "Something seems to be wrong with your nurse. I think she has a case of hysteria."

Lisa snorted. Tried to stop. Snorted again. "I'm sorry, doctor. I"—hoot—"apologize. I—uhm. If you'll excuse me a moment. I'll be right back." With that, she fled the room.

Dr. Williamson watched her leave, then looked at Jack. "That's quite a talent you have. I thought there was a real monkey in here."

"I wish I could tell you where I learned that."

"Perhaps today will give us some clues. If nothing else, maybe I can sign you up for a Vaudeville show."

"It's good to know I have options."

Dr. Williamson chuckled and reached a hand to help Jack stand. "Do you think you can walk to the front door? I left the wheelchair there in hopes you were up for some exercise. But I can get it if you'd like."

"I can make it. I need to build up my strength."

"Something told me you'd say that. I'll let you try on your own, but I'll be right here if you need to grab on."

It was humiliating, this needing to rely on strangers for every little thing. And right now, everyone in the world was a stranger. His muscles hollered at him with each step, but every inch forward made him feel a little more like a man, less like a child. He decided to distract himself from the aches and pains by bringing up the idea of a job.

"Say, Doc, I was wondering... I mean, I know I can't do much right now. But I need something to make me feel useful. How long will it be before I can look for some kind of steady work?"

"Well, I did mention Vaudeville."

"Not exactly what I had in mind, but thanks."

They made it to the bedroom door, then into the hallway. The front door was a sharp left turn and about thirty feet ahead. And there, waiting, with the light from the window behind her outlining her like some kind of angel from heaven, was Lisa. Jack reminded himself to stand up straight.

Dr. Williamson was talking, and Jack had to pull his attention back to what the man was saying. "I'm sure we can find something for you to do here at the orphanage. We can test you out in the kitchen. Martha can always use an extra set of hands. You seem to be well-educated too. Perhaps you can tutor some of the students in reading and math."

Jack groaned. "I don't know why, but the thought of doing math gives me a bigger headache than I already have."

"Duly noted," the doctor said. "When you're ready, we could talk to Mr. Joske. He owns a large department store here in town. He may have something for you sooner than you think, if, as you say, you're willing to accept whatever's available."

"I'll do anything. I've counted every dot on the ceiling of my room, and now I'm connecting those dots to make animals. It's not the most challenging task."

They reached Lisa, and she fluffed a pillow in the wheelchair before Dr. Williamson helped ease him in. Jack was so tired of people hovering. Not that he didn't appreciate it. But although he had no idea who he was, he was pretty sure he wasn't the type of person to enjoy being fussed over.

Unless it was by Lisa. That had its perks, for certain.

When he was comfortably seated, she handed him a basket.

"Are we going on a picnic?" he asked.

"Not today. Not us, anyway. But I thought your horse might

enjoy some treats as you get to know her again. There are a few carrots, an apple, and some sugar cubes."

"How thoughtful. Thank you."

Outside, someone had added a temporary ramp on one side of the stairs. This time, Dr. Williamson pushed. He turned Jack around and pulled him backward down the ramp before settling him on the sidewalk.

They fell into a quiet rhythm, walking down the sidewalk to the livery, soaking in the warm San Antonio sun, and Jack's heart sped up. Would his memory come back when he saw his horse? What if it did?

What if it didn't?

He took a deep breath, then another and tried to ease his anxiety. The sounds of the busy street—the clop-clopping of horses, the rumble of wagon wheels, the snippets of strangers' conversations—soaked into his spirit. Some might have described the scene as busy, even chaotic. But after being cooped up for more than a week—how many days had it been? —it offered a calm serenity. The air, the space—it smelled a bit like freedom.

He almost wanted to hold onto that feeling a little longer, to prepare himself for the best, or the worst, or the in-between. But too soon, they arrived at the livery, where Dr. Williamson spoke with the owner, a middle-aged black man.

Lisa stooped to speak into Jack's ear. "The doctor has arranged with Mr. Carson, the owner, for you to see your horse out back, where there's a paddock away from the other horses."

Jack nodded. Excitement blended with something like nausea. Soon, Carson motioned for them to follow, and Lisa pushed the wheelchair around the building.

There, on the other side of a fence, was the horse. Mr. Carson said a few more words to Dr. Williamson and Lisa before disappearing through a side door, but Jack wasn't listening.

He stared at the horse.

Nothing. Nothing about her stirred any memories.

She was a beautiful horse. Appaloosa? Was that the name?

But the horse's actual name, if she had one, was lost to Jack.

The horse whinnied. Approached the gate, pawing like she was excited.

Lisa started to push him closer, but Jack waved her off. "I'd like to stand."

He handed her the basket and pushed himself up before taking the treats back. Reached inside, grabbed a carrot. Held it out as he stepped close to the fence.

The horse nuzzled his neck, then took the carrot.

"Hi, girl. You remember me, don't you?"

She snorted again but kept chewing the carrot.

"What's your name? I wish you could tell me." He ran his hand along her muzzle. "I wish you could talk. You could probably answer a lot of my questions."

She nosed toward the basket, and he pulled out another carrot. But the horse bypassed Jack's hand and tried to get into the basket on her own.

"You want the apple?" He dropped the carrot back in and grabbed the fruit, holding it out, hand flat. She took the whole thing and chomped loudly. "You like that, do you? Somebody needs to teach you some manners. They can hear you chewing back at the orphanage."

Lisa laughed, that beautiful, low laugh.

The doctor moved beside him. "Is anything coming back to you?"

"Not a thing. I don't recall ever seeing this horse before."

"That's okay. She clearly knows you. We'll stay as long as you like, and you can visit as often as you want."

"I don't understand. Why can't I remember anything?" Jack was aware of Lisa on his other side, rubbing the horse. He didn't care that she was listening. He just wanted answers.

Dr. Williamson shook his head. "I'm not sure I fully understand it either, son. I've been reading everything I can get my hands on about this condition. It was probably brought on by your concussion. When that happens, your brain gets bruised, and there may even be some swelling. When the swelling goes down, most likely, your memories will return."

"And if they don't?"

"Why don't we swim that stream when we come to it?"

"I think we're there. I mean, I can talk. I can read. I remember how to do all kinds of things. I just don't remember anything about my past."

Dr. Williamson leaned on the fence and gave the horse a pat. "There is another condition this could be. I've been reading about the works of Drs. Charcot and Souques. They say amnesia can occur when there's something traumatic about one's past that they don't want to remember. It's kind of a defense mechanism. The mind blocks out important information, causing gaps in the memory. If you've had trauma in your past, it could be that your concussion triggered a deeper condition."

Jack studied the horse as he tried to process what he'd just heard. "I need to sit down."

In nearly the same moment, Lisa was there with the wheelchair, and Jack eased into it. He locked eyes with the horse. *What do you know, girl? Tell me who I am.*

His thoughts turned to that voice, deep in his spirit. *Who am I, God? You keep telling me not to be afraid. How am I supposed to be okay with this?*

"Fury." Lisa said the word while looking at the horse, then turned and met Jack's gaze. "I think her name might be Fury."

"Fury?"

"I'm so sorry. I...I think I'm right. I've gone over and over our brief meeting in my mind, at the river, but that didn't come back to me until just now. You were leaning down, talking to your horse when I first saw you. I think you called her Fury."

Jack's gaze swung to the horse. "Is your name Fury? You don't seem furious. Then again, you're technically to blame for the state I'm in, so maybe it is an appropriate name."

The horse nickered, as if to apologize.

He felt Dr. Williamson watching him, but Jack didn't take his gaze off the horse, as if by staring hard enough, he could bring forth some key to his past.

After a time—he wasn't sure how long—he spoke. "I think I'm ready to head back."

The doctor rested a hand on Jack's shoulder. "I'm sorry, son. I know you wanted this to offer a breakthrough for you."

Jack nodded.

The physician addressed Lisa. "Do you think you can handle getting him back on your own? I'm due for another appointment."

"Of course, Doctor."

The older man took his leave, and soon Jack felt himself being pushed in the wheelchair, back toward his home-away-from...who knew where? He slumped in the chair. It felt like he'd been gut-punched, creating a leak in his spirit where all the hope seeped out. He wasn't even embarrassed to be pushed around in this chair. He didn't care.

But before they arrived at their destination, Lisa turned into a small building with a sign that read *Harvey's Mercantile.* Inside, it looked like a general store. Maybe she needed to do some shopping, but all he wanted was his bed, though he doubted he'd sleep. He really just wanted to disappear, like his memories.

She wheeled him all the way to the back of the store, through a doorway that led to some kind of café. When she parked him at a table and sat across from him, he met her eyes.

"This place has the best medicine known to mankind. Outside of the medical profession, that is."

"Is that so?" Jack couldn't even muster a smile in response to hers.

"Yes, that's so. They sell the best vanilla ice cream I've ever tasted. Although to be honest, it's the only ice cream I've tasted. They also make these wonderful, chewy chocolate chip cookies, and they serve them with the ice cream, and it's—well, you'll see."

"I'm not hungry."

"You don't have to be hungry to eat this. Trust me. It will make you feel better. Temporarily, anyway."

He wanted to argue with her. Wanted to tell her he didn't want to feel better. That he wanted to wallow in his frustration. But she looked so hopeful that he just nodded and looked away.

"Wait here. I'll be right back." She disappeared behind him.

Wait here? Was that supposed to be a joke? It wasn't as though he could go very far with his head pounding and his arm in a sling and his chest all wrapped so that it ached every time he took a breath. Even if he tried to get away, without a memory, he'd have no place to go.

He heard her telling someone they'd like two of whatever she was ordering.

After a moment, she returned to her seat and rested her elbows on the table, chin on her fists. "This has always been my favorite place to go when I was down about something. Papa—Father Hidalgo—brought me here when I was a little girl whenever one of my brothers or sisters was adopted."

"So you had siblings?"

"Not blood related. The orphanage was my family. When one of them left, I knew I'd probably never see or hear from them again."

He knew what she was doing. The ice cream hadn't yet

arrived, but just thinking about something besides his own problems already caused his head to pound less. "That must have been difficult for you. I'm sorry."

"Don't be. My childhood may not have been traditional, but it was a good one."

An aproned man delivered ice cream in two stemmed glasses, each centered on a plate with a chocolate chip cookie. Jack had to admit, it looked good. He waited for her to take the first bite, and a look of pleasure flooded her face. She closed her eyes for a moment, and he wished he could capture that exact picture and keep it with him. She was beautiful.

She opened her eyes and looked at his spoon, still unused. "What are you waiting for? Dig in!"

Jack obeyed. First, he broke off a piece of the cookie. It was still warm, and it melted on his tongue. It was his turn to close his eyes in satisfaction. Something about it seemed familiar, but no specific memory surfaced. When the last of the chocolate dissipated, he scooped some ice cream onto his spoon and took a bite.

Immediately, a scene flashed through his mind. He was sitting at a table, much like this one, only nicer...fancier. White tablecloth.

Several people sat at the table with him, but he couldn't make out their faces.

They were laughing.

This flashed in his memory and was gone just as quickly. He froze, trying to hang onto the moment, but it faded to nothing, like the last remnants of a dream you want to recall but can't.

"That good, huh?" Lisa pulled his attention back to the present.

"I...I think I just remembered something."

She set her spoon down and leaned forward. "Tell me."

"I've had ice cream before. I was with other people, and

they were talking and laughing. I couldn't see them clearly." He leaned back, trying to process what had just happened. "It was just a flash...just a moment, and then it was gone."

"That's wonderful news, Jack! It means your memory is starting to wake up. I'll bet the memories come faster now."

He hoped she was right. This piece of the puzzle was much more pleasant than the nightmare he'd had several days ago. But at this rate, he'd be an old man before he figured out who he was. He picked up the cookie, took another bite. No new memories appeared.

They ate the rest of their treat in silence. Thankfully, Lisa didn't feel the need to fill every moment with chatter. Right now, he just needed to be alone with his thoughts.

CHAPTER 9

Lampasas

Riley heard his brother's voice from the sidewalk and tried to locate its origin. There—the post office. He pushed open the door and stepped up to the counter next to his brother. The clerk, a wiry, balding man whose thick glasses hung on ears too large for his head, stood on the other side, eyes wide, taking the verbal lashing.

"I've sent four telegraphs in four days with no response. I have no choice but to believe the telegraphs aren't going through. Either your machinery isn't working, or you're sending them to the wrong place." Colt's voice boomed through the small room, and he pounded his fist on the counter in rhythm with the words.

"What seems to be the problem?" Riley kept his voice low and neutral. He knew his brother, and he didn't want to escalate his anger even further.

Colt swung his head around, and his eyes held familiar fury. "I'm trying to find out about Jackson. I've sent message after message to the post in Cuba."

The clerk spoke up, his voice timid. "The telegrams were received. I have receipts here to show it."

Colt slammed his open palm on the counter. "Liar! Roosevelt is a personal friend of mine. He would not ignore my messages."

Riley placed a gentle hand on his brother's back, only to have Colt recoil from the touch.

"I don't need to be mollycoddled. I need this imbecile of a postal worker to do his job!"

"Colt. There's a war going on. I'm sure Roosevelt is in the field with his men. He'll respond when he's able."

"That's not good enough!" Colt's voice shook with a combination of anger and frustration.

This time, his brother's behavior stemmed from fear for his son. "When did the last telegraph go through?" Riley asked the employee.

"Yesterday."

"Let's send another one. Just repeat whatever yesterday's said." Riley dug some cash from his pocket and handed it to the man.

"Yes, sir."

Riley pressed his hand on Colt's shoulder, gently turning him toward the door. "I'm glad I ran into you. Do you have time for cup of coffee at Grace's Cafe?"

"I suppose."

They walked silently across the street to the small restaurant. Colt opened and closed his fists, clearly trying to get hold of his emotions. After they were seated at a corner table and had ordered their coffee, Riley leaned back and looked at Colt.

What could he say?

How could he make this better?

He couldn't. He remembered what Emma's father had once told him. Sometimes, the less said, the better. Just be there.

Colt looked out the window. "Allison's a mess with worry."

"I can imagine. Emma plans to stop by this afternoon."

"It's appreciated."

They sat in silence for a few minutes, until the waitress delivered their coffee.

Colt cleared his throat. "This is my fault."

Riley's eyebrows lifted, but he schooled his expression before Colt looked his way. For Colt to admit fault in anything was unusual.

"We fought before he left. He wanted—it's ridiculous, Riley. Jackson wants to be a trick rider. Can you imagine that? He's a Stratton. And he wants to be some glorified circus performer."

Riley measured his words carefully. "He certainly has a talent."

"A talent for what?" Colt shifted in his seat, obviously agitated. "What possible use can you think of for standing on a horse's back and riding around in front of an audience like a clown?"

"Entertainment? Inspiration? Education?"

"He's a Stratton, not Buffalo Bill!"

"He's his own person, Colt."

Colt held Riley's eyes but said nothing.

Riley added some sugar to his coffee and stirred. "It's easy for us, as parents, to think of our children as extensions of ourselves. But God doesn't use cookie cutters when He creates us. We're all unique. I know it's been hard for me to let my own children choose their paths. If it were up to me, Skye would live next door, not several hours and a train ride away."

There was a tense pause. Colt's racial prejudice and bigotry was the reason Skye, their half-Coushatta Indian niece that Riley adopted after their brother Donnigan's death, left in the first place. It was something they'd never really addressed, but now wasn't the time.

Colt took a sip of his coffee. "Jackson is my only child. It's his duty to take over the ranch. It's what I did when you and Donnigan took your own paths."

Riley pushed down the lump that always seemed to form in his throat when he thought of their deceased brother—Skye's birth father, Donnigan. Such a waste. Yet Riley would always be grateful for the chance to be a father to Skye.

He leaned forward. "It's what you *wanted* to do, Colt. No one forced you." He was one of the few people in the world—maybe the only person—who could speak so openly with Colt. Not that Colt would listen. But he probably wouldn't seek revenge on Riley just for speaking his mind.

"Jackson's mother coddled him. If only I hadn't let him spend so much time with those blasted horses... He should have been out on cattle drives, learning the trade."

Riley let the silence settle before responding. "He has a gift, Colt. Why do you think I keep asking him to work with my guests in the summer? He loves horses, and they love him. He has a way with people too. I'm not sure he'd be happy doing what you do, no matter how much you groomed him for the job."

Colt gulped the last of his coffee and set the mug down a little too hard. "Was there a reason you wanted to have coffee? Did you need something?"

Riley grinned. "Yeah. I was trying to protect that poor fellow at the post office."

Colt huffed and stood up, ready to leave, but a hint of a grin poked through his countenance. "He needed protection, I suppose. I'm good now."

Riley tossed a few coins on the table and followed suit. When Jackson came home, he might need some protection too.

CHAPTER 10

The next few days brought no new memories. Sometimes Jack awoke with the acrid taste of a vivid dream, but when he tried to recall it, it vanished into a fog. Each time, he felt like he'd stepped out of an Edgar Allen Poe short story.

But at least he'd been given some light kitchen duties. Today he sat alone at the worn table trying to mash some potatoes. He held the bowl with his weak hand and smashed the spuds with his strong arm. Martha could do this faster, for sure, but he was grateful for the distraction, and she was probably grateful for the break. The smell of roast chicken comforted him and made his stomach growl.

Most days, he sat with some of the boys in the afternoons and helped them with their schoolwork, and even read to them out of his borrowed copy of *Tom Sawyer*. Each day, he returned to the livery to spend time with Fury, always bringing her a treat, always hoping for a new recollection to appear.

Maybe if he could ride her...but with his injuries, that wasn't a good idea. Not yet.

Next week, he'd talk to Mr. Joske about a paying job. He felt like a freeloader.

Come to think of it, maybe he'd walk over there this afternoon. Yes, that's what he'd do.

"Those are some pretty deep lines on your forehead." Lisa stood in the kitchen doorway.

He pushed aside the bowl. The potatoes were lumpy, but it was the best he could do. "Just thinking about my future."

"Anything I can help with?"

"Dr. Williamson mentioned that I might find temporary work in Joske's department store. I was thinking of going over there this afternoon and asking for a job."

One pretty eyebrow lifted, then dropped. "You feel up to that?"

"I'll see if he needs someone part time for a week or two. Hopefully, after that, I'll have a better idea of who I am. If not, I'll need a job, anyway. Maybe he'll take me on full time."

She crossed her arms and leaned against the door jamb. "That sounds like a good plan. I'd think the more you get out, the more experiences you have, the more likely you are to trigger your memory."

"You would think." Jack tried to keep the frustration from his voice. He had much to be grateful for. What would have become of him if he hadn't ended up with these people who were willing to take in a stranger, knowing nothing of his past?

"Would you like me to go with you? To Joske's, I mean. Do you know the way?"

"I think I can manage on my own, but I wouldn't mind the company."

"So yes? You'd like me to come? I've always wanted to shop there."

"Only if it's not an inconvenience. I feel like I've taken so much of your time. How are your colleagues? Are they recovering well?"

She pulled out the bench and sat across from him at the worn wooden table. "Yes, but it's slow. Fortunately, it was caught early, and they were kept hydrated. But it's a dreadful disease and causes such drastic weight loss that it takes a while to build up strength again. Hopefully, in another month, we'll be able to reopen the hospital."

Jack was afraid to ask. But he needed to know... "What should I do when that happens? I can't stay here forever. I need to come up with a plan. That's one reason I need a job."

"Papa and I have discussed this. The children love you, and you're not in anyone's way. It's nice to have another man around. You're welcome to stay here until you're completely on your feet."

Some of the tension left his shoulders. Still, he couldn't rely on charity indefinitely. One day, maybe he'd be wealthy enough to donate to the orphanage. And the hospital. But right now, he didn't have much choice but to rely on the kindness of others.

~

Lisa left Jack in the kitchen and eyed the clock in the entryway. If she hurried, she could slip home and change into a nicer dress. The last time she visited Joske's, she was treated like a peasant. She didn't want to give that snooty woman another reason to snub her, though her wardrobe would probably make little difference in the woman's poor manners. Still, it had been several weeks since she wore anything other than her nurse's uniform out in public, and she needed a break. Needed to feel like a regular person again, if only for an hour.

She walked the half block to her small home as fast as her legs would take her. As soon as she shut her door, she peeled off her white nurse's apron, then stepped out of the blue hospital underdress even before removing her shoes. She knew just what she'd wear. It wasn't her first choice, but the Texas heat made her favorite—the heavy floral brocade dress she'd sewn in March—impractical. She selected a white pleated cotton blouse with lace trim and puffed sleeves. A thin green satin ribbon was woven through the lace at the neck and elbows. She buttoned it, pulled on a vivid green cotton A-line skirt, then tied a wide satin ribbon belt around her waist.

Already, she felt like a new person.

A quick look in the mirror and she laughed. She was still wearing her nurse's cap. She took it off, unpinned her hair, and brushed it out. She twisted it into fat curls, secured them in a pile on top of her head, and pulled out a few loose strands to frame her face and neck. Then she stood at her closet door, peering up at her three nice hats. After selecting a wide-brimmed straw one with white trim, she opened the sewing box on her dresser and extracted some leftover green ribbon. She pulled it around the rim and tied it into a bow, with long streamers hanging from the back. A few hairpins secured it in place, and she was ready to go. She grabbed the green calico-print reticule she'd made from scraps and tucked a few coins inside.

She was going *shopping.* At Joske and Sons.

As an afterthought, she selected the cameo brooch from her jewelry box. It had come with the house. She assumed it once belonged to Pastor Smith's wife. Now it was hers, and she was ever so grateful. Once the brooch was pinned over her top blouse button, she stood at the mirror and admired her reflection. Following weeks without a break, it was nice to feel like a girl again.

Next to the mirror, a tall vase held her one parasol—white chiffon with a fishnet lace overlay, bordered with rows of white chiffon ruffles. It wasn't an expensive parasol, but it was pretty. She'd bought it with her first paycheck from the hospital but had yet to use it. She'd never carried one before.

Why not today?

She grabbed the fancy umbrella and glanced at the wall clock. Not bad for twenty minutes. She took her time on the short walk to the store, enjoying the sights and sounds of her city, using the parasol as a walking stick. She didn't quite have the courage to open it yet. The thought both thrilled her and made her feel like an imposter.

Just before she turned the corner to the orphanage, she mustered her pluck, opened the ruffled sunshield, and rested the handle on her shoulder as she'd seen other ladies do. A smile bubbled up from her heart to her face. What would Papa say? What would *Jack* say?

Why did it matter what Jack would say?

She didn't have time to examine her thoughts further, for there in the porch rockers sat the two men in question, deep in conversation, each holding a glass of lemonade.

They continued their conversation as she approached, only turning when she made her way up the stairs.

"May I help you, Miss?" Papa directed the question at her as if she were a stranger. An instant later, recognition dawned on both their faces. "Evelisse? I did not expect to see you this way. You look beautiful. What is the occasion?"

Jack remained silent, but his eyes hadn't left her, as if he were soaking in the change.

"No big occasion, Papa. I told Jack I'd accompany him to Joske's, and since I haven't been out of my nurse's attire in weeks..."

"You look..." Jack paused, as if he couldn't find the word he searched for.

Different?

Ridiculous?

"Beautiful," Jack breathed.

For several seconds, her eyes locked with his until Papa cleared his throat.

"Si. *Muy hermosa.*" Papa stood. "I need to refill my drink. And I believe Jack is ready to be on his way." He took Jack's glass in his other hand, then edged the screen door open with his foot. "You two have fun. I hope you get the job, Jack."

And with that, Lisa was left alone on the porch with Jack's clear green eyes on her.

What was he thinking, really? Did he think she dressed up for him?

Did she dress up for him?

Jack used his good arm to push himself up from the chair, then held it out for her to take. She placed her free hand in the crook of his elbow, and they made their way off the porch and onto the sidewalk, as if they were a normal couple, enjoying a normal summer day in San Antonio.

~

If Jack had been concerned about his memory loss before, he was doubly concerned now. Apparently, his tongue had grown to twice its size and he couldn't form words. And even if he could, he couldn't think of a single coherent thing to say to the woman by his side. Lisa was beautiful. He already knew that. But seeing her like this, it...it...he didn't know. He felt like a fool for admiring her beauty, forever thinking she could see him as anything but a patient. She was far out of his reach. He was wasting his time.

Yet here she was, sharing an afternoon with him as though it was her choice, as though there was nothing she'd rather be doing.

Of course, it was her choice. She'd done little but tend to his needs and wrangle children for the last several weeks. It didn't mean she held any special interest for him. Only that she wanted to shop in a department store. He couldn't remember details about his past life, but he knew women liked to wear pretty things. And they liked to shop. It had nothing to do with him.

The only way he'd have a future he could be proud of was to grab hold of every opportunity. And he'd be crazy if he didn't grab this opportunity to get to know the beautiful creature by his side. If he could only find words.

"It's a beautiful day." The words sounded dull, even to him. Was that the best he could do?

"It is."

"I...like your dress. It's very pretty."

"Thank you. I made the blouse and skirt myself."

"A nurse *and* a seamstress. You're a woman of many talents."

"Sewing was part of my curriculum during my time at the orphanage. I'm so glad the nuns taught me well."

How could he keep the conversation going? "Did you...design the clothes yourself?"

"Oh, heavens, no. I copied them."

He tilted his head. "Copied them?"

"I study pictures in ladies' magazines. Then I buy similar fabric and copy the designs."

"That's brilliant."

"Not really, but thank you. It's a common practice among people whose taste exceeds their budget."

He laughed. This woman was delightful. "It sounds brilliant to me. I guess I need to learn to sew if I ever want to wear anything besides the three shirts that were in my saddlebag."

She squeezed his arm. "You look fine. If Mr. Joske gives you a job, you may get an employee discount. Then you'll be able to afford as many new shirts as you want."

Too soon, they were inside the department store. He glanced around, amazed at the sheer amount of merchandise. This was no general store. It was an emporium.

A woman approached them, and Lisa stiffened on his arm.

"How may I help you?" She focused on Jack, her voice kind, accommodating.

"I'd like to see Mr. Joske, please."

Lisa added, "Mr. *Alexander* Joske."

The woman's brows lifted. "Do you have an appointment?"

"No."

Lisa spoke up again. "He's a friend of Dr. Williamson's."

The woman's attention shifted to Lisa, and something in her expression changed, as if she recognized Lisa. Her gaze trailed up and down Lisa's body, stopping at her face. The customer-friendly smile dissipated, replaced by a disapproving stare. "I see. Wait here."

When the woman disappeared through a door, Jack whispered, "Do you know her?"

"Not really."

Jack didn't press. But he got the distinct feeling that something foul was afoot. He tugged Lisa toward a display of men's shirts, folded and stacked in a pristine arrangement. "Could you copy these?"

She picked one up and unfolded it, examining the buttons, the seams, the collar. "Yes. Would you like me to make you some shirts?"

"Oh! No. I wouldn't ask that of you. I'm just curious about your sewing talent. What about these?" He led them across the aisle to some children's clothing. "Could you copy any of these?"

She examined a girl's dress with an oversized collar and big ruffled sleeves. "I could but I wouldn't. It's too confining. Girls need just as much freedom to run and play as boys do."

This woman was fascinating. "What would you make for a little girl to wear?"

She browsed the racks of hanging clothes until she found a simple dress. "Look at this one. The sleeves are straight, so they won't get caught in everything. The dress is full enough to run in. You could cover it with a pinafore to protect it. It's so much more practical for a child than those miniature adult versions."

"That shows how little I know about girls. I figured they all just sat around playing with dolls."

She turned an almost comical expression on him. "I believe you've just revealed a clue about your past."

"Really? What do you mean?"

She laughed. "I'm pretty sure you do *not* have a sister. Yes, girls like to play with dolls. But they also like to play stickball and climb trees and get muddy, just like little boys."

"I see. You may be right." He would have spent more time pondering her insight, but the woman appeared in the doorway.

"Mr. Joske said he's not aware of any orders from Dr. Williamson. The last order was delivered weeks ago." There was that disapproving expression again. "However, he will see you. He's in his office. Down this hallway, third door to your left."

Lisa took a step back. "I wish you the best."

"Aren't you coming?"

"You don't need me. I'll stay here and shop." She raised her voice a bit. "I need to buy a few things. I'll be here when you're done."

Jack felt protective of her. He wasn't sure he wanted to leave her with that vulture of a woman, but he didn't argue further. With a nod and a smile, he left her in the children's clothing department and went in search of Mr. Joske's office.

When he read the man's name on a sign outside a door, he knocked.

"Come in!"

Jack entered. A dignified, balding, middle-aged man stood, offered his hand. "Hello. I am Alexander Joske. What can I do for you?" He sat back down and gestured for Jack to take the chair across from his desk. His accent was thick, but Jack couldn't quite place the origin.

Jack settled in the chair. Cleared his throat. "Well, sir... I'm a patient of Dr. Williamson's. I had an accident a few weeks back, and I'm still recovering. The doctor suggested I talk to you about a job I can do while I continue the recovery process."

"I see. Does your recovery leave you with any limitations?"

"I tire easily, but I'm getting stronger all the time. I was hoping you might take me on part time for a while. Maybe I could transition to full time in a few weeks."

"What are your skills?"

Jack froze. What *were* his skills? How did someone without a past know what they were good at? "I'm good with people." He thought that was right. "I can read and write pretty well. I'm willing to do anything you need, sir."

The man swiveled his leather desk chair back and forth. "On Dr. Williamson's recommendation, I will hire you. I need a clerk for my men's department. We'll start you at two to three hours a day for the next week, if that is agreeable. How soon can you begin?"

It was that easy? Jack wanted to jump from his chair, whoop and holler. Might have, if it wouldn't have aggravated his sore ribs. "Tomorrow?"

"Tomorrow it is. You will train with the woman you met earlier—Mrs. Clark."

A little of the spark seeped out of Jack's enthusiasm. "Yes, sir. What time would you like me to be here?"

"Nine in the morning."

Jack stood, offered his hand to the man again. "Thank you so much, Mr. Joske. I'll do my best to make you glad for your decision. I'll be here in the morning."

"I look forward to working with you. I'll walk you out. I'm headed that way, anyway."

Jack exhaled a sigh of relief, maybe a little too loudly, but

Mr. Joske didn't let on that he noticed. Jack followed him down the hallway. He had a job! He couldn't wait to tell Lisa.

~

Lisa examined the gloves. Then she moved to the housewares section and looked at the teapots, making sure to touch each one in view of the rude clerk. When the woman approached, Lisa turned her back and moved to the linens, lifting the price tag on a lovely tablecloth.

"I'm not sure that's suitable for someone on a nurse's income. Perhaps you'll find something in the clearance section more appropriate to your taste and budget."

Lisa's heart pounded, but she worked to keep her expression neutral. "Thank you for your help, but I'm not in need of assistance at the moment."

The woman let out a low *hmph* and continued following Lisa around the store. Did she think Lisa might steal something? In all her years of enduring piteous stares from strangers, she'd never felt as flustered or as offended as she did right now.

Please, God. I know it shouldn't matter what this woman thinks. But please let me find something in my budget. Something I want and need. Something to shut this woman's mouth.

Her eyes fell on a display of small silver teaspoons. She had a chipped china teapot with two matching teacups. Each morning, she enjoyed her tea from one of those cups, and it made her feel like such a lady. But she was using a plain tablespoon. How fun it would be to stir her tea with one of these delicate, embellished spoons. She held her breath as she turned one over.

Ten cents. She had that in her reticule! She picked up the teaspoon and marched to the counter. "I'm ready to check out, ma'am."

The woman scowled, her mouth creased and pinched. She picked up the spoon, turned it over. "These are sold as a set. Would you like all twelve? That will be a dollar and twenty cents."

Lisa's heart fell. That far exceeded her budget. And what would she do with twelve teaspoons? Now she'd have to slink away from this woman. But wait... "If they're sold as a set, why are they priced individually?"

"That was a mistake."

"I see. And who placed the price tags individually on each teaspoon? That seems like a lot of wasted work."

"Do you want the set or not?" The woman's haughty demeanor sent a chill through Lisa. What had happened to her, to make her so cruel?

"No, thank you."

"Is there a problem, Mrs. Clark?" Mr. Joske's German accent was easy to identify.

Lisa looked at the man with Jack slightly behind him, then quickly at her feet. She didn't want him—or Jack—to see her red face.

"This woman wanted to break up the set of teaspoons. I was just explaining that she'd have to purchase them all."

The man picked up the spoon in question. "I believe you're mistaken, Mrs. Clark. The sets come in a box, along with other utensils. These spoons are sold individually."

Now it was Mrs. Clark's turn to flush. Only, her flush seemed more from anger than embarrassment. "My mistake, sir. I do apologize."

"Everyone makes mistakes. Think nothing of it." He turned to Lisa. "To make up for your troubles, please accept this as my gift to you."

"Oh, no. I'm happy to pay for it."

"Save your money for something else. Enjoy your teaspoon

with a nice cup of tea. And shop with us again." He handed the spoon to Mrs. Clark. "Wrap this for her, please."

Under her boss's watchful eye, the woman wrapped the spoon with careful detail, folding it into delicate sheets of paper and placing it inside a beautiful red box with *Joske and Sons* printed on the lid. Mrs. Clark handed it over, and Lisa took it, almost reverently. Never in her life had she had something so special, so new, so out of reach. She'd use the spoon. But she'd save the box forever.

"Thank you, sir. You're very kind."

Jack touched his good hand to her elbow. "And thank you for the job. I'll see you in the morning."

~

He and Mr. Joske had witnessed more of that scene than Jack would ever admit to Lisa. Watching the way Mr. Joske handled the situation raised Jack's respect for the businessman even more. He was proud to work for him.

He also made a decision. One day, he'd buy Lisa something extravagant. He didn't know how or when. But she'd spent the last month of her life taking care of him. Had chosen a profession geared to serving others without expecting anything in return. One day, he would repay her as best he could.

He led Lisa to the exit and onto the sidewalk before speaking. "Are you all right?"

"Of course. Why do you ask?" She wouldn't meet his eyes.

"Oh, no reason in particular. That clerk just seemed kind of...uppity."

She heaved a sigh. "You noticed it too? I thought it was just me."

"Oh, no. She's a piece of work. And she'll be training me in my new job."

Lisa stopped. Her mouth dropped open, and she looked up

at Jack with eyes the size of silver dollars. "Jack! No. Please tell me you're joking."

"I am not. But I'll be okay. She doesn't scare me. Much."

Lisa laughed at that, and he loved hearing the sound. Loved turning her mood around. As a matter of fact, the more he was with her, the more he loved everything about her.

Which brought him back to the knowledge that she was too good for him. Out of reach.

But one good thing about having no past was that he could make the future anything he wanted. And whatever that looked like, he wanted Miss Ivelisse Garcia to be a part of it.

CHAPTER 11

The next morning, Lisa sat at her small dining table, stirred her black tea with her new silver spoon, and watched the sun rise out her window. The spoon made her feel so fancy. Not that she needed *fancy*...but this spoon was one of the many reminders that God *saw* her. He *loved* her. And time after time, He gave her the desires of her heart.

From where she sat, she could almost see her whole house. The small parlor held a worn, cozy sofa and two overstuffed chairs. New fringed pillows she'd made from fabric scraps offered a cheery touch, and the faded rug added to the room's comfortable warmth. The cotton floral curtains were old, but she'd freshened them up with some ruffled edges in a coordinating blue. The stone fireplace made a lovely focal point, and she'd placed some mismatched china dishes along the mantel, along with some dried flowers.

Beyond the parlor, her small bedroom held a wooden bedframe carved with delicate roses. Small matching tables flanked either side of the bed. A white quilt, embroidered with burgundy roses and green leaves, was Lisa's favorite thing in the house. Lace curtains allowed soft, filtered light to stream in, and opposite the bed, a delicate, mirrored dressing table held a porcelain pitcher and basin.

She had everything she needed.

This morning, Lisa was up earlier than usual, dressed in her brown cotton twill riding skirt. If only she could wear the comfortable pants-like skirt every day, but that would be frowned upon. Still, she enjoyed the freedom it gave her to ride astride instead of side saddle—which she'd never mastered.

It had been a while since she visited the livery across the street to exercise the horses for Carson. That had been her unofficial job since she was old enough to ride a horse, and he'd patiently taught her how to mount, ride, and care for the horses. Why he'd taken such an interest in her, an orphan, she never understood. But honestly, she never gave it much thought. His interest was simply another way God chose to show His love for her.

She finished her tea, rinsed her cup and spoon, and set them on the sideboard to dry. The thought of riding added a bounce to her step. One day, maybe, she'd have her own horse.

When she entered the livery, Carson's face lit up. "There you are! I thought you'd abandoned me in favor of your other job."

She laughed. "Never. We've just been shorthanded, and time has been sparse."

"I know. But the horses miss you. Which one do you want to ride today? Take your pick. They're all itching for a trot."

She walked from stall to stall, rubbing her hand across muzzles and speaking lowly to each animal. She stopped at Fury's stall. "Can I ride her?"

"I don't see why not. As long as there's no gunfire to spook her. Shouldn't be a problem in this part of town."

Lisa felt a little guilty as she led the Appaloosa out of her stall. Jack should be the one riding her. But with his ribcage still healing, she was pretty sure Dr. Williamson wouldn't approve of that. Not yet.

Carson pointed out Fury's tack, and the mare stood perfectly still as Lisa got her ready. She was well trained, but when at last Lisa stepped into the stirrup and straddled the horse, Fury stomped her feet in excitement.

In the paddock, Fury trotted as close to the fence as possible, as if she wanted more than anything to run free. Clearly, the horse was holding back, yet she never once seemed out of control. Jack had trained her well.

She spent about a half hour riding in circles, taking advantage of the limited space. When she finally led Fury back to her stall, Lisa felt exhilarated. She couldn't wait to tell Jack she rode his horse.

She looked at her watch. 7:30 am. She'd better hurry if she wanted to see him. He had to be at his new job at nine.

A half hour later, she was dressed in her nursing clothes, her cap hastily pinned in place, taking the front steps to the orphanage two at a time.

Jack stood in the entryway, looking in the mirror and straightening his collar. He smiled when he saw her. "Good morning! How do I look? Do you think Mrs. Clark will approve?"

Lisa took a moment to catch her breath from her hurried walk. When she finally settled her gaze on him, she lost her breath again.

How did he get even more handsome with each day? She pressed her lips into a sly grin. "You'll do."

Jack tried to look offended but then laughed. "I suppose I'm grateful for that. I also need to find a barbershop. My hair looks kinda scraggly."

She didn't see a problem with his hair. As a matter of fact, now that he'd drawn her attention to it, an urge to touch the thick golden waves in the guise of putting them in place nearly overpowered her. But she restrained herself. "I think your hair is fine, but there's a barbershop on the corner, just past Joske and Sons. Or..." She paused. Should she offer?

"Or...what?" His eyes held hers, waiting for her to finish the thought.

She sighed. She'd have to offer now. "I could cut it. When you grow up in an orphanage, you learn to do a lot of things for yourself. I've cut the other orphans' hair...and Papa's. I mean...if you want me to."

He glanced at the wall clock. "Could you do it now? I'd really like to look my best, since it's my first day and all."

"Of course." Shuffling sounds came from upstairs. Any minute, the children would head down for breakfast. "Let me grab some scissors. Meet me on the back porch."

Soon, she had him seated on a ladder-backed chair, an old sheet draped around his shoulders. She held a rat's tail comb between her teeth while she ran her fingers through his hair. Oh, my.

She'd never enjoyed anything more. This felt awkward and intimate and exciting, and her heart thrummed in her ears. Could he hear it?

After a few deep, concentrated breaths, she forced her mind toward the goal—a haircut. She measured this curl, then the next, trimming each piece to match that around it, making sure it lay right. It didn't take long before she dusted off the sheet and handed him a small handheld mirror. "What do you think?"

He turned one way, then the other, reaching up to touch his golden locks. His eyes met hers in the mirror. "You're truly a woman of many talents. I'm impressed."

She flipped the sheet off his shoulders and shook it into the wind. "Thank you. I do what I can."

He stood. He still had a few minutes before he needed to

leave. He grabbed the other end of the sheet and helped her fold it.

Lisa cleared her throat. "I went to the livery this morning."

"Really? Why?"

"I ride the horses there for exercise. I've been doing that since I was ten. Carson's always been great. He knew I was interested in horses, so he taught me how to care for them. He let me spend my free time there and do what I could."

"That's nice."

"I haven't had much time to do it recently, but this morning, I got up early..."

He nodded. "Sounds like a pleasant way to start the day."

"I rode Fury."

He froze. Was he mad? Had she crossed a line?

But he didn't look upset. Only curious. "How was she?"

"She's a delight. You did a wonderful job training her." She placed the scissors, mirror, and sheet in a stack and scooped them up.

"Hmm. I wondered about that, considering she threw me."

"Well, there wasn't any gunfire this morning." She almost winked, then caught herself. That might seem flirtatious.

"I'd like to watch you ride her, if that's okay. I'm anxious to ride her myself, but I'm not sure I could make it into the saddle yet."

A flush warmed her cheeks at the thought of Jack watching her. But she was being silly. He wanted to observe the horse, not her. "When would you like to go?"

"This afternoon?"

She hesitated before answering. "You'll work all morning, and you're not used to being up and about for more than a couple of hours at a time. Why don't we see how you feel when you get home?"

"Good point. And speaking of work, I'd better get moving.

The last thing I want is for Mrs. Clark to punish me for being late my first day."

"That would be awful."

They held gazes for a moment before she looked away. This man did funny things to her heart. Pleasant things... but it wouldn't be pleasant when he regained his memory and recalled a girlfriend or fiancée from his past. Or another life that didn't include her. As much as she told herself to proceed with caution, her heart seemed to have other ideas.

He shifted from one foot to the other. "Well...goodbye. Thanks again for the haircut."

"Have a good first day."

And with that, he was gone. And she was left on the back porch, holding the scissors and comb and trying to sort out her mixed-up feelings.

~

For the first time since he awoke from the accident, Jack wasn't focused on the dull throbbing in his ribs with each movement. It was still there, but today, as he walked to work, something else took up the whole of his thoughts.

Lisa's fingers in his hair.

That she was unaffected was clear. She moved her fingers here and there, measuring, snipping, combing... She was doing a job. But with each stroke, each touch, something like electricity coursed through his veins. He wanted to reach up and pull her into his lap, wrap his arms around her and kiss her, but thankfully, despite his memory loss, he knew that would not be okay. Still, if she only realized what her touch did to him, she would have stopped. Probably slapped him. Never spoken to him again.

He was falling for this woman. Truth was, he'd already fallen hard. And he was in no position to court her.

Which set his mind spinning in an effort to come up with a plan. How could he become worthy of her attention? He had a job. That was a step. But as hard as he planned to work, something told him that *department store clerk* was not his true calling in life.

Right now, it was his only option.

Jack nodded to a man on the street who'd tipped his hat at him, then sank back into his thoughts. He needed a strategy. He needed to figure out what he was good at. Just thinking about it dredged up that infernal headache, and he *didn't* need that right now, at the beginning of a new job. *Think pleasant thoughts.*

But the most pleasant thought he could find was the feel of Lisa's fingers in his hair...and that brought distraction that was certainly not conducive to concentrating on work. He turned his mind to Fury.

He was anxious to get to know the animal. So far, she was the best key he had to his past. After work, he'd eat some lunch, take a nap, then head to the livery with Lisa. For now, that was the most long-term plan he could handle. He arrived at Joske and Sons, did his best to clear his mind of Lisa, and pushed through the glass door that led to his new job.

~

Lisa wasn't sure what to do with herself now that Jack was gone. What was a nurse with no patient? She'd updated Jack's chart and read the articles Dr. Williamson had given her about working with amnesia patients, and now she was left twiddling her fingers.

She walked to the hospital. The quarantine sign was still on the door, so she didn't go in. She should probably see how she could help at the orphanage, but until yesterday, she hadn't taken time off since late May. For her own sanity, she needed to take advantage of this chance to just breathe.

Her feet wandered, almost of their own accord, back to the river where she first met Jack. The hydrangeas were still in bloom, so she broke off several full purple-blue blossoms. The black-eyed Susans had awakened since her last visit. She admired them but left them alone. They tended to wilt by the time she put them in a vase.

Before long, she found herself at her favorite resting spot—a large flat rock nestled in the shade of a weeping willow, right on the edge of the water. She unlaced her sensible, ugly nursing shoes and set them aside, inched up her skirt, and rested her feet in the cool, gurgling stream. She leaned against the tree trunk and just listened to the sound of peace.

All around her, a symphony of frogs click-clicked a peaceful chorus. In the oak tree to her right, two redbirds hopped from branch to branch. She watched them for a time, then closed her eyes, letting the soft sounds lull her spirit.

God, I'm tired. But it's a good kind of tired.

For a moment, she felt guilty about not spending more focused time with God recently. But just as quickly, the guilt dissipated. In the past days, she'd carried on a start-and-stop conversation with the Almighty, with quick snatches of thought-prayers as they entered her mind. God understood.

Please help Nurse Jacobs and Phyllis get better. Soon.

She paused, trying to form the right concepts in her mind, even though she knew God heard her heart even when the words failed.

My feelings for Jack confuse me. He's so handsome...but it's more than that. How can I be drawn to a man who doesn't know who he is? There's something about him...something about his spirit that calls to me. As much as I try to stay professional, I know I'm falling hard. If he's not good for me, change my heart before it gets broken.

Heal his mind and his memories. And if it's okay, I think I'd really like to be a part of his future.

Was she crazy to fall for a man with no past? Maybe. But it helped to talk things out with God. Philippians 4 said, *make your requests known to God.*

But the next verse didn't promise fulfillment of those requests. It promised peace. Sitting here, baring her soul to her Maker, she did feel peace—even if she didn't have any idea what lay in store.

CHAPTER 12

By the time Jack left work at noon, his arm ached. His ribs throbbed. But his spirits felt better than he had since he woke up from the accident. At least today, he'd taken a step toward independence. He'd worked hard. He'd learned how operate a cash register and how to greet customers.

Mrs. Clark was cool and professional in a clipped, better-than-you way. She didn't mention the incident with Lisa the day before, and neither did he. He just respectfully listened to her instructions and tried to help as best he could, considering his injuries. He even sold a pair of pants to a man who came in knowing exactly what he needed, and he helped a mother and her young son choose a pair of shoes.

But now he was exhausted, which frustrated him to no end. Who got tired after three hours of soft labor?

When he arrived back at the orphanage, the children were already seated around the large dining table, their chatter echoing through the halls. He waved as he passed, then slipped into the kitchen. Hopefully, he could eat a few bites there and escape the din of questions they'd have about his morning. Lisa was there, her back to him, arranging flowers in a milk pitcher.

"Beautiful," he breathed, before he realized he said the word out loud.

She turned. "They are, aren't they? I picked them near the river—the same place where you and I met."

He didn't correct her on the object of his admiration. "I'd like to visit there."

Her face lit up. "It's my favorite place. Maybe we can plan a picnic there. Tomorrow afternoon?"

"Sounds perfect."

"How was your day? Sit down. Let me fix you something to eat, and you can tell me about it."

The energy it took to talk over the echo of children's voices coming from the next room taxed him, but at least it was balanced with the pleasure of spending time with Lisa. He shared the highlights of his morning between bites of green bean and ham.

Her eyes held concern. "You've pushed yourself, I can tell. You should rest. Maybe we should go to the livery another day."

"No! I want to go. I want to watch you ride Fury. Just give me a couple of hours to lie down, and I'll be fine."

She leveled a look at him, as if judging his well-being.

He grinned. "You've got that scary nurse expression."

Her mouth dropped open. "Scary? I'm not sure how to take that."

"I think any good nurse keeps a good dose of intimidation in her back pocket. You just pulled yours out."

She laughed, then scrunched her face into an ominous expression.

It was his turn to laugh. "It doesn't work if you try too hard. Now you just look cute."

She grinned, and a pretty blush crept into her cheeks. "That wasn't the look I was aiming for."

He laughed again, and it caused his head to hurt more. How

could your head hurt and your heart sing at the same time? That's what she did. She made his heart happy.

"Thank you for the meal. I'll go rest. If I don't feel better after a nap, we won't go. But if I do, we will. Deal?"

There was that look again, as though she wasn't sure if she should agree to something that might not be in his best interest. "We'll see."

"You're a tough one."

"That's my job. Can I get you anything else? Would you like something to help you sleep?"

"Goodness, no! You'll have me sleeping until tomorrow morning." He stood, walked his plate to the sink, and leaned against the counter. "Thank you for all you've done for me." He really needed his bed. He pushed his weight forward and trudged out of the kitchen, down the hall, and into his room where he nearly fell onto the mattress.

The next thing he knew, he jerked awake. The remnants of a dream echoed in his thoughts—and this time, they were more vivid.

The same man was there, though he couldn't see the face. Jack was a child, maybe six or seven years old. The man's voice was the same as the last dream. Only this time, he yelled, "You little idiot! You left the gate open. Again! You are killing me, boy. I mean it. Do you see all those cows in the road? That's just the ones we can see. Who knows how many are down in the woods somewhere, or off on somebody else's property?"

He got down on one knee, held a finger in Jack's face. "When I lie cold in that grave, boy, you'd better not shed one tear. Are you listening to me? Not. One. Tear. Because you'll be the one who put me there."

Jack's head pounded. What time was it? Four p.m.? Five? He shifted, rubbed a hand across his face, then pushed himself to a seated position. That's when he realized he'd fallen asleep with his shoes on.

Good thing. It saved him time now. The question was, would his nurse-protector send him back to bed? Was it too late to visit the livery?

Hopefully not. He needed the distraction from this most recent nightmare. A sense of urgency pushed him forward. He had to figure out how to unlock his past, and right now, that horse held his only key.

~

Lisa looped her hand through Jack's arm, trying to ignore the thrill his touch sent. She'd gone home and changed back into her riding clothes after lunch. But when his nap went on for four hours, she'd thought they may have to postpone.

She studied his profile, looking for signs of exhaustion or stress. "Remember, this is a short visit. The minute your head starts hurting again, we're leaving."

"Aye-aye, Cap'n." Despite his wrinkled clothes, his grin assured her he felt refreshed after his nap.

At the livery, Carson greeted her with his gentle smile. "Twice in one day? I must have done something right."

"Mr. Carson, you remember Jack?"

"I do." The older man reached a welcoming hand toward Jack. "No need for formalities. You can call me Carson."

Jack gripped it in a strong handshake. "Nice to see you again, sir. I'd like to spend more time with my horse."

"She'll be glad to see you, I'm sure. Take your time. I'll be in the back."

When Fury spotted them, she whinnied in pleasure, and Lisa dug in her pocket and pulled out some sugar cubes. "Here you go," she said, and placed them in Jack's hand instead of feeding them to the horse.

Maybe as the animal took the treat from his flattened palm,

it would bring him a flash of memory. If it did, he didn't let on. His expression remained stoic, unreadable.

Lisa ran her hand down Fury's neck. "Want to go for another ride, girl? This will make two today." She led the horse out of the stall toward the various sets of tack hanging on the back wall, chose Fury's, and began to ready the animal.

Jack just watched. Even if he'd wanted to help, his injuries still limited what he could do. But then, his countenance changed. Did he remember something?

"You need to slide her saddle back some. It's too far forward." He motioned with his hand where the saddle needed to go.

"Really?"

"The lowest part of the saddle needs to sit at the lowest part of her back. Otherwise it will be uncomfortable for her...and for you."

Lisa looked at him, a slight smile parting her lips. "Another clue."

His face registered a series of expressions she couldn't quite identify as he processed this information.

"I don't know how I know that," he said. "But I'm sure I'm right."

She adjusted the saddle, put her foot in the stirrup, and climbed up. "Can you lead us to the paddock?"

He took up the reins and led them out the side door into the exercise yard, then handed them to her. "I'll watch from here."

She nodded and directed Fury into a trot. The ride was smooth—the saddle placement did make a difference.

Jack stepped into the yard a few feet. "Try using your feet to direct her instead of the reins."

Lisa kept the reins steady and gently nudged the horse's flank with her left foot. The mare turned to the right. She tried it with her right foot, and the horse turned left. "Wow! I thought I was a decent rider. But you clearly know what you're doing. Hopefully, you'll be able to ride her yourself soon."

He walked back to the fence and leaned against it, arms crossed, face full of concentration.

After a couple of loops around the paddock, she directed the horse back toward the stable. "I think that's enough for today."

Jack followed her inside and silently did what he could to undress Fury.

Lisa respected his need for quiet. He'd talk when he was ready. In silence, they replaced the tack and urged Fury back into her stall. She gave the horse a couple more sugar cubes and closed the gate.

They made the short trip back to the orphanage in silence. Once there, Jack sat in one of the porch rockers and motioned for her to sit in the other one.

"I know about horses. I can't come up with any specific memories...but the knowledge is there. I'm certain of it."

She said nothing. Didn't want to interrupt his train of thought.

"I'd like to ride her. I'll go easy, but I think sitting in the saddle may stir something up." He moved his gaze from somewhere in the distance to her face, waiting for a response.

"I'll talk to Dr. Williamson. I can't let you do that without his permission, but hopefully, he'll be okay with it. As long as you're careful."

He nodded, then retreated back into his thoughts. She sat there with him, gently sending up prayers and wondering...if he found his past, what would that mean for their future?

CHAPTER 13

June 23, 1898
Lampasas, Texas

Riley folded the newspaper and pushed it across the breakfast table, toward Emma. "Apparently, when the cavalry arrived in Florida to set sail for Cuba, they didn't calculate the space they needed for the horses. The animals were left behind."

Emma's jaw dropped. "What? I don't understand. It's Jackson's skill on horseback that's given me hope for his safety. He'll be fighting on foot?" A trickle of sweat glistened on her forehead.

Riley stood and crossed the room to open a window. "It seems so. They trained as cavalry but will fight as infantry."

Emma rested her face in her hands for a moment, then dropped them to her lap. "I don't know what to say."

"Just keep praying."

"I haven't stopped."

A thumping noise under the table told him his wife's foot

bounced out of control. Her nervous habit was both endearing and telling.

"Why don't we head over to Allison and Colt's with something delicious from the inn?" Food might comfort his brother and sister-in-law. The task would also temporarily occupy his wife's nervous energy and help her feel as though she were doing something, when there was little to be done.

"Excellent idea. I'll get started on that right now." Her chair scraped against the wood floor, and her skirt rustled as she hurried from the room.

He watched out the window as she jogged the distance across their yard to the back porch of the Big Skye Inn. She would summon the chef, and soon she'd have several baskets of deliciously prepared meals ready for transport. It would surely be more than one couple could consume...but Emma Stratton wasn't known for doing things partway. He only hoped that if his brother was there when they arrived, his temper would be under control.

An hour later, they pulled up in front of Riley's childhood home. Allison sat on the porch, handkerchief in hand, eyes red and swollen. Emma jumped from the wagon and bounded up the stairs. She knelt in front of her sister-in-law and wrapped her arms around the woman.

"I guess you saw the paper?" Allison said, choking back a sob.

"We did." Emma's voice was low and soothing. To think, Allison once did all she could to keep Emma and Riley apart. Emma had more grace than anyone Riley knew.

Allison watched as Riley clutched a basket in each hand. "I can only imagine what that is. You're always so kind."

"Just a bit of comfort food," Emma told her. "It won't solve anything, but I hope it provides a temporary distraction."

"Thank you." Allison's eyes followed Riley up the porch stairs. "Colt's in his study."

Riley nodded and continued to the kitchen, where the latest maid—he couldn't recall this one's name—said she'd take care of the items. Riley left them with her and made his way through the wide hallway to Colt's study—once their father's study. It was hard to be in that room without dredging up bad memories. But that was all far in the past. Right now, he needed to offer what little comfort he could to his brother.

Colt sat behind the desk, leaned back in his chair, his eyes set in a lost gaze out the window. The open newspaper was splayed across the desktop.

Riley cleared his throat, and Colt's head came around, slow, as though he was in a daze. "Oh. Hi." His watery eyes told Riley all he needed to know. Colt never cried. He yelled. He hit things. But cry?

Wow. What could Riley even say?

"Hey."

Colt turned his head again, in that same, slow movement, shifting his gaze back out the window. "I can't fix this, Riley. I have as much money as any man I know. I have friends in some of the most powerful positions in the United States. I have favors to call in. People owe me things. But there's not a blasted thing I can do to bring my son home safe."

For a long time, the only sound in the room was the tick-ticking of the grandfather clock. After a while, Riley said, "Emma brought pie."

Colt let out a halfhearted chuckle, swiped the back of his hand across his eyes, and swiveled his chair to face his brother. "What kind?"

"I'm not sure. Let's go find out."

The next week brought a more rapid recovery—at least physically. The first three days of working part time were hard. But after that, the increased movement seemed to work out some of the kinks in Jack's muscles. His energy increased. In a way, he felt more clear-headed.

Friday afternoon, Jack sat on the side of his bed, shirt off, while Dr. Williamson examined him.

"Lift your arm."

Jack lifted it as far as he could, which was higher than last week.

"Twist your torso to the left, as far as you can. Good. Now to the right. That's good."

Letting out a slow, quiet breath, Jack waited for the verdict. He still felt some pain, but it was nothing like what it had been. And he really, *really* wanted the go-ahead to ride Fury.

"All right. You can get in the saddle, but only for a slow walk around the paddock. Too much jostling could lead to a major setback. Understood?"

Jack smiled so big, he could feel the stretch in his cheeks. "Understood."

"Get dressed. I believe there's a pretty nurse waiting to take you to see your horse." The man stood and replaced his medical instruments into his bag. "I hope it stirs up some recollections. Keep me posted." He shut the door behind him, leaving Jack to care for his own needs.

Each day brought more physical independence, but he wouldn't feel totally free until his brain was healed. Once he was presentable, he stepped into the hallway. There was Lisa, resting against the opposite wall, a cat-ate-the-canary grin on her face.

"Dr. Williamson told me the good news. The children have a surprise they've been saving for this moment."

"Really?"

"Come with me."

She led him down the hallway into the dining room, where he was greeted by a chorus of "Surprise!" and "Hooray!" and "Congratulations!"

Strung across the far wall was a banner—a string with multiple pages clipped to it. "We've been working on these for days!" Lucy grabbed him by the hand and pulled him to the banner. "This one's mine."

She pointed to a juvenile picture of a spotted horse. Under the picture it said, *I hop yor memry comes bak.*

"Thank you," he told her. He studied a few other pictures and notes before saying, "Thank all of you."

The children cheered again. Tiny arms encircled his waist. Lydia clung to him, looked up at him with her soft smile, and whispered, "I love you, Jack."

His heart melted, and he knelt and looked her in the eye. "I'm honored to have you say that, Lydia. I love you too. And all your brothers and sisters here." His gaze swept the room. "I don't believe I could have recovered so quickly at any other place."

Lisa held a hand up and called the room to order. "Okay, children. Jack's had enough excitement for right now. Everyone back to your classes."

A series of groans brought another smile to Jack's face. Yes, they were excited for him, but this was as much about getting out of schoolwork as it was about his recovery.

Once the room was cleared out, Lisa put her hands on her hips. "Ready?"

"I've been ready. Let's go!"

~

As ready as he'd been, Lisa watched Jack in the paddock, straddling Fury's saddle with a look not unlike fear on his face. What was he thinking? What was happening in his mind? Never would she have imagined her nursing duties would require her to oversee a horse-riding session.

"Do you want me to lead, or would you rather do this on your own?"

He shook his head. "I've got it. Just give me a minute."

She stepped out of the way but kept her eyes focused on his expression. Dr. Williamson had told her to watch both for signs of physical pain and emotional exhaustion. She wasn't sure what the latter might look like, but she'd do her best.

Soon, Jack leaned forward and said something low into Fury's ear. The horse must have understood because she nodded her head. It was amazing what these animals could comprehend.

He nudged her with his foot, as he'd taught Lisa to do, and the horse moved forward, gentle and slow, as though she knew her rider wasn't at his best. Lisa hopped up onto the fence without regard for what might be considered ladylike. To keep her eye on Jack, she needed to watch from a higher vantage point.

Sounds from the street provided a nice, easy background for the session as Jack and Fury got to know one another again. After about ten minutes, Lisa relaxed. Jack was doing just fine. She let her attention wander to a low bush of mint, next to the building, where several honeybees took turns circling and landing. Did they have a hive close by? And maybe some honey?

Something in her peripheral changed, and she looked back at Jack, sucking in a breath at what she saw. Jack was *standing* on the saddle, and Fury trotted along as if it were the most normal thing in the world.

She couldn't cry out. Jack might fall. Had he lost his mind? Had his concussion caused more mental damage than they'd realized?

She slid down from her perch. "Jack..." She fought to keep her voice calm. "What are you doing?"

He didn't answer her. Just kept riding, fully erect, with a crazy grin on his face.

"Jack, I need you to get down. You'll hurt yourself. This isn't what we agreed to."

He let out a low whoop. "I know. But this is great!"

"Jack...no. It's not great. It's dangerous. You don't want to injure yourself more, do you? Nice and easy...you need to sit back down in the saddle."

He met her eyes for a moment, flashed a mischievous smile. "I'm okay. I'm not going to fall."

She was just about to run for Carson when Jack bent his knees, lowered himself into the saddle, and reined Fury to a stop in front of her.

She exhaled, and it felt like all the breath left her. Very few times in her life had she been stunned into silence...but she was now. She couldn't even find words.

Jack brought one leg across the saddle before sliding to the ground in front of her. "It's all right. I'm okay. I'm more worried about you right now than anything."

That's when a million words—none of them pleasant—flooded her mind. When she got him home, she'd shower him with a good many of them. For now, they needed to get Fury back into her stall. And she needed to get him to a padded room.

CHAPTER 14

The following afternoon, Jack sat at the kitchen table across from Lisa, Dr. Williamson, and Father Hidalgo. He felt like he was in the Spanish Inquisition. And it irked him that he could remember everything about the Spanish Inquisition yet still couldn't recall anything concrete about his life before he came here.

Father Hidalgo spoke in his soothing, broken English. "Tell me one more time, Jack. What led you to feel the need to stand up in the saddle?"

Jack shrugged. "I don't know. It just felt...right. As though it was something I'd done with Fury a thousand times before. And I must have! She didn't flinch. I know it sounds crazy. But somehow, I knew just how to do it."

Lisa ran her finger back and forth across a dent in the worn tabletop. "When we went earlier this week, you instructed me on saddle placement and leading with my foot. You clearly have a deep knowledge of horses and riding. And considering you came here to be part of Roosevelt's cavalry, I wonder if you were a riding instructor of some kind."

"Maybe." Jack sighed. "But I just can't remember. It's like I know stuff, but I don't remember how I learned it."

Dr. Williamson scribbled something in a folder and shut it. "Standing up in a saddle is odd behavior, for sure, but it's not unheard of. I believe this gives us reason to hope. I'm prescribing an hour of riding each afternoon. Keep going to your job in the mornings, come home and rest, and then ride. Who knows what else you may recall. But please...be careful. I'd really rather not start over with you, with more broken ribs."

"Me either, sir. I'd like to leave the paddock, though. I felt confined yesterday."

The doctor shook his head. "Not yet. The limited space will keep you from going too fast or doing anything crazier than you did yesterday. Let's take it slow. We'll reevaluate things in a week.

Jack nodded, though reluctantly.

The two older men pushed back their chairs and dismissed themselves. Lisa and Jack stayed in the kitchen.

"You nearly gave me a heart attack," she said. Her eyes held part humor, part accusation.

"Yeah. Sorry about that."

"I forgive you. At least now I have a little warning that you might do something crazy."

"I could teach you..."

"No! Thank you, but no."

"Aww, come on. You're a natural in the saddle. I've never asked. Do you own a horse?"

"No, but I've always wanted to. And Carson has always been so kind to me. The livery was my second home as a child. He taught me to care for the horses and how to ride them in the paddock, but my whole life has been spent within these few blocks—other than a brief time for nurse's training. I haven't needed my own horse. Even the orphanage doesn't have one. Father rents a horse and buggy when needed."

"You may be right. Maybe I was a riding instructor." Jack ran his fingers through his hair, leaving it sticking up in odd spikes. "But where? Are there any places near here that offer riding lessons?"

"You're not from around here, remember? You asked me for directions."

"Oh, yeah."

They both sat there, elbows on the table, trying to puzzle out this new piece of insight into Jack's past. After a time, Lisa stood. "Well, you heard the doctor. An hour a day. We'd better get going."

He didn't have to be told twice. Yesterday's jaunt was the first time he'd felt like himself—whoever that was—since his accident.

~

For Jack, the next days settled into a comfortable routine. Work in the mornings. Back to the orphanage for lunch and a nap. An hour of riding, then home for dinner, and back to bed. He still felt like something of an invalid, but at least he was out and moving around now.

Still, he wanted more. He'd saved up a little money from his job. He offered Father Hidalgo some of it to cover his expenses, but the man wouldn't hear of it. He tried to pay Dr. Williamson, but the doctor told him Roosevelt had set up an account to cover his expenses, since he was injured during a training exercise. He had no place to send money home to...so he saved it.

He stowed all his cash and coins in a damaged cigar box he brought from the department store. At some point, he'd need some money.

He lay in his bed, staring at the ceiling, listening to the children play outside his window. Each day, the twins continued to check on him like miniature nurses. If only he could do something for the orphans, to make their lives a little brighter.

That's when it hit him. He could give riding lessons! Why hadn't he thought of it sooner? He'd developed a pretty solid relationship with Carson. Maybe there was a way to use the paddock for lessons. He'd talk to the man today.

Right now, as a matter of fact. He had another hour before his daily riding appointment. But now that the idea was brewing, he couldn't take it back to a simmer.

He sat up, slipped into his boots, and studied the worn, stitched leather. They looked expensive. Why hadn't he thought to examine them before? He tucked that thought aside, ran a comb through his hair, and scribbled a note to Lisa to meet him at the livery. He closed the door on the page, leaving it sticking out where she'd see it. Then he made the short trip with more bounce in his step than he'd felt in a long time.

Carson greeted him with a handshake. "You're early today. Where's your partner?"

"I wanted to talk to you alone."

"Oh...is there a problem?"

"Not at all. It's just...even though I'm still struggling with my memory, I know horses. I know riding. And I was wondering if it would be possible to give riding lessons to the children from the orphanage."

The man's face lit up like a fireworks display. "I think that's an excellent idea! Of course, I'm only part owner. We'll have to clear it with the other owner...and that may take a little time. I'll see what I can do on my end and get back with you when I know something."

Jack's shoulders sagged. He'd hoped for a clear yes, for permission to start tomorrow. But if there was one thing he was learning in this odd season of his life, it was patience. The only way to build patience was to wait for something you wanted right now.

And right now, patience-building was turning into his life story.

~

Emma sat in Papa's office twisting the small sheet of paper in her hands. Dr. Williamson's message that he needed to meet with her privately—that he didn't have a lot of time and could she please be waiting for him—had her unhinged. Had she done something wrong? Was she in trouble? The doctor had never requested a private meeting before. If he needed to speak with her, he simply took her aside. Their conversations rarely lasted more than a few sentences.

Why did he need an office? Why the special message?

The door opened, and Papa leaned in. "The doctor is here. I'll leave the door cracked open for propriety."

That he'd be concerned about propriety between herself and a man in his fifties showed Papa's protective heart toward her. He had the same love for all his "children," but Lisa knew she was special. She was his family, and he was her Papa.

A moment later, Dr. Williamson entered and sat behind the desk in Papa's chair. "Thank you for being ready."

"Certainly, sir. I hope I haven't done anything—"

"Oh, no! I'm sorry if my message caused you concern. I have good news. Our cholera patients are recovering well. I'm hoping to reopen the hospital in about a week. Since Jack has shown such remarkable improvement—in no small part due to your excellent efforts—I'd like to move you back to your main post. You'll still come here each afternoon to check on Jack. I don't want to move him from the orphanage. He seems comfortable here, and Father Hidalgo has agreed to let him stay. But I'll lean heavily on you at the hospital until your colleagues return to their full strength. I'll start them each with just a few hours a day, much like Jack's work schedule."

Lisa's mind reeled as she took in the information. She was happy her friends were recovering—the outcome could have been very different. She was glad to return to the hospital...but truth be told, she'd become spoiled to her schedule of the last few weeks. Getting to spend each day in her childhood home with Papa, with the children...with *Jack*...she'd miss it.

But Dr. Williamson was right. This was good news. "That sounds...wonderful. One week, you said? Is there anything I should do to prepare for the reopening?"

"Not at the moment. I'll limit the patients until we have a full working staff. In a few days, I may need you to help ready the beds with fresh linens, check the supplies, and do some other preparations. Doris will be available to help you, but as you know, she's a volunteer. You'll be the only full-time nurse with formal training for a while. Because of that, I'd like to make you temporary head nurse. Do you think you can handle that?"

Honestly, she didn't know. As a new nurse, she hadn't really thought about advancing yet. But she wouldn't tell him that. "I'll do my best, sir. Thank you for your faith in me."

"I know these last weeks have been taxing, and you've worked far more hours than anyone should be required to work. I appreciate your willingness to do what's needed. When this is all behind us, I'll make sure you're rewarded with a nice vacation."

"That's not necessary, sir. I'm just glad to help."

The doctor nodded, thanked her again, and excused himself. His footsteps retreated down the hallway. He and Papa spoke to one another. Then Papa's familiar, heavier footsteps approached.

He entered the office and plopped into his chair. "Good news, I hope?"

"Yes. The hospital will reopen soon."

Papa's face fell, just a little. "I've enjoyed having you here. It's almost felt like old times."

"Me too." She leaned forward to stand, but Papa motioned for her to sit back down.

"Don't leave. I need to talk to you."

How much more news could she take? "What about?"

"Why the wrinkled brow, my dear? The news is good."

"That's what Dr. Williamson said. But his news involves me being the new temporary head nurse. I'm not sure I'm ready for that responsibility."

"Don't be silly. You're the most capable, intelligent young woman I know. He may make your position a permanent one."

"Oh, goodness, I hope not! I still have much to learn."

"Your humility becomes you, my dear. If God gives you a responsibility, He will equip you to fulfill it."

She wasn't sure Papa's—or Dr. Williamson's—confidence was well-placed. But as she'd told the doctor, she'd do her best. "What did you want to tell me, Papa?"

"Oh, sorry. As I said, it is good news. You know that Pastor Smith left everything to you in his will."

"Yes. I'm so grateful for my home."

"Well, there's more." The smile on his face got bigger. "He set up a trust for you, which you'll have access to when you turn twenty-one. Your birthday is coming up this fall."

"A—a trust fund?" What could that mean? The old pastor wasn't a wealthy man. What could he have possibly left her besides the house?

"That's right. In addition to being a minister, he owned half of a local business. He was a silent partner. He invested money in the beginning, and the other man invested his knowledge and skill. All these years, Pastor Smith's share of the profits have been set aside for you. It's amassed into a tidy little sum."

She opened and closed her mouth several times, trying to form words, but none would come.

Papa leaned back in his chair and watched her, giving her time to process.

"How much?"

"In the beginning, the business didn't turn much of a profit. Don't get too excited...you're not an heiress in the sense that you can quit your job and buy a mansion."

"Okay. But how much?"

Papa smiled. "You have around two thousand dollars."

She popped out her chair. "Two thou—what? That's more money than I make in a year as a nurse! Two...two thousand dollars?"

"Sit back down. There's more."

"More?" Her pitch lifted an octave. "How could there be more? I can't handle more, Papa. This is too much." Her voice shook with emotion, and her eyes moistened. She didn't deserve such goodness.

Dropping into the chair, she shut her eyes and tried to recall what her nurse's training had taught her about calming an overly excited patient so she could use it on herself. She sucked in a long, slow breath, counted to ten, then exhaled just as slowly. After repeating that a few times, she opened her eyes and looked at Papa. "Okay, tell me."

"You own half of the business. So you'll continue to receive profits."

With all the books she'd read in her lifetime, how was it possible that she couldn't find one word to respond? Not a single word. Her heart pounded in her ears. Heat spread in her neck and face, and she knew if she had a mirror, she'd see red splotches. She always got red splotches when her emotions ran high.

Outside, a wagon rumbled past. From the next room, the children raised their voices, reciting a poem they'd memorized. All around her, life continued as usual. But this...this changed everything about who she was, or who she thought she was.

She had money.

She was a business owner.

It didn't seem real.

She tried to gather her thoughts into some coherent pile.

Papa just looked at her, arms crossed, with that sweet half smile he gave her so often when he was waiting for her attention.

All of a sudden, she found her words. One sentence, precisely. "What is the business?"

CHAPTER 15

July 5, 1898
Lampasas, Texas

Riley watched his wife's expressions change as she read the article, then read it again, then looked at Riley, her face drained of color.

July 1, 1898

The Lampasas Leader Volume 10, No. 32

On June 27, General Joseph Wheeler officially notifies the war department that Americans dead in Friday's battle number 22 and the wounded and missing about 80. Thirty-nine Spanish dead bodies have been found, but their loss is believed to have been much heavier.

Sgt. Hamilton Fish, Jr. was the first man killed by the Spaniards. He lingered 20 minutes and gave a lady's watch to a comrade. He shot one Spaniard.

Captain Capron, after being mortally wounded, sent a parting message to his wife, then knelt down and shot two of the enemy.

Excepting Capron, who was buried at Juragua, the killed rough riders were buried Saturday morning on the battlefield. Their bodies, each wrapped in a blanket, were laid in one trench. Palm leaves lined the trench, and were heaped on them. Chaplain Brown read the solemn burial service of the Protestant Episcopal church, and as he knelt in prayer every trooper with bared head did likewise. The men sang "Nearer, My God, to Thee," the trench was covered and the chaplain marked the place. He has a complete record of where they lay.

They didn't have to speak. Riley felt what Emma was thinking. He couldn't have formed words even if he'd had any. The boulder in his throat—in his chest—made it impossible to talk.

Emma broke the silence. "We don't know for sure. Names haven't been released. He could be fine."

Riley struggled to swallow, to clear a way for speech. "You're right."

"We can't assume the worst. That's the opposite of hope. Until we know for sure, we'll keep praying. Keep believing God will protect Jackson—that he'll come home safe and sound."

Riley nodded. "We should check on Colt and Allison."

"I'll get my things."

Soon, they pulled into Colt's circle drive, not even bothering to see to the horses. Emma clutched a single box of chocolate chip cookies as Riley helped her down. After knocking, Riley didn't wait for an answer. Just opened the door and entered.

"Hello?" he called.

The maid entered from the direction of the kitchen. "Oh, hello. I...uhm..." She looked nervous, as though she might get in trouble for them being here unannounced.

Allison's voice echoed from the top of the stairway. "It's all right, Clara." She still wore her night clothes with a silk robe. Her hair was uncombed. "Colt and I will be down shortly. Make yourselves at home in the parlor. Clara, please get them some coffee."

"We don't mean to intrude, Allison. We just...wanted to be near you." Emma's voice trembled with emotion.

"No...I'm glad you're here." She looked as though she wanted to say more, but didn't. Just turned and disappeared in the direction of the master bedroom.

Emma handed Clara the box of cookies before the woman retreated to the kitchen. Riley took her hand, and together they entered the parlor where they'd shared some of their first moments of falling in love.

Allison had changed the decor since then. Still, if those walls could talk, they'd have a lot of stories to tell. Some happy. Too many of them, sad. Today, one of the saddest to date.

But no, Emma was right. He had to cling to hope. They didn't know for sure.

Even if Jackson was okay, twenty-two men—sons, husbands, fathers, friends—lay in a shallow grave in Cuba, wrapped only in a blanket and covered in palm leaves and dirt. Even more were missing—possibly dead without any kind of burial. It made Riley sick to think of it.

A short time later, Allison and Colt entered the parlor. Allison was now dressed, her hair combed and pulled back away from her drained face, and she looked a decade older than she was.

Colt looked even worse. He clutched the weekly paper in one hand. "I'm going."

"Going?" Riley asked. "To Cuba?"

"Yes. I have to see for myself."

Riley dropped into one of the overstuffed chairs, hoping Colt would do the same. "When?"

"As soon as possible."

This was a delicate matter, and Riley knew to proceed with caution. Somehow, he had to convince his brother without alienating him that this was not a good idea. "There's still a war going on, Colt."

Colt slammed the paper down on a side table. "I don't care what the bloody he—"

"Colt!" Allison put her hand on her husband's chest. "I can't handle this. Please."

Colt looked at his wife, then shifted his gaze to the family portrait over the fireplace. His lips were tight, the skin around them white. "I don't care what's going on down there. I need to get my son and bring him back."

Emma's voice, soft and soothing, broke into the tension. "I believe Jackson is fine, and that he will come home to us. Until we hear otherwise, we mustn't give up hope." She paused, let her words sink in.

Colt kept staring at that portrait. Allison dropped to the settee and placed her head in her hands. Fat tears fell beneath her, onto the expensive carpet.

Clara saved the moment by entering with a large tray holding a silver tea and coffee service, porcelain cups and saucers, and the cookies, now displayed on a china platter. She took turns asking each of them, "Coffee or tea?"

Riley didn't want anything, but he took some coffee and a cookie, anyway, just to have something to do with his hands. After Clara had served everyone, she left the tray on the center table and exited the room.

Emma, who had been in the chair next to Riley, moved next to Allison and placed a hand on her back. "I wish there were something I could do."

"Just being here is enough. Thank you for coming." Allison's voice sounded wooden, hollow.

They stayed there for a while, Colt resting one hip on the edge of the sofa, the rest of them sitting, sipping from their cups.

Once again, Emma spoke, her voice almost a whisper. "I'd like to share something I've learned, if that's okay. It's helped me get through some difficult times." She waited for permission to continue.

Allison offered a slight nod.

"There's no right or wrong way to wade through times of uncertainty. But during a very dark, bleak time in my life, God showed me that hope is the opposite of fear. Hope is the belief that good things are in store. Fear is the belief that bad things are coming. Over and over in the Bible, we're told not to fear. Time and again, we're told to hope in God. It's that reminder, that belief that God loves me and has good things waiting for me, that's gotten me through."

As Emma continued, Colt gradually turned his head toward her.

"I'm not being glib when I say that I choose to believe Jackson is okay. It's a choice for faith. It's a choice not to jump ahead. I read the papers, like this morning, and my stomach gets all in knots. But when I turn to God, I don't know... I don't know anything for sure. But this morning, as I've prayed, I have a peace. As though God is taking care of him, and he's okay."

Allison placed a hand on Emma's knee. "Thank you for that. Your faith has always been stronger than mine."

Riley set his cup aside, ready to intervene should Colt lose his temper as he was so prone to do.

Instead, Colt said, "I hope you're right." Then he stood, set his own cup on the mantel, and left the room. The front door opened and shut.

After a few minutes, Riley went in search of his brother. He found him in the stables, feeding one of the many thoroughbreds from a bucket of oats. "I hope Emma didn't say the wrong thing, Colt. Her faith is real."

"No. She didn't say anything wrong. I've always admired the faith both of you have. I wish I could find something like that for myself."

Riley rested his arms on the stall gate. "'Seek me and you will find me, when you seek me with all your heart.'"

"I guess that's the problem. I've never spent much time looking for God. Too many other things on my mind."

Riley wasn't sure how to respond to that, so he didn't. Instead, he focused on the horse. "You've always had the best horses. I can see why Jackson loves them so much."

Colt swiped his eyes. "That's all he wanted to do. That's why he left. I wanted him to live life on my terms, and he wanted to go his own way. I told him he needed to grow up. Take his rightful place as a cattleman, as the heir to Stratton Ranch. I said some awful things to him, Riley. When did I turn into our father?"

Riley remained silent.

"You don't have to answer that. I know I've made a lot of mistakes. And your family has been on the receiving end of a lot of them. I don't even know why you're here right now." His voice wobbled.

This was a side of Colt Riley hadn't seen. He wasn't sure what to do with it. He reached up, rested a hand on Colt's back. "Because you're my brother."

~

July 10, 1898

Jack looked at the sky. It was well past six o'clock. Where was Lisa? She was usually punctual. Hopefully, she'd found his note. He'd been riding for about half an hour, taking it easy. But the longer he rode, the more he felt the need to do something crazy. At least, Lisa would think it was crazy. But somehow, he felt confident in his ability and in his relationship with this horse.

Maybe it was time to just give in to his instincts. To stop

holding back. He urged Fury into a faster pace—as fast as she could go in the paddock. He twisted his left ankle around the stirrup, brought his other leg over the saddle, and leaned over the side, still holding the reins, until most of his body projected out in a ninety-degree angle from the horse.

His concentration was broken by a gasp somewhere in the background, but he ignored it. He had to remain focused, for his own safety and that of his horse. He took his time, found his rhythm, worked out the steps in his mind before pulling back up to a seated position. Then he reined Fury to a stop in front of Lisa, who stood on the other side of the paddock fence and looked as though she might lose her lunch.

He smiled, hoping she'd find the whole thing entertaining.

She did not.

"Get off the horse. *Now.*"

"Aww, come on. I'm fine! See?" He held up both hands so she could examine him. Considering the blaze in her eyes, he wasn't about to let on that his ribs were on fire. That particular trick really wasn't his best decision.

She pointed to the ground and stamped her foot. "Off!"

He heaved a sigh, patted Fury on the neck, and whispered, "Good girl." Then he swung out of the saddle and faced his nurse. His judge and jury.

"That was the stupidest thing I've ever seen. If you weren't already injured, I'd throttle you."

Lisa's fury reflected his horse's name, and he tried not to laugh at the irony.

"You think this is *funny?* I assure you, sir, it is not. It's one thing to care for a patient who is hurt by no fault of his own. It's another thing, entirely, for a person to intentionally put himself in danger. Your behavior leaves me concerned for both your mental *and* physical well-being. No more riding sessions. Period."

He stiffened. "I'm pretty sure you don't have the authority to make that decision."

"I'm pretty sure I do."

Jack wasn't amused anymore. He was a grown man, and he wasn't going to let some slip of a nurse dictate his actions. But then he noticed her face—all red and splotchy, and her eyes were shiny. Oh, man. Was she going to cry?

He didn't know how to deal with a crying woman. Especially not Lisa. She'd been so good to him, and here he was acting like a donkey's backside.

"Is everything all right?" Carson must have heard their voices, which had elevated more than Jack intended.

Jack looked at Lisa, and she looked at him, and neither said a word for a long moment. Then Jack said, "Yes, sir. Everything's fine. I was just finishing up here."

He led Fury out of the paddock, into her stall, and proceeded to undress her. His side was killing him. His head pounded. And his heart felt confused.

Despite all that, a small sense of hope built inside. He still had no specific memories of his life before the accident. But now he knew—somewhere, somehow, he'd learned to trick ride. Maybe he could contact some rodeos or traveling shows and see if they could help him with the missing puzzle pieces.

CHAPTER 16

Lisa followed Carson into the livery office and sat down. The man pulled a worn bandana from the pocket of his denim overalls and handed it to her, and she promptly blew her nose. "I'll wash this before returning it."

He chuckled and took the other chair. "Take your time. I've got plenty." He waited for her to take some deep breaths and regain her composure. "Want to talk about it?"

"I'm not sure. I know I acted unprofessionally out there. He's a patient, and I should have shown more restraint."

"Judging by the way you look at him, and the way he looks at you, he's more than just a patient."

That infernal blush took over, and Carson pointed a finger and nodded. "See? You can't deny it."

"Oh, Carson. I don't know what to do. I met him briefly before his accident, and now he can't remember anything from that time. It's absolutely wrong of me to have feelings for that man...but I do. Did you *see* him out there? He could have died."

"Yeah, I saw him. But Miss Lisa, you've gotta let a man be a man. And sometimes, well...we do things that seem foolish to you women. Appears to me, Jack's just trying to figure out who he is. And that horse is the only one who really knew him before his accident."

She nodded. "I know. You're right. I probably owe him an apology."

"I'm sure you two will work things out. You were just being who you are—a caring nurse. And today, that went against his chance to be who he is...who he's trying to figure out."

Her shoulders drooped. "I'm just feeling overwhelmed today. I've had so much to process. And then coming here and seeing him like that—anyway. I have something else to discuss with you."

He eyed her expectantly.

"Papa talked to me today. I can't believe it, Carson. All these years, and neither of you told me. I own half of the livery?"

"That's right. Knew he planned to talk to you soon, with your birthday coming up. It's been a closely guarded secret. Father Hidalgo wanted to keep you near. If you'd been adopted, your adoptive parents would have assumed control of your trust fund, and he could never have been sure it would be handled with your best interest in mind. I even looked into adopting you at one time, but that was a short journey. No one would have let a single black man adopt a little girl."

"Wow. It's starting to make sense now. I always wondered why I wasn't given a chance at adoption...but I never resented it, either. The orphanage was my family. Papa was my family. And Martha, and you."

Carson leaned back in his chair and looped his thumbs beneath his overall straps. "I'm glad you see it that way. It's how we felt, for sure and certain."

"It's a lot to take in. Papa thinks I should become a silent partner, as Pastor Smith was. He said that because I'm a woman, and because of my age, people might try to take advantage of my position."

"I have to say, I agree with him."

"I don't have a problem with that. I'm just so grateful. To you, to Papa...to God. To Pastor Smith, though I barely remember him." She brushed at her eyes, trying to push the moisture back. "I don't know what I've done to deserve something like this."

"That's the beauty of love. God chooses to love us even though we don't deserve it. It's not something we have to earn."

Emotion pumped thick through Lisa's veins. "True. Still, I don't feel worthy."

"None of us is worthy. But as far as worthiness goes, I think you're a pretty good choice."

"That's kind of you to say."

"So now that you're aware of your role in the company, I do have some business to discuss with you."

Lisa shook her head. "Please, no. I've had enough big news for one day. I don't think I can handle any more."

"I think this will make you happy. Before you arrived, Jack and I talked. He said he was interested in giving riding lessons to the orphans. I told him I'd discuss it with my partner."

Her jaw dropped. "Meaning...me?"

"That's right."

"Wow. I don't know. I mean, the children would love it, and it would be so good for them. But after what I've seen of Jack's riding style, I'm just not sure."

He nodded. "I see your point. How about I tell him that I need to observe him riding consistently in a safer, more conventional manner before I make a decision?"

"I...suppose that would at least give us some time to consider it. And allow Jack to prove he's not insane."

"You really think that? That he's insane?" Carson looked skeptical.

She huffed. "No. I don't. I've just never seen anyone act like that on a horse."

~

An hour later, frustration pulsed with every beat of Jack's heart. He lay on his bed, fully clothed. Outside his open window, a pesky squirrel chased a cardinal to another tree. He wished he could chase away his problems so easily.

If he had a place to go, he'd pack his things and leave. Not out of anger. He just wanted to track down who he was. He was tired of being a charity case. But he knew he wasn't ready...not yet. Here, he had Dr. Williamson and Father Hidalgo and...and Lisa, though he didn't know if she'd ever speak to him again, after his shenanigans.

And he had a job. Not his dream job, for sure. But he was earning a paycheck. He'd even found ways to feel useful here at the orphanage.

What he didn't have was a past. So far, the clues he'd been able to put together didn't make much sense. Was he some kind of circus performer? That didn't feel right. But his actions—his weird knowledge of trick riding, indicated...what?

In the past month, he'd listened to that voice in his head. God's voice. But he hadn't talked back. Maybe it was time.

If only he knew how to pray...

Uh, hey God. It's Jack. Jack who, I'm not really sure. But I guess You know, don't You? Since You're, uh...God. Thank You for taking care of me. For giving me this great place to stay, with these kind people. I'm really grateful.

But God, please help my brain wake up. Help me find out who I am. I'd really like to know.

Uhm... thanks.

Amen.

He lay there a few more minutes before a soft knock sounded at the door.

"Yeah?"

"It's me. Lisa. May I come in?"

He climbed off the bed, smoothed the covers, and opened the door. "Sure." He left the door wide, pulled out the desk chair for her, and sat back down on the mattress.

She fidgeted with her nurse's apron. "I wanted to apologize. I was harsh with you today. I know you're just doing your best, trying to figure things out."

"No. I'm the one who needs to apologize. I told Dr. Williamson I'd take it easy, and I didn't. It's your job to carry out his orders, and I made that difficult for you."

Lisa paused before answering. Sucked in a long, slow breath, as if measuring her next words. "You're very talented. It must have taken a lot of training to learn those tricks."

"It must have. I wish I could remember. I think that's why I need to see what all I can do. I'm hoping it will unlock something."

"That makes sense. But why don't you give your body a chance to heal a little more before trying anything else." She said it as a statement, not a question.

All the aches and pains he'd reawakened today confirmed the wisdom of her suggestion. "You're right. I won't do anything like that again until the doc gives me the go-ahead. I promise."

At first, doubt clouded her features. But a twinge of a grin started at one cheek, and she looked at him with those golden-honey eyes, and he wondered how he could ever be upset with her. "I'm just worried about you," she said.

"I know. And I appreciate that."

Neither said anything for a moment. Then she chuckled. "You nearly gave me a heart attack."

"I know." He laughed. "You should have seen your face."

She rolled her eyes, but the smile held.

For now, everything would be okay.

~

Lisa stood in her small kitchen and measured flour and sugar into the bowl. Then she cracked several eggs and added the other ingredients for a cake. She hadn't spent much time in this kitchen in a while. Other than a quick breakfast, she'd taken her meals at the orphanage. But this evening, she needed some time to herself. She needed to think. To process her new status. She'd always only identified herself, first and foremost, as an orphan. Even with her nurse's training, she still felt like the poor girl everyone looked at with pity. Like some part of her deserved to be treated as Mrs. Clark, Joske's clerk, treated her.

Well, not *deserved.* The woman offended her, for sure. But somehow, she identified with the pauper, the beggar, the outcast. And for the first time, she realized she needed to address some of those feelings with God—sort out the knot of tangled strings one by one and deal with them. It would take some doing, for sure.

She saw herself as unwanted because someone, so long ago, abandoned her.

But God had shown her, time and again, that she *was* wanted. First by Pastor James Smith, who took her in. Who left her everything he owned. Then by Papa, who cared for her when Pastor Smith died. By Martha. And by Carson. And by the nuns who came and went but who always treated her with such tender care.

She saw herself as unworthy, as less than, as though she had to prove herself through hard work. As though she had to be perfect, or she'd be rejected again.

But today, she was reminded that she didn't need to prove anything. She was worthy of love and care simply because she was God's child.

God's child...

The orphan title had singed itself on her heart. But she'd

never been an orphan—not really. For God had never ceased to care for her as a loving Father. And from her first moments on earth, He'd surrounded her with others who cared for her too.

And now...now He poured out His love so abundantly. She was an *heiress!* Maybe not a wealthy one, by earthly standards, but still. Never again would she have to depend on others for her wellbeing. She could stand as tall as any royalty, for that's what she was—a daughter of the King.

Emotion rose, inch by inch, and spilled onto her cheeks like riverbanks during a flood. Moisture coursed down her jaw, but she just kept stirring the batter in front of her. Twice, she had to refocus her vision to read the lemon cake recipe, to make sure she was measuring right.

It was Mrs. Smith's recipe, from the box Lisa had found tucked in the back of the cupboard. This woman she'd never met, who died before she was born, yet in Lisa's mind, this was her cherished grandmother.

So many thoughts... Her mind felt like a jigsaw puzzle, and she jumped from piece to piece trying to fit it all together.

When all the ingredients were well-blended, she poured the batter into a greased and floured, cast-iron fluted cake mold —also a relic from the Smiths—and placed it on the counter while she checked the oven's fire. After shaking the ashes through the grate to the ash box below and adjusting the damper, she used her apron to shield her hand while opening the oven door. Carefully, she slid in the cake, moving it as far away from the fire side as possible to avoid burning.

She wasn't a great cook. Yet. Martha had prepared all her meals growing up, and while she did have some lessons in simple meal prep, her experience since moving into her small home was by trial and error. Meal by meal, cake by cake, burned biscuit by burned biscuit, she was improving.

Please let this cake turn out, Lord.

She couldn't put into words why the cake's success was so

important to her. Somehow, she saw it as an act of worship, of praise, of thanksgiving for all God had done for her. Her hope was to take it to the orphanage in the morning. Even though she couldn't share about her fortune publicly, she could offer this private celebration. Much like the heavy emotions she tried to sort through, her joy bubbled over and needed a place to spill out.

CHAPTER 17

July 20, 1898

Time passed, and Jack's memory stalled. The hot Texas July was halfway over, heading toward a sweltering August. He now worked full days, two days a week, at the department store, avoiding Mrs. Clark's sour attitude when possible. Fortunately, the store stayed busy enough that he kept to his domain—the men's department and tools sections—and she remained occupied in the women's and housewares sections.

Lisa had returned to full-time work at the hospital, only checking on him when she stopped by in the evenings. He missed her. But she was out of reach, at least until he made something of himself. He was starting to accept the possibility that his past might be lost to him forever. He might as well focus on his future.

On Monday and Thursday evenings, Jack taught the orphans basic horse care and riding instruction. Lisa joined them when she was able, which was most of the time. The younger ones—five in all, including the twins—had their turns on Mondays.

"Mr. Jack, why don't you have a last name? Are you an orphan like us?" Lucy studied him with her big, curious eyes from atop Dusty, the docile gray gelding.

Jack lifted his hat brim and wiped away the sweat that dripped into his eyes. "Uh...that's a good question. I'm not sure I have an answer."

Tommy, a boy one grade ahead of the twins, spoke up from beside the quiet Lydia as they waited on the other side of the paddock fence. "It ain't that he ain't got no last name. Or even that he ain't got no parents. He just can't 'member nothin'."

"Tommy, watch your grammar. You know how to speak correctly." Lisa's voice was low and gentle but firm.

"But I'm not in school right now. Why do I gotta talk like I am?"

"You should always speak correctly. It's important to communicate well, so people can understand you."

"Jack understands me just fine, don't ya, Jack?"

Jack locked eyes with Lisa. If he said no, he'd be lying. If he said yes, he'd be in big trouble with the pretty nurse he wanted to impress. Swinging his eyes to Tommy, he said, "Nurse Lisa is right. People will judge you by the way you speak. It doesn't matter if they understand you or not. You want them to know you're smart. And some people may think you're not smart if you don't use correct grammar." He glanced back at Lisa to see how he'd fared.

She smiled and offered the slightest nod.

He continued with the lessons, allowing the children to take turns riding, instructing them on posture and technique. It was getting late. He swatted at a mosquito that buzzed near his head. The evening lessons protected them from the beating sun, but the nasty insects were the unfortunate tradeoff.

"All right, children. It's time to head back and get your

baths. You always smell like wet, sweaty puppies after these lessons." Lisa's comment brought giggles amid the protests of not wanting the lesson to end.

With all of them helping, it didn't take long to remove the tack, put it away, and care for Dusty's needs. Jack gave the horse a treat and slipped an apple slice to Fury on his way out. Did *he* smell like a sweaty dog? Probably so. He'd hoped to ask Lisa to take a walk with him after the children were settled, but maybe he should wait until another time.

The problem was, he'd been trying to work up the courage to ask her to take a walk with him for weeks now. Not as patient and nurse, but as man and woman. And every time, he lost his nerve. Sweaty or not, tonight, he was going to do it.

As was their routine, she led the group of children at the front, and he headed off the rear. The evening of their first lesson, Tommy had slipped away when he spotted a stray kitten between two buildings, and a panic ensued for a good ten minutes until they located him.

Once all the children were herded back into the orphanage, the nuns on duty took over. Lisa offered brief hugs and cheek-kisses to each child, and Jack felt a little jealous. If only he were eight years old...

She sat on the entryway bench and gestured for him to join her. "Still nothing new to share?"

She was all business. Every now and then, he thought he saw something akin to attraction in her expressions or body language. But it always disappeared behind that mask of professionalism.

"Well, there was something... I was hoping you'd take a walk with me. So we could talk. That is, if you don't mind that I smell like the livery."

Her laugh felt like a thousand feathers tickling his skin. "I don't, if you don't mind that I'm in my nursing uniform."

That's when it dawned on him. As long as she was in

uniform, she'd keep that distance. "I have an idea. I've been hoping for some more of that vanilla ice cream since the day you first took me to Harvey's. I noticed they stay open until half past eight during the summer. Why don't we both take a few minutes to change, and I'll take you there? My treat."

A dozen expressions flashed through her eyes in an instant, and he couldn't read any of them. Uncertainty? Longing? Amusement?

He hoped not amusement. Was she laughing at him? Did she find his suggestion ridiculous?

"That sounds lovely." She stood, and the smile she gave him was brighter than a thousand suns.

She said yes! He tried to control the goofy grin that took over his face. "All right. It's 6:45 now. What do you say I pick you up at your place in a half hour?"

"I'll be ready." She returned his grin, and he tried not to hope too much. After a small wave, she let the screen door shut behind her.

He sat there for a couple of minutes, soaking in the shock that she'd agreed to have ice cream with him. But he shook himself to his senses and headed for his room, straight for the washbasin, grateful that he'd purchased new shirts and pants with his employee discount last week. And even more grateful for the bottle of men's cologne with the dented metal lid that wasn't suitable for customer purchase. He'd gotten it for the manufacturer's cost. Tonight, he'd use it for the first time.

~

Just before she'd bid Jack goodnight, Lisa was ready to go home, chuck off her shoes, and fall into bed. But with his invitation, excitement had kicked in, and she couldn't wait to change into—what? She stood in the middle of her small bedroom, three rejected dresses strewn across her bed. She didn't want to look like she cared *too* much about her appearance. This outing wasn't about courtship, after all. He simply wanted to talk to her, a medical professional, about his condition. Still, her heart wanted him to see her as more than his nurse.

She finally decided on a dress of white cotton lawn. It was the coolest thing she owned and perfect for the sweltering summer heat. It was also quite pretty, with tiny buttons up the front and eyelet lace at the hem, sleeves, and neck. It even had an open overskirt that made a deep V from her waist to just below her knee line, and when she walked, that top layer fluttered.

She scrambled into it, checked the clock, then did the best she could with her hair, tying it back in a loose bun at the nape of her neck and adding a simple brimmed hat with floral trim. Patting her cheeks and biting her lips for color, she examined herself in the mirror above her dressing table. Not bad. As an afterthought, she grabbed the bottle of lavender scent she kept on her dresser for special occasions, pulled out the stopper, and dabbed a bit on her wrists and neck.

The knock at the door caused her heart to flutter even more. She took two deep breaths, grabbed her reticule, and shut her bedroom door behind her. She'd be mortified if he caught a glimpse of the mess she'd made! "Be right there," she called.

When she opened her front door, she nearly lost her breath again. He looked every inch like one of the newspaper advertisements for the Joske and Son's men's department. His hair was immaculately slicked back beneath a straw boater hat. He wore a dark-green striped vest and trousers, and a white shirt with a starched collar and cuffs. A thin brown tie finished the look.

She exited, shut and locked her door, then took the arm he

offered her. "My, Jack. You certainly look dapper tonight." Was that too forward?

"Thank you. I wanted to at least try and look worthy of walking through town with such a beautiful lady, though I know I could never reach such a level."

Was he flirting? She smiled, looked down at the sidewalk in front of her, and murmured a low, "Thank you. You're very kind."

They strolled along without saying anything for a time, and Lisa desperately tried to think of an appropriate topic of conversation. Why was she so nervous? Why were her palms so moist? Perspiration soaked through her white lace gloves.

She'd never been out alone with a gentleman before. Not like this. Though she'd walked Jack to various places, it had been as a nurse helping a patient. But this? This wasn't about her nursing duties at all. "How is your job coming along?" *Really?* She couldn't do any better than *that?* She asked him about his job nearly every day.

"It's not as much fun as riding a horse, but it brings in a paycheck. And I get some pretty good deals there too. I was getting tired of wearing the same old clothes all the time."

By this time, they had arrived at Harvey's. She was a little in awe of her surroundings. The town was alive in a way she hadn't seen it before. As a child, she'd been in bed by this time. And since working at the hospital, she'd gotten home weary each evening, eaten a quick dinner, and gone to bed. Though this was her hometown, she'd never taken much part in the social culture.

A barbershop quartet gathered a crowd on the sidewalk, singing, "Wait Till the Sun Shines, Nellie." The tune sounded vaguely familiar, though Lisa couldn't recall where she'd heard it. Maybe during her training in Austin. They stood there listening until the song finished, then made their way through Harvey's to the cafe. This was much different than the last time they'd visited. Nearly every table was full, and a large group of teenagers waited in front of them.

A waitress greeted them. "Just the two of you?"

"That's correct," Jack said.

"Follow me. Fortunately, we have a small table on the patio."

Jack placed his hand on Lisa's back as they wound through the tables, and she was so distracted by his warm touch flowing through the thin fabric of her dress, she nearly tripped. Twice.

Once seated, she could still feel the place where his hand had rested, and she missed the contact. Goodness! What was wrong with her? This man had her addlepated.

The waitress handed them each a menu and left them to decide.

"What are you in the mood for?" Jack asked her.

"I'm not sure. What are you having?" Why did she feel so nervous?

"Vanilla ice cream, of course. Although this time, I may have the ice cream sundae. The fellow at the table behind you has one, and the chocolate sauce looks delicious."

"Oh, that does sound good! I think I'll have that too." Oh, no. Would he think she didn't have a mind of her own?

Jack motioned for the waitress, and the woman took their orders. He also ordered them each a glass of lemonade. "Unless you'd prefer something different to drink?"

"Lemonade is fine, thank you."

She couldn't help but notice Jack's impeccable manners, his confidence in this new social situation. He'd never shown *poor* manners. But she'd never witnessed him like this, all dressed up. He possessed a quiet self-assurance that doubled—no, tripled—his attractiveness. And it made her wonder how different his background was from hers.

Somehow, she needed to get hold of herself.

"So what did you want to talk to me about? Have you had a new memory?"

For the briefest moment, confusion flashed in his eyes, so quick she thought she might have imagined it. Then he leaned back in his chair and stretched his long legs out to the side, toward the edge of the patio where no one would trip. He rested one arm on the back of his chair. With his other hand, he played with the napkin that still rested on the table. "I...uh...did say I wanted to talk to you, didn't I?"

"Yes. What's on your mind?"

He grinned at her, then shifted his eyes to the napkin like he was embarrassed. "I just wanted to talk. Not about anything in particular. I just...wanted to spend time with you. I hope I haven't overstepped my boundaries."

A thrill coursed through her, and as hard as she tried to remain dignified, she couldn't stop the smile. Or the heat that flooded every part of her, that she knew was now evident on her face and neck. "I see."

He drew his legs back in and sat up straight. His expression moved from confident to repentant. "I'm sorry to have misled you."

"No! Don't be sorry. I'm...glad you asked me. I'm having a nice time."

Outside, the tight harmony of the quartet drifted through the night air. They now sang a song Lisa hadn't heard before, about a woman named Annie Rooney.

> She's my sweetheart, I'm her beau;
> She's my Annie, I'm her Joe.
> Soon we'll marry, never to part;
> Little Annie Rooney
> Is my sweetheart!

Lisa swayed to the music, and Jack joined her. For a

moment, they locked eyes, and there was a shared understanding. At least, she thought there was. She liked him. And he liked her. And somehow, the words to that song seemed personal. She wanted to be his sweetheart. And from the way things looked, he wanted that too.

The waitress interrupted the moment when she brought two oversized sundaes and two lemonades on a tray and set them on the table. "Enjoy!"

They looked at the volume of ice cream, then at each other and burst into sweet laughter.

"Next time, we'll know to share one." After she said it, she realized what she just implied.

But he saved her from embarrassment when he reached across, took her hand, and said, "I'd like that very much."

CHAPTER 18

Lampasas
Friday, July 22

"Riley! Cordell, Anita! All of you—come look at this! The Spanish have surrendered. The war in Cuba is over!"

At his wife's cry, Riley descended the stairs of his home two at a time, holding onto the rail to make sure he didn't slip in his eagerness.

Emma stood in the entry hall, her head buried in the newspaper that must have just been delivered through the mail slot. A couple of other envelopes and catalogs were still on the floor by the door.

He peered over her shoulder to read as their two youngest children joined them from the kitchen.

"Does this mean Jackson's coming home?" Anita asked, her hands clenched at her chest.

"Yes. That's what we hope," Emma answered and handed the paper to Riley.

"This is a long article. We might as well get comfortable."

Riley stepped into the parlor, and his family followed him. He and Emma sat on the sofa, eighteen-year-old Cordell on the sofa arm, and fourteen-year-old Anita plopped on the floor at her father's feet.

The Lampasas Leader

[July 18]—The American flag is floating in triumph over the governor's palace in Santiago de Cuba. ...Gen. Chambers McGibbon has been appointed temporary military governor.

... At 12 o'clock sharp yesterday the United States flag was hoisted over the civil building, a salute of twenty-one guns fired, and a detachment of cavalry and infantry presented arms while the band played national airs. Gen. Wheeler said it would have cost 5,000 American lives to have taken Santiago, so perfect were the Spanish entrenchments.

...The ceremonies customary to surrender were duly observed, and there was absolutely no friction. Our flag waves over Santiago and its principal fortress, El Morro, and the American army is triumphant in all Eastern Cuba.

...The final report of casualties in the army, since it landed in Cuba three weeks ago, has been forwarded to Washington. It shows an aggregate of 1,914 officers and men killed, wounded and missing. The number killed 246, of whom 21 were officers; wounded 1,584, of whom 98 were officers; missing 84, of whom none were officers. Of the wounded, only 68 have died.

Col. Pope, the surgeon-in-chief, says this is a remarkably small number of fatalities, considering the large number of wounded. In the field hospitals, there has been a remarkably small number of septic wounds and but two cases of gangrene have developed, one of which resulted fatally.

When Riley finished reading aloud, none of them said anything. Just absorbed the hope and uncertainty of the moment.

Finally, Anita said, "Are you going to Uncle Colt and Aunt Allison's? I'd like to go."

"Me too." Cordell stood up and moved toward the door.

"Let's load up," Riley said. "Maybe Colt finally received a telegram."

A short time later, they arrived to find Colt riding out on one of his prize horses. "I'm headed to the post office to see if I've had word," he said.

Riley pulled the horses to a stop as they passed him, jolting the wagon. "Hold up. I'll go with you."

"I'm kind of in a hurry. I'll go on ahead. You can meet me there. Take one of my horses if you want. I don't care which."

"Go on, Dad," Cordell told him. "I'll take care of the wagon and horses."

Riley hopped down and headed for the stables. He looked over a chocolate-brown Arabian and a shiny black Friesian and chose the Friesian. Arabians were too hot-blooded for Riley's taste. A stable hand helped him dress the horse, and within minutes, Riley was following Colt's tracks.

When he arrived at the post office, Colt sat on the bench outside, holding a piece of paper, all color drained from his face. Riley sat next to him. Without a word, Colt handed over the telegram.

NO RECORD FOUND OF JACKSON STRATTON. UPON INVESTIGATION, LABELED MIA. DEEPEST SYMPATHIES. –T. ROOSEVELT

Riley read the words a second time. A third time. He felt like he'd been gut-punched. "I don't know what to say."

Colt stood, balled his fist, and punched the cast-iron hitching post. The post didn't budge, but his brother's knuckles were now scratched and bloodied. Colt climbed on his horse, dug his heels into the mare's flanks, and took off in the opposite direction of home, pushing the mare as fast as she could go.

Should Riley go after him or head back to his family? As much as they had a right to know, Riley didn't want to be the one to bear this news. Not yet, anyway. He swung back into the saddle, flicked the reins, and once again followed his brother. Only this time, he had no idea where they'd end up.

It didn't take long to catch him. He'd taken a narrow trail just outside of town toward the river. Riley spotted him riding full speed along the bluff, dangerously close to the edge. If the horse slipped, they'd both go down. And if he pursued his brother, it would only push Colt to ride faster. He'd have to get ahead of him somehow, cut him off.

He led the horse down the steep bank, into the shallow water. It didn't get very deep in this section of the river, so where the bluff curved, he could ride straight.

"Colt! Stop." He yelled over and over until his voice was hoarse. If Colt hadn't been acting recklessly, Riley would have let him be. But the last thing Allison needed—any of them needed—was to lose Colt and Jackson in the same day. "Colt!"

Finally, his brother heard him. He reined in his horse. Circled back. Looked at the sky.

"Why, God? Why would you do this?" Colt's fist shook at the heavens. "I'm the sinner. I'm the one who's done wrong, time after time. Why Jackson?" The sky seemed to eat his words. They were greeted with an eerie silence.

Riley slid from his saddle, looped the reins around a low tree branch on the bank, and climbed the slope to get to his brother. When he arrived, he rested both hands on the horse's back and lowered his head to the horse's side. What could he say?

Colt just sat there. The horse stomped his feet a few times, but otherwise let them be. After a long time, Colt said, "Jackson's a good boy. He's not like me. It should have been me."

Riley wiped his eyes. By the grace of God, he'd never lost a child. But this—losing his nephew—was one of the hardest things he'd faced in a long time. He couldn't even imagine what Colt was feeling right now. Or how Allison would respond.

He had no words of wisdom or comfort for his brother. Not because he didn't want to give them. But in this case, he was no different than Colt. Riley had nothing to say because he was at a loss. This was one of those awful things he didn't think he'd ever, in all his days, understand.

CHAPTER 19

The hospital would reopen today. Lisa had spent two weeks making sure everything was ready to go, and now she'd step into her role as head nurse. *Temporary* head nurse. She was grossly underqualified, but she'd do her best.

As she walked down the street, a local band played patriotic tunes. Men stood around, smoking cigars and poring over newspapers. Women joined them, some with papers in hand, others holding on to small children. If she didn't know better, she'd think all the hoopla was about the hospital reopening. But she'd read the papers this morning and knew Spain had surrendered.

Only a few short weeks ago, Roosevelt's Rough Riders had left San Antonio to make their way to Cuba. Now, the war was over.

She made her way through the crowd toward the hospital, a spring in her step and a smile on her face. Whatever God's reasoning, Jack *hadn't* gone to Cuba. And in spite of his injury and memory loss, she couldn't help but be grateful that he'd stayed here. For the last several weeks they'd spent together, her life had taken on newer, brighter color.

She pushed through the double hospital doors to find a tall, thin woman in nurse's garb, her back to the door, studying a clipboard.

"Hello," Lisa said. Dr. Williamson hadn't said anything about hiring new nurses.

"Lisa!" The woman rushed to her, wrapped her arms around Lisa's neck. She only got a brief look at the woman's face, but from the voice, she knew... "Phyllis?" Had her voluptuous blond friend really become so gaunt?

Phyllis stepped back. "I know. All my clothes are hanging on me, and I haven't had the energy to alter them yet."

"No...you look great. We'll put some weight on you in no time. I'm just glad you're back! I have so much to tell you."

"Good. Because I've been bored out of my skull. At least the last few weeks, the doc let me recover at home, so I had my family to keep me company. But that was only after he was sure I wasn't contagious. I've missed you so!" She dropped to a chair and caught her breath. "But I'm not my old self yet. I still tire easily, and it's frustrating."

"I'm sure it is. Do what you can, and Doris and I will handle the rest."

"That's right! Doc told me you're the new Nurse Jacobs. In that case, I'd better be on my best behavior around you."

Lisa laughed. "You've never been on your best behavior for anybody. Speaking of Nurse Jacobs, is she around?"

Phyllis's face fell. "No. Didn't you hear? She's still not ready to come back. The doctor wants her to rest a while longer."

"No, I wasn't aware. I guess we'll have to make do with the three of us, then. Dr. Williamson said to expect patients around noon today. He's limiting it to five, to make sure we can meet the demands. So I'm sure they'll be his five most serious cases. I'm going to start by checking the men's ward one last time to see if it's ready. When you've caught your breath, would you mind doing the same for the women's?"

"Certainly."

"When Doris arrives, send her to me."

They parted ways, and Lisa felt a new surge of anxiety. With one fewer nurse than expected, that would surely spell longer hours again, at a time when she was hoping for extra free time to spend with Jack. Hopefully, he'd understand.

~

Jack pushed his way through the crowded street, making his way to Joske and Sons. By the looks of things, business would be good today. People were out and about, which meant they'd stop by the store. They were celebrating, which meant they'd make pleasure purchases. This much he'd learned in his few weeks working in retail.

Spain had surrendered. This had to be one of the shortest wars in history. The news brought mixed feelings for Jack, but he didn't have time to sort through them right now. These thoughts would probably keep him up most of the night, and he'd be tired tomorrow.

Of course, he was happy the war was over and the U.S. troops would come home. But the knowledge that, if not for his unfortunate injury, he'd have been over there... What would he have seen? What would he have experienced?

Would he even be alive?

Was his injury God's way of saving his life? And if so, why him? He wasn't any more deserving of that kind of protection than anyone else.

He pushed through the employee's entrance to be greeted by a sour-faced Mrs. Clark. "Better get ready for the masses. They're sure to arrive in hordes, as soon as the doors open."

"Good for business, right?"

She glared at him. "Good for the Joskes. You and I get paid the same, no matter what. Today, we'll be folding and refolding, cleaning up customer messes, wearing a fake smile when people are rude. I'm not looking forward to it."

Jack bit back the words that wanted to spew out. *You mean your normal smile? And customers who are ruder than you are?*

Mrs. Clark grabbed a box of women's hats and headed for her department. "I'll need you to man the jewelry counter. Watch out for con artists—they work in pairs. They'll try to get you to take out several pieces at once. Then one will distract you while the other swipes a piece. They're sure to be active on a day like today. Oh! And I've pulled several pieces to be marked for clearance. They're in the locked cabinet below the register."

Jack took in her barked orders and responded with a simple, "Yes, ma'am." The less he said to that woman, the better. She tended to take any comment and turn it into a cat fight.

He deposited his hat in his small locker and made his way to the jewelry counter. His keyring jangled as he unlocked the cabinet and pulled out the clearance items. There were three boxes, one marked for ten percent, one twenty-five percent, and one fifty percent off. In a short time, he had the first two boxes tagged with their new prices. He opened the last one, for half off, to find only one item inside. A small silver charm in the image of a horse. The original price was seventy cents.

He wanted to buy this for Lisa.

Would it be inappropriate to give her jewelry at this stage in their relationship? He hadn't even asked Father Hidalgo's permission to court her—he planned to do that this evening. Still, at this price, with his twenty-five percent employee discount on top of it...that was what? Around twenty-six, twenty-seven cents? He couldn't afford *not* to get it. It had Lisa's name all over it. He could save it for a future time, a time he hoped would soon come. Her birthday?

That was in early October. The twins were already whispering and giggling about the surprise party they planned. Maybe by then, he could give her jewelry without it seeming presumptuous. And by Christmas...who knew? With no memories to look back at, Jack was already looking forward to making new holiday memories—recollections he could build a life on. Maybe by Christmas, Lisa would agree to be his wife. Because more and more, his past was becoming less important to him. Foremost in his mind was that he wanted Lisa in his future.

He couldn't complete the transaction on his own. It was against the rules. He found Mrs. Clark. "I know you're busy, but I'd like to make a purchase before the doors open. I'm afraid if I don't buy it now, someone else will."

She rolled her eyes. "Can't you just set it aside for later?"

"I'd rather take care of it now." Could the woman be any more unpleasant?

She slammed down the stack of shirts she was folding and headed for the register, mumbling under her breath. "Hand it over. I don't have all day."

He gave her the charm, and she rang it up. "That is a good deal, if I say so myself. It's been here for over six months. I'm surprised no one's purchased it by now. I assume it's for your *nurse* friend. I'm sure it will be the nicest thing she's ever owned."

Jack didn't comment. How she could turn a simple transaction into what felt like an insult to Lisa, he wasn't sure.

"Here's the receipt. I'll let you wrap it yourself. We have seven minutes before customers will swarm the place."

He quickly added the charm to a box and tied a white silk ribbon around it, then hurried to place it in his locker. He made it back to the jewelry counter just as the doors were opening.

~

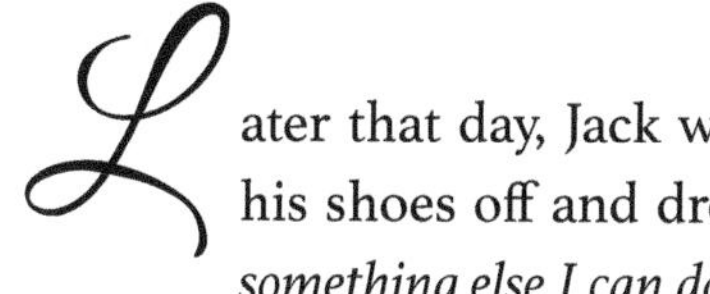

ater that day, Jack wanted nothing more than to kick his shoes off and drop into bed. *Please, God. Show me something else I can do to make a living.*

He was grateful for this job and for the generosity Mr. Joske had shown him. But if working in a department store was the way he'd spend the rest of his days...well, he just hoped that wasn't the case.

Despite his weary state, he bypassed his room to find Father Hidalgo. The man was out back, watching the children play a game of badminton. "When you have a moment, I'd like to speak with you about something, sir."

"I have time now. Have a seat."

Did he really want to ask permission to court Lisa out here, where anyone could listen in? Then again, the children were occupied. Martha and the nuns were inside getting dinner ready. And this kept him from having to hold awkward eye contact for the entire conversation. If the man wasn't happy about Jack's request, at least Jack could feign watching the game instead of fidgeting with his hat or something.

He sat in the chair next to the old priest, with a small table between them, and stretched out his legs. Rotated his ankles, to relieve the soreness from standing all day.

"What is on your mind, son?"

Jack rolled his shoulders. Rolled his neck. He'd rehearsed this conversation in his mind, but all the words left him. But the quickest way through a thing was straight on, so he jumped in. "I'd like your permission to court Lisa."

He cast a quick glance at the older man, who kept his eyes on the children. His eyebrows lifted, then lowered. Then his brow furrowed before Jack looked away. He wasn't sure how to interpret those expressions.

Father Hidalgo didn't answer for a couple of minutes, though those two minutes might have been hours. He clapped for something one of the children did. "Good job, Alice! You're getting it."

Had the man not heard Jack? Should he repeat the question?

After a time, the priest turned to face Jack. "You seem like a nice young man. And it's clear Lisa is fond of you. But I'm concerned. What happens when your brain injury heals? You could have a sweetheart you want to return to. Or who knows? You could be a wanted criminal with a sordid past."

Jack remained quiet. How could he argue without any facts to the contrary?

"Why don't you wait a little while longer? See if your memories return. As of now, none of us really knows you. You don't even know yourself."

Jack's heart turned heavy in his chest, like a cake that went flat. "I respect what you're saying, sir. And I understand your concerns. I can't control what happened to me. I can't control when—or if—my memory will return, but I do know my own mind. I know I'll never meet another woman like Lisa, and my intentions toward her are honorable. I believe she has feelings for me, as well."

The priest crossed one foot over his opposite knee. "I am very protective of Lisa. But she is an intelligent young woman and can make her own decisions. If she feels the same as you do, I will give you my blessing to court her. But I would like you to respect some boundaries. I want you to take things slow."

Jack nodded.

"And if you recall anything from your past that might hurt Lisa, talk to me first."

Jack exhaled. "Of course."

The old priest studied Jack, as if trying to decide if he was worthy of Lisa's attention. After a time, he cleared his throat. "All right. You have my permission."

A smile broke out on Jack's face, and his heart went from flat to soaring. "Yes, sir! Thank you, sir."

Father Hidalgo chuckled. "You sound as though you're addressing a military captain, not a priest."

Jack laughed, stood up, and saluted. "As you say, sir."

~

Lisa plopped down in the chair in Nurse Jacobs's office. She felt strange sitting in the woman's place...but for now, it was Lisa's office. She'd been here since nine a.m.—for nearly twelve hours—and wasn't sure when she'd be leaving. Five patients—three women and two men—had arrived around noon. Doris and Lisa got them settled, and they left the light chores to Phyllis.

In theory, the tentative schedule would have worked, with Lisa and Doris each taking an eight-hour shift and Phyllis and Nurse Jacobs splitting the third shift. But with no one to split a shift with Phyllis, the extra half shift fell to Lisa. And with what Lisa observed of Phyllis's energy levels, she wasn't even ready to be left alone for four hours.

They needed backup. She'd talk to Dr. Williamson in the morning. For now, Doris—bless her!—had agreed to sleep in one of the empty rooms in case Lisa needed assistance in the night. She even offered to spot Lisa if she became too weary to work.

That she'd missed supper with Jack upset her more than anything. She'd looked forward to it all morning and into the afternoon. But around four p.m., she realized she wasn't going anywhere, anytime soon. She hadn't even had time to send word. She felt horrible for standing him up. Hopefully, he'd understand.

A light rap sounded at the entrance—just outside her office. Anxiety swelled and took over. Visiting hours closed at eight p.m., and at that time, Lisa had locked up the building. What should she do? What if it was a stranger? Taking a few deep breaths, she drew up to her full height, approached the door, and mustered a stern and foreboding demeanor, imitating Nurse Jacobs when she dealt with a difficult patient.

"We're closed for the night," she called through the closed door. "You'll have to come back in the morning. Visiting hours begin at nine a.m." She tried to sound forceful, but there was a bit of a wobble. Perhaps the person on the other side of the door didn't notice.

"Lisa, it's me. Jack."

Jack! She unlocked the door and there he was, in his boater hat, those dimples framing his roguish grin, holding a single daisy. He handed it to her, and she couldn't control her smile. She went from weary to energized in just those few seconds. "Thank you. Come in. I've been swamped, and I can't leave yet. Phyllis isn't as strong as we'd hoped, and Nurse Jacobs isn't even back."

"I figured it was something like that. Is there anything I can do?"

"Unless you want to don a nurse's cap and apron, probably not. I'm hoping some of the nuns can volunteer, or perhaps we can invite some students from Austin to finish their training here. Until then, I doubt you'll see much of me." She led him inside and shut the door.

"I'm not sure about wearing the cap, but I'm serious. I can pour a glass of water and fluff a pillow as well as the next guy. I'm happy to help."

If she hadn't already been drawn to Jack, she would be now. "You are so kind. I may take you up on that offer. But for now, the patients are all asleep. I'll check on them again in a half hour or so. Would you like sit and talk until then?"

"I'd love to."

She gestured to the small bench in the hallway. He took a

seat, and she retrieved a drinking glass and added water, then the daisy, and placed it on her desk before joining him.

"Tell me about your day," she said, cringing at the way her voice echoed in the quiet hallway.

"We had more customers than we have since I've worked there." Jack leaned back on the bench and extended his long legs, crossing them at the ankles. "Mrs. Clark and I were kept moving the whole time, as well as some temporary workers Mr. Joske hired during the day. Even he was on the floor, waiting on customers."

"Oh, my."

"It was worth it. Mr. Joske was so happy with all the business we did today, he gave both me and Mrs. Clark a raise. Two whole cents more an hour."

"That's wonderful! Congratulations."

They grew quiet then. They'd never been this alone before. They were always together at the orphanage, or the livery, or at a restaurant or walking on the street. Even though they were in a hospital with Doris a few doors down and five patients, this felt...intimate. Suddenly, she didn't know what to do with her hands.

Jack must have felt it too. He moved on the bench until he faced her completely. When he spoke, his voice was low and husky. "I talked to Father Hidalgo today. About you. About...us."

She sucked in a breath. "About... us?"

Jack grinned. Ducked his head, looking sheepish. "I asked if I could court you. With your permission, of course."

Her heart sped up, and she felt tingles all over her skin. "What did he say?"

"He was concerned about my memory issues. And I don't blame him. But I assured him I have only the best of intentions toward you."

She smiled. Looked down at her hands.

He took one finger and placed it under her chin, lifted it until her eyes met his. "He agreed to let me court you, if that's something you'd like. With some stipulations, that is."

"What are they?"

"He wants us to take things slow."

She nodded. "I see. Anything else?"

"If my memory comes back and I recall something that may hurt you, I have to talk to him first. Then we'll talk to you together."

"Oh." How should she feel about that?

"He's very protective of you. And so am I. I don't think that will be an issue, but I promised him—and I'm promising you—I won't keep anything from you. You have my word."

"I appreciate that. I trust you."

"So does that mean yes, you'd like to start courting? Officially?"

She held his gaze. "Yes," she breathed, the sound almost lost by the time it escaped her lips.

His hand still cupped her chin ever so gently. He leaned forward and brushed her lips with the softest, feather-like kiss, then pulled back. She couldn't move—just stayed there, stunned, wanting to freeze this moment in time.

"I'd better go." He stood and pulled her to a standing position. Ran one hand across her cheek and whispered, "Good night, Lisa."

"I..." Her brain was in a fog. A beautiful, glorious fog, where she couldn't find her words.

He smiled, placed his hat on his head, and let himself out.

She stood there in the hallway, listening to his retreating footsteps. After a time, she locked the door behind him and leaned against it. Good thing she was on duty. Because even if she'd been home in her comfortable bed, she wouldn't have slept a wink tonight.

CHAPTER 20

October 12, 1898

Weeks turned into months, and the summer heat gave way to a short spell of autumn-like weather, a relief from the infernal Texas sun, only to return in full-force Indian summer. Despite the changes in weather, Jack's life took on a comfortable routine, and the sameness of his days became a source of contentment.

Carson had invited Jack to work afternoons at the livery. The man said his partner wanted to try some new things, and they needed another set of hands. It didn't pay as much as Mr. Joske did, but Jack's calling lay with horses.

So each day, he worked mornings at the department store, then after a quick lunch and a change of clothes, he went to the livery, where he cleaned stalls, groomed, and did whatever else needed to be done. At three p.m. each day, four days a week, he offered beginner riding classes. Two of those days were reserved for the orphans, and the other two days were open to the general public. It didn't take long for the classes to fill up.

Each evening, Lisa shared dinner with him at the orphanage. It wasn't the most romantic setting, but it provided opportunities for them to get to know each other. On weekends, they went to dinner at Market Square or on picnics by the San Antonio River, and on Sundays, they attended church at La Villita, the protestant church where Lisa had been left as an infant.

Jack's nightmares had not returned. Maybe it was because his heart was so full of Lisa, or because he was so grateful to God...but he was at peace, and he wouldn't question it.

With the nightmares disappearing, so did any progress toward recalling his past. So for now, and maybe forever, he would simply be Jack. Maybe he'd take on Father Hidalgo's last name. Or if he and Lisa married, he could become Jack Garcia. The thought left him feeling both empty and full, sad and happy, leaving him in a state he couldn't quite put words to.

But that was a worry for another day. Today was Friday, and tomorrow was Lisa's birthday. He had a special treat planned for tonight—just the two of them. Dr. Williamson had finally given him the go-ahead to take Fury outside the paddock. Carson told him about a local riverside trail where he and Lisa could ride, and yesterday, Jack tested it out. The trail led right to the shady spot by the river where they'd first met. They'd gone there a few times, but they'd never *ridden* there. This evening, away from the litter of nosy children, he planned to give her the horse charm.

"Good morning, Mrs. Clark," he said to his coworker as he entered the store.

The woman answered with a low *hmph.* The more pleasant Jack was, the more irritated she seemed. Goading her with his good nature had become a favorite part of his morning.

"I don't see what's so good about it. Walking in this heat is going to be the death of me. Just look! My dress is soaked through. Good thing I keep an extra dress in my locker." She disappeared into the area reserved for female employees.

He'd carried rather than worn his coat, so his appearance was acceptable. He walked around his various departments, straightening merchandise and shining countertops. When he got to the jewelry counter, he unlocked the clearance drawer so he could label and display the merchandise. There, in the twenty-five percent-off box, was a simple silver necklace chain. It was just the right size for the charm. He set it aside and waited for Mrs. Clark to return so he could pay for it.

He could hardly wait for this evening.

~

Lisa could barely recall the last time she'd had a full day off. Since before Jack came, which was around the time the cholera disaster happened. Good thing Dr. Williams had taken every precaution. They hadn't lost a single patient. At long last, Phyllis and Nurse Jacobs were back to their full-time schedules, along with two new recruits from the Austin Nursing College. Lisa was now number two in charge, which she felt far more comfortable with.

With a full staff in place at last, Dr. Williamson had insisted she take the weekend off. She doubted the man knew it was her birthday, and she didn't tell him. She was just grateful to have a day to sleep late, read a good book, and spend some time with Jack.

After making a last round to check on patients, answering questions from the new nurses, and giving the supply room a final onceover, she entered the office she now shared with Nurse Jacobs. The woman sat at her desk, checking over some files.

"Do you need anything before I leave?" Lisa asked.

Nurse Jacobs smiled. "Not a thing. I hope you enjoy your time off. You've earned it. I don't know what would have become of things if you hadn't been here."

"It was definitely a learning experience. I'm just glad you and Phyllis made full recoveries."

"Me too. Have a wonderful weekend, and I'll see you on Monday."

Phyllis waved Lisa down before she could exit the building. "What do you and Jack have planned?"

"I don't know. He's been very mysterious about this evening." Lisa couldn't keep the grin from stretching her cheeks.

"Mysterious, huh? Do you think he'll pop the question?"

"Oh, stop it! You're such a romantic, Phyllis. I think—at least, I hope—he'll ask me one day. But I don't think it will be this soon. I really hope he can regain his memories first. He doesn't talk about it much, but I know it frustrates him not to know his past."

"But...what if he doesn't?"

"He will. In my heart, I know he will. And if he doesn't, we'll figure it out."

Phyllis got a cat-ate-the-canary gleam in her eye. "What if he's a millionaire? Or a prince from a foreign land? Wouldn't that be great?"

"If he were from a foreign land, he wouldn't have a Texas drawl. And if he were a millionaire...well, I doubt that's the case. He's a trick rider. How many millionaire trick riders do you know?"

"It could happen."

Lisa snorted. "Goodbye, Phyllis."

"Enjoy your mystery time!"

With a wave, Lisa pushed through the door and headed to her home.

Once there, she kicked off her shoes and collapsed onto the worn blue tapestry sofa. It was her favorite piece of furniture—the perfect place for a nap or curling up with a book. But today, she didn't have the luxury of a long break. Fifteen minutes—then she'd have to get ready for—what? Jack had been so secretive about their evening, she had no idea what to wear. She leaned her head back and closed her eyes...but despite her weariness, her excitement made it impossible to rest.

When she opened her eyes, she noticed a piece of paper on the floor by the door, as though it had been slipped under. She must have stepped over it when she came in. She uncrossed her legs and reached her foot toward it, stretching her toes, hoping she could slide it over without getting up.

Almost... There. The page made a scratching noise on the floor as she pulled it toward her. She nearly fell off the sofa trying to pick it up. There in Jack's writing were three words.

Wear riding clothes. ~J

If any three words could get her heart pumping and blood flowing, it was those. She hadn't ridden since the hospital reopened. A couple of times, she'd had her break at the time the children were in their riding lessons with Jack, and she'd walked down to observe. He was a gifted rider and teacher, and the kids loved him. And that made her love him even more.

A look at the clock told her she needed to hurry. He'd be here in a half hour. She scooted out of her nurse's garb, took a few minutes to clean up, and slipped into her riding clothes. If nothing else exciting happened this weekend, getting to ride would be enough! She unpinned and repinned her hair, secured her riding hat, and was just making a final check in the mirror when a knock sounded at the door.

She opened it, and there was Jack, somehow even more handsome than usual, holding a single yellow rose.

"For you," he said.

"It's beautiful. You're always so kind." She placed the rose in some water, then took his arm and let him lead her toward the livery. “I almost missed your note. I’m so excited we’re going to ride.”

“Not only are we going to ride—we’re going by the river.”

She stopped. “What? Dr. Williamson gave you the go-ahead?”

Jack nodded. “I’ve known for several days now, but I wanted to surprise you. He said that physically, I’m healed. As long as I don’t do anything stupid, I’m free to ride where I want.”

“Which means no trick riding, I suppose?” Lisa tugged his arm.

“He didn’t say that, exactly.” Jack laughed at her lifted eyebrows. “Trick riding is only stupid if you don’t know what you’re doing...which I clearly do.”

She rolled her eyes. Huffed.

That only made him laugh harder, and his joy was contagious.

“After all the time I’ve spent nursing you back to health, if you fall hit your head again, I’ll...I’ll...”

“Kiss it and make it better?” he asked, a gleam in his eye.

“You are cheeky. Come on. I’m anxious to get back in the saddle.”

“That makes two of us.”

They picked up their gait, and soon they were at the livery. Carson already had Fury and Dusty saddled and ready to go. In addition to her saddle, Fury carried a pack, and Lisa wondered what was inside. But she didn’t ask. For now, it was enough to relish the feel of being on a horse.

She leaned forward and rubbed Dusty’s neck and whispered in her ear. “Are you ready for a fun evening, girl? Because I am.”

The horse whinnied in response.

When Jack was settled on Fury, he looked at Lisa, his smile lighting up every part of him. “Follow me.” Slowly at first, he guided them down the street to a side path that led to the river.

Once they were away from the traffic, he increased to a moderate trot, and she followed suit.

Rarely had she ridden outside the paddock. As she didn't own a horse, Carson always wanted her to keep the borrowed animals close. The gentle sway, the wind in her face, the fragrance of trees and flowers and grass, even the earthy scent of horse sweat filled up her senses. It felt magnificent.

The trail took them a different way than she was used to going. Her little walking trail took the shortest path from home to the river, but this path looked to be more for horses than foot traffic. It wound in and out of trees, always in sight of the river. It felt both familiar and new. They passed a few other riders, cantering along, each nodding a greeting as they enjoyed time away from the bustle of San Antonio city life.

After about ten minutes, they veered off the trail to a secluded spot, and she knew exactly where they were. "How did we end up here?"

"We took the long way." Jack reined in Fury and slid down, then held out his hand to help her. Once she had her footing, he secured both horses where they could easily drink or munch on fat clumps of dandelion and clover. Then he dug through Fury's pack and pulled out a blanket, which he spread on the ground, and a cloth tied up with what she assumed was their dinner.

"Wow. You've thought of everything." She watched him for a moment, then took some deep, relaxing breaths. "This is just what I needed."

"Good. Because it's just the beginning." He swept his arm out like a knight with his lady. "Have a seat."

She smoothed out a place on the blanket and sat, tucking her legs to one side. "How was your day?"

"It was pretty standard. Business was slow at Joske's. Busier at the livery. Carson told me he and his partner want to add onto the paddock, maybe invest in a few more permanent horses. The beginner riding lessons have proven to be a good business move. Since tourism is growing in San Antonio, they'd like to add the option for some guided tours on horseback."

She shifted her eyes to the river and watched the water move over the stones. She loved the way his eyes lit up when he talked about his work at the livery. What would he think when he found out *she* was the partner? Should she tell him?

But Papa had advised against it. Would Jack feel ashamed if he knew she was helping pay his salary? Would he feel misled? Lied to?

She'd have to tell him sometime. But finding the right time, the right place...that was proving difficult. She pushed the thought to the back of her mind and met his eyes again. "How do you feel about that? Do you think it's a good idea?"

"I do. I've never met anyone who doesn't like horses. Even if they're afraid of them, they're almost always fascinated. They're gentle giants. There's something almost therapeutic about them."

"I agree. Someday, I hope to have my own horse."

He smiled at her as though he knew a secret. After a moment, he fumbled around in his pocket. "I was going to save this for later, after we eat. But I can't wait any longer. I know your birthday isn't until tomorrow, but I got you something."

He pulled out a little box with the familiar Joske and Sons bow. She sucked in a little breath, looked from the box to him, held his gaze a moment, then looked at the box again. Had Phyllis been right? Was he going to propose?

"Don't look so flustered. It's not a ring."

Her eyes jerked back to his. Could he read her mind?

His face held a combination of humor and excitement. Holding the box out to her, he said, "Open it."

Lisa laughed, a nervous little chuckle. Her heart still galloped in her chest. She took the box, untied the bow, and met his eyes once more before removing the lid. Inside was a dainty silver necklace. The charm was a horse, lifting its front leg in a prance. Its mane and tail billowed out behind, as if caught in the wind. "Oh, Jack. It's beautiful! I love it."

"Here. Let me help you."

She turned, and he fastened it around her neck. When it was in place, she fingered the tiny grooves. "Thank you so much. This is the nicest birthday gift I've ever received."

"It's not nearly as pretty as the lady wearing it. I'm glad you like it." He reached out, clasped her hand, and pulled it to his chest. Then he dipped his chin and kissed her fingers.

They sat there, soaking in the sweet, intimate moment. Oh, how she loved this man. She really needed to tell him about the livery soon. She didn't like keeping things from him. The closer they grew, the more wrong it felt.

But not now. Not today.

Soon he pulled out a well-thought-out bachelor's feast, with thick slices of soft bread, a wedge of yellow cheddar, a flask of lemonade, and a couple of moon-shaped hand-held apple pies. They enjoyed their food leaning against the old willow tree, laughing at each other's stories. Once finished, he showed her how to skip rocks, then she showed him how to skip them better. They held hands and strolled the banks, and he picked her a gold chrysanthemum and tucked it into her hair.

The sun was just about to kiss the horizon when he said, "We'd better head back before *Papa* Hidalgo tans my hide."

This was the best birthday she'd ever celebrated. And it wasn't even her birthday yet.

CHAPTER 21

The next morning, Lisa slept in later than usual. The evening had ended in an odd way. She told Jack she'd be by in the morning and asked him to let Papa know she needed to speak with him about something. Jack had reacted with a flash of surprise, then something like discomfort in his eyes, as though he didn't want her to come.

"Oh…I, uhm…almost forgot. Father Hidalgo wants to talk to you too. He said he'd meet you here in the morning, around ten-thirty. No need to come to the orphanage."

A wave of disappointment swamped her. Why wouldn't Jack want to see her? He hadn't mentioned tomorrow at all. After they said goodnight, she sat in the dark in her small parlor for a long time, fingering the horse charm. But no…she was being silly. He'd made tonight so special. Clearly, this was meant to be her birthday celebration with him. Maybe he had to work at Joske's tomorrow, though he hadn't said that.

Still. She refused to let anything ruin the memory of a perfect night. Once she got in bed, exhaustion from too many weeks without a break took over, and she fell fast asleep.

Now she opened her eyes, and the sun was high in the sky.

Panic overtook her briefly, as though she'd overslept, and then she remembered. Today was her day off.

Her birthday gift to herself? To do as little as possible.

She stretched her arms over her head, stretched her legs and toes to their full length, then pulled the covers up to her chin. She'd have to get up soon to dress before Papa arrived. But she wanted to lie here a few more minutes, in her soft bed with her soft pillow, under her soft quilt. This was heaven.

Next thing she knew, someone was rapping at the door. She'd fallen back asleep!

"Just a minute," she called, bolting upright. Her head spun from getting up too fast, and she grabbed her robe and tied it around her before stumbling through the parlor to crack the door open. "Hi, Papa."

"Ivelisse Maria Garcia! Were you still in bed?" His words were stern, but his eyes laughed at her.

"I think I've earned a sleep-in. Have a seat on the porch. Or come inside and fix yourself some tea. I think there are cookies in the pantry. Give me five minutes."

"Take your time, *mija*. I'm in no hurry."

She smiled at the endearment. *My daughter.* Their adoption may not be official, but they'd certainly adopted one another. She closed her bedroom door, grabbed her softest, threadbare day dress off the hook, then changed her mind. It was her birthday, after all. Even if no one saw her but Papa, she would make herself look nice. She pulled out a dress she'd made last spring but only worn a couple of times—pink calico, with tiny blue and green flowers and a wide, scooped neckline that created the perfect frame for her necklace. After running a brush through her hair, she tied it back with a pink ribbon and slipped into her shoes.

A quick look in the mirror reminded her—this was the dress she wore the day she met Jack. She smiled and ambled to the parlor, where Papa sat in her rocking chair, cradling a teacup.

"You're as pretty as a spring meadow," he said.

"Why, thank you. Did you find something to eat?"

"I'm not hungry, but I made us both some tea. I also brought you one of Martha's hot rolls from breakfast, though I'm not sure it's still hot."

Her mouth watered. "You know her rolls are my favorite," she called over her shoulder as she entered the kitchen. The roll was on a plate covered with one of her dish towels. Next to it was her favorite teacup, filled with steaming tea. She picked up both and reentered the parlor, then sat cross-legged on the sofa.

Papa let out a chuckle. "You look like a grownup lady, but you have the heart of a child. Don't ever change."

He referred to the way she sat. "I won't. At least not with you. But don't worry—I know how to behave around other people."

He sipped his tea. "Jack said you wished to see me?"

"Yes. He said you wanted to see me too. You go first."

He laughed. "I merely wanted to wish my favorite young lady a happy birthday. This is the first year you haven't woken up down the hall from me since you came to live there. Twenty-one years old. I don't know where the years have gone."

His eyes got all shiny and wet.

"Don't worry, Papa. I'm just down the road from you."

He ran the back of his hand across his eyes. "I know. It is just hard to let go. But I suppose it is time."

For a long moment, the only sounds were the ticking of the clock on the mantel, the creak of his rocking chair, and a dog barking somewhere down the road.

Lisa heaved a sigh. "Okay, my turn. I think I should tell Jack about the livery. I feel strange keeping that information from him... like I'm being dishonest. But I promised I wouldn't say anything until you agreed."

The nostalgic expression on his face turned to one of concern. "I'm still not sure that's wise."

Her stomach muscles tightened, and she grabbed hold of her skirt, twisting and wrinkling the fabric. "Can you share your reasons? I know Jack can't recall his past...and who knows if he ever will? But he's proven himself to be steady and true. He's kind, reliable, and hardworking. What is it about him you don't trust?"

"No, mija. It's not that I don't trust him. But you two have only been courting a short time. You may think you know him, but he came to us in May. He was incapacitated through most of June. It was late July when he asked to court you. So a little over two months...and you're still enamored with each other." He paused, as though considering his next words. "Getting to know a person is a marathon, not a sprint. Jack is a good man. But he is still healing, and you're both young. You have plenty of time. Enjoy your courtship."

She frowned. Everything he said made sense. But it still didn't feel right keeping this from Jack. "I feel like I'm lying to him."

Papa exhaled. "There's another reason. Pastor Smith requested in his will that you remain a silent partner. If people find out a woman owns half the livery and a black man owns the other half...well, some of them will take their business elsewhere. As it stands, most customers don't even know Carson's status. They think he works for someone else. People can be cruel. Pastor Smith wanted us to show wisdom in this matter, and I agree with him."

Lisa didn't know what to think. She felt nauseous. But she could see his point. "Still, we can trust Jack. He won't tell anyone."

Papa leaned forward. "I'll tell you what. Give it until Christmas. If you feel the same and you want to tell him, I will give you my permission. I only want what is best for you."

"I know."

He placed his hands on each arm of the rocker and pushed himself up. "Okay. Let's go."

"Go? Where?"

"I'm taking you on a birthday stroll. You look too pretty to stay inside all day reading a book, which is what I know you'll do if I leave now."

She eyed the stack of novels on her side table and laughed. "What's wrong with that?" Without waiting for an answer, she retreated to her bedroom. "Let me get my hat."

To strangers, they must have made an odd pair on their morning stroll, her in her pink dress, with her flowered hat and parasol, and him in his priestly garb, ambling arm in arm through the streets of San Antonio. They visited the business district, just a few blocks away, where she loved to window shop.

They paused in front of a confectionary. "Choose something," he said. "My birthday treat to you."

"You just want to fatten me up and rot all my teeth so Jack will lose interest."

"Ah! You're onto my plan."

After entering the small shop and studying the selection of candies, she chose a string of black licorice—her favorite.

"Get more than that, mija. You don't have to choose the least expensive thing."

"I like licorice!"

"I know. Get some lemon drops too. I'm hoping you'll share —and I can't stand licorice."

The clerk laughed at their exchange and added lemon drops to the bag.

Lisa's stomach rumbled. "I guess it's licorice and lemon drops for lunch."

"Save them for later. You'll get a sick stomach." He led her out of the store and back toward her home—or so she thought. Instead, they turned at the orphanage.

Did he want her to drop him off? Should she go in? Was Jack here? He'd acted so odd about her coming tod—

"Surprise!"

Lisa gasped. Her hand flew to her chest. Everywhere she looked, children popped out from behind bushes and benches. Lydia and Lucy held a hand-painted sign that read, *Happy Birthday, Miss Lisa!* in childlike print. Echoes of "We tricked you! You were so surprised!" surrounded her as children lunged at her skirts, wrapping her in hugs.

Standing to one side of the porch was Jack, wearing a Cheshire grin.

He winked.

She blushed.

She felt herself being pushed along by little hands and arms. "Come inside, Miss Lisa. Miss Martha made your favorite lunch, and cake for dessert!" She succumbed to the miniature mob, following the crowd into the dining hall. It was decorated with paper chains and homemade flag banners with *HAPPY BIRTHDAY, LISA* spelled out.

Mismatched tablecloths covered the tables, and flower petals lined the center of each. The children clamored around her.

"Sit here! You're the guest of honor."

"Your dress is pretty."

"Does this mean you're old?"

So many voices spoke at once, Lisa had a hard time keeping up with who said what. She sat at the head of the center table, and soon she was surrounded by boys and girls on either side, fighting to sit near her. Her eyes searched for Jack. He leaned against the doorjamb, Papa next to him, both looking smug and self-satisfied. She flashed them a grateful smile and turned her attention back to her small admirers.

This party certainly took some organization, and she wished, for a moment, that each child here could have such a moment of love, at least once in their lifetimes. Papa and Martha and the nuns did their best, but they didn't even know the birth dates of more than half the children. She'd have to put some thought as to how to bring more parties to this place...but for now, none of them seemed concerned with their own parties. They were just happy to be a part of this one.

All those years growing up here, Lisa had secretly wished for a home of her own. Looking around, she realized this *was* home, and she was blessed.

CHAPTER 22

Lampasas
October 15, 1898

If Emma hadn't watched the progression her sister-in-law had undergone over the last couple of months, she wouldn't have recognized Allison on the street. The normally stylish woman looked gray and gaunt. It wasn't just the severity of her black dress and hat against her pale skin. It was the lack of the subtle lip and cheek stain Allison used to wear. It was her hair—still neat, but instead of stylish pin curls and hair jewelry, it was pulled back in a tight, low bun. She'd gone from elegant to severe.

In addition, Allison had dropped probably twenty pounds. Since the day they'd received Roosevelt's telegram, she had simply stopped caring. About everything.

Emma sat next to her sister-in-law in Allison's dark, dusty parlor and offered to refill her tea. Allison had even dismissed the servants.

"No. Thank you."

What could Emma say to someone who'd lost her only child?

How could she pull Allison out of her hopeless tunnel when Emma had no way of understanding what she felt?

She couldn't. All she knew to do was be here. Sit with her, so she wasn't alone. Should she even broach the subject she'd come to discuss, or leave it for another time?

She was about to say something when Allison spoke. Her eyes fixed on a place somewhere in the distance, as if she were just talking—not necessarily to Emma. Just saying her thoughts out loud.

"It's the *not knowing* that's killing me. I know Jackson's gone. He's not coming home. At least, the logical part of my brain knows that. But..." She used her embroidered lace handkerchief to wipe her tear-streaked cheek. "But there's this tiny part of me that hopes...that he just got lost, and any day we'll get word. Any day, he'll come walking up those front steps yelling, "Mama! What's for dinner? I'm star—'" Her voice broke.

Emma waited, her heart twisting with pain.

After a time, Allison continued. "It's that hope that aches more than anything. I don't think I'll ever finish grieving him as long as there's even the tiniest chance he's alive. And since I'll probably never know, I doubt I'll ever be whole again."

If hearts could literally break in two, Emma's would be in pieces right now. She reached over, rested her hand on Allison's. Didn't say anything. There was nothing to say.

After a few moments, Allison cleared her throat. "I'm sorry. I know I'm not much fun to be around right now."

Emma squeezed Allison's hand before returning her own hand to her lap. Gave herself a few deep breaths and a hundred silent prayers for wisdom. Finally, she decided to jump in. "I have a favor to ask."

Allison pulled from her trance long enough to meet Emma's eyes.

"The décor at the inn is dreadfully outdated, and I need to redecorate. But I'm not good at that sort of thing. *You're* the one with the excellent taste. I'd really appreciate it if you'd go with me to choose new curtains, paint colors, wallpaper, furniture... I get a catalogue from a furniture maker in San Antonio. His name is Wenzel Friedrich, and he makes furniture using the discarded horns from cattle. Doesn't that sound fascinating? They sell a bit of everything, and from the illustrations, they have some beautiful choices. But I refuse to order from a catalogue without seeing it in person. And I really don't want to spend that much money only to have it look drab. Or worse—garish." *Please, Lord. Let this work.*

Allison lifted one eyebrow—the first sign of any expression other than complacent sadness Emma had seen in weeks. "Horns? I thought you didn't want garish."

Emma laughed. And then—miracle of miracles—so did Allison. A small, half-hearted chuckle, but it was something.

"You're probably right, but I thought we could go have a look. Apparently, this type of furniture is all the rage in Europe. If it's awful, there are several other furniture stores in San Antonio, as well." Emma held her breath and waited. Prayed.

The décor was fine. And Emma's taste had never been questioned. But Allison needed a *project*. One that would distract her from her pain. Just for a time, so the wounds could close—even a little.

Allison sighed. "You don't need me."

"But I do! You don't know what a hard time I had when we decorated the first time. Please? The train just opened a new route down through Waco and over to San Antonio. It's four hours. It could be fun."

The woman offered a half smile that didn't go all the way to her eyes. "I'll talk to Colt. When did you have in mind?"

"Whatever time is best for you. Riley said he'd come along. Invite Colt! We'll make it a family affair."

As she spoke, Emma didn't miss the irony of her words. Though they were civil, there'd never been much love lost between the siblings or the sisters-in-law. But this was different. They were all mourning Jackson's loss in their own ways. Better to support one another through the pain than have everyone suffer alone.

"As I said, I'll talk to Colt." Allison stood. "I think I need to lie down now."

Emma felt dismissed, as was Allison's way. This time, Emma wasn't offended. "Can I get you anything before you go? Would you like the tea tray brought to your room?"

"No. Just leave it. I'll see to it later."

Emma nodded and watched Allison leave the room, her steps heavy, her shoulders sagging. When she disappeared from view, Allison picked up the tray and took it to the kitchen, picked up a rag, and began washing dishes.

~

Sunday morning, Jack sat next to Lisa on the third row from the back, in the tiny La Villita church where she had been left as an infant. No wonder this felt like home to her. After attending each Sunday for the past couple of months, it was starting to feel that way to him too. The fact that the pastor left his home to Lisa, and that members of this church had cared for the empty home until she was able to live there, seemed like something out of a fairytale.

The tiny organ at the front of the church signaled the closing hymn, and they all stood. For some reason, Jack remembered the words to the song as if it were embedded deep in his soul.

> Blessed assurance, Jesus is mine!
> Oh what a foretaste of glory divine!

Heir of salvation, purchase of God,
Born of His Spirit, washed in His blood.

This is my story, this is my song,
Praising my Savior all the day long;
This is my story, this is my song,
Praising my Savior all the day long.

As the congregation continued the following verses, Jack went quiet. Last night, he'd had another dream. This one was actually pleasant. He was a child—maybe eight or nine. He rode on a horse with a man—his father. It was nighttime, and the stars were bright against a black sky. His father pointed out various constellations. While Jack might never recover his full memory, he was glad for at least one happy image to cling to.

Did he have parents out there somewhere? Siblings? Were they worried about him?

He pulled his thoughts back to the present. He loved hearing Lisa sing—her rich alto reminded him of soft butter on warm bread. With honey.

He also thought about those words he'd just sung... *Blessed assurance.* He'd lost his memory, which left him feeling as though he'd lost his footing. Did God offer assurance in this time of uncertainty? Could Jack accept that he may never know his past, and trust God with his future?

The chorus cut especially deep. *This is my story...*

Jack didn't have a story. Could God be his story? As the song said, could Jack find meaning and purpose in God?

The song ended, and the people in the small congregation shuffled to gather their things.

Jack placed his hand on Lisa's back. They spoke to a few people as they left. Once outside, he asked, "Where would you like to eat lunch today? There's a new café downtown."

"That sounds nice. Or we could eat leftovers at the orphanage." She grinned. Her birthday meal yesterday had been her favorite—roast beef with potatoes and carrots.

"Let's do that. But I would like some time away from little ears later. Perhaps we can go for a walk? I have something I'd like to talk to you about."

She took his arm as they walked away from the church. "Now I'm curious. Maybe we should go to the café, after all, so I don't have to wait as long."

Jack laughed. This woman filled up his heart. "Naaah. Now I want roast beef. It's nothing to get too excited about. Just an idea I have."

"The best way to get a girl excited about something is to tell her not to get excited. Let's go." She released his arm and grabbed him by the hand. "Maybe we can get there before the children return from mass."

Sure enough, they were just finishing up a shared slice of her birthday cake—a moist carrot cake—when they heard the children coming up the sidewalk.

"Hurry!" Martha called from the kitchen. "You can make your escape out the back."

Jack and Lisa laughed. It was good to have Martha on their team. Soon they walked arm in arm toward the livery. He wasn't really planning to go there, but both sets of their feet seemed to head that way of their own accord. Which was appropriate, given what he wanted to discuss.

"I have an idea," he told her. "And I'd like your feedback before I present it to Carson."

"I'm all ears."

"I told you he and his partner want to expand to include some draws for tourism."

"Yes...you said that."

"What would you think about a rodeo?"

She stopped in her tracks, right there on the sidewalk, hungry churchgoers bustling past them. "A rodeo?"

"Hear me out. The children love riding horses. Some of them really have a knack for it. What if I trained them for a children's rodeo? No bull riding or anything dangerous. Just some basic tricks. We can put them in costumes, have them carry flags—stuff like that makes anything look more impressive. We could call it the *St. Joseph's Benefit Rodeo* and charge for entrance. The money could help support the orphanage. Plus, it will give the children a sense of pride and purpose."

She didn't say anything for a moment. Just stood there, looking at him like he—well, he wasn't sure what her look meant. "If you think it's a terrible idea, just say so. I'd rather know now than make a fool of myself, talking it up to Carson."

One side of her mouth quirked up, then the other. She stood on her toes and planted a soft kiss on his cheek. "I think it's a wonderful idea."

"Really?" Relief washed over him. "I mean, it will be a lot of work. And I'll have to convince Carson and his partner. That guy's a real mystery. Likes to remain silent, Carson said."

Lisa shifted her gaze to the livery and began walking again. "I think it sounds like an excellent way to use your gifts and help others at the same time."

"Thank you. That means a lot. I...guess I'll talk to Carson about it tomorrow."

"Let me know how it goes."

He grabbed her hand and pulled her closer. "Hey."

She looked at him.

"Thank you."

"For what?"

"For believing in me. For encouraging me."

"Of course." She smiled, and the afternoon sun caught the gold flecks in her eyes, and his heart felt as though it did a backflip into his stomach.

"Since we're here, why don't you and Fury show off one of

your fancy tricks for me?" Her voice was part childlike, part womanly.

"Really?"

"Really. Just don't hurt yourself. I don't have my nurse's bag with me."

CHAPTER 23

The next day, Lisa and Phyllis shared the same shift. Lisa was glad for some time with her friend, even if they were working. Unfortunately, they had several needy patients. And those who weren't needy were cranky, so the two of them didn't get much time together.

When their replacements signed in, they exchanged a look of relief. "Want to come to my place for dinner?" Lisa asked. "Nothing fancy, but I have stuff for sandwiches. Jack's staying late to talk to Carson about a project."

"Oh, I get it. I'm just the backup." Phyllis tried to look offended.

"You are. Sorry. Your shoulders just aren't broad enough for my taste."

They shared a laugh as they made the short walk. Once there, they enjoyed a comfortable camaraderie, with Phyllis fixing a pot of tea while Lisa put together the simple meal.

Lisa really wanted to talk to someone about her dilemma with Jack, about not telling him of her part-ownership in the livery. And though Papa had told her not to share that information, she didn't think he meant Phyllis. What harm would it be for her to know?

"I need some advice. Or at least, I need to talk something through." She placed plates, teacups, and saucers on the small kitchen table, along with flatware.

"What's on your mind?" Phyllis poured the tea and placed the teapot between them.

"Well...I have some news..."

"You're engaged!" Phyllis clapped her hands. "I knew it. I knew he was going to propose. Oh, this is wonderful!"

Lisa shook her head and laughed. "No. Not that. You can calm down."

"Oh." Phyllis picked up her sandwich. "In that case, tell me what's on your mind."

"You know how the pastor who found me as a baby—James Smith—left me this house?"

"Yes. It's lovely."

"Well...that's not all he left me."

If Phyllis's eyes had gotten any bigger, they would have rolled onto the floor. "Do tell!"

This was one of the many reasons Lisa loved Phyllis so much. She had a way of making Lisa laugh, even when things were stressful.

"Apparently, he fronted the money for the livery, and Carson provided the work. They became fifty-fifty partners." She sipped her tea, then set the cup back in its saucer. "When Pastor Smith died, he left everything to me in his will. I thought this house was all he had, but I was wrong. My share of the profits from the livery have been put in trust all these years, to be made available when I came of age."

Phyllis slammed her sandwich onto her plate and spoke with her mouth full. "No!"

"Yes. I'm not independently wealthy, by any means. Those early years didn't see much profit. But with Carson's hard work, the business has grown. And I didn't just inherit money. I own half the business."

"Lisa, that's wonderful." She threw her hands in the air." It couldn't happen to a better person. So...what do you need advice about?"

"Well, you know how protective Father Hidalgo is of me."

"Yes. I'm surprised he's letting Jack court you. In his eyes, no one will ever be good enough for you."

"Apparently, Pastor Smith wanted it kept quiet. He was afraid we'd lose customers if people knew a woman and a black man were the owners. And Father Hidalgo thinks I ought to get to know Jack better before I tell him. He said to give it until Christmas."

Phyllis picked up her sandwich again and held it, elbows on the table. "Honestly, Lisa, I can see Father Hidalgo's point."

"I can too. But since Jack is now working for the livery...I mean...it's like I'm lying to him. I don't want to disregard Papa's advice. But I also feel guilty keeping this from Jack."

"From what I know of Jack, he'd be happy for you. What's the problem?"

"It's not that. I just wonder if, since he's working there, when he finds out I've been paying his salary and he didn't know...don't you think that might bother him? Won't it be better to tell him sooner, rather than later?"

Phyllis chewed, then swallowed. Took a sip of her tea, then dabbed at the corners of her mouth with her napkin. "I'd say you're in a tough spot. If he truly loves you, he'll understand."

A deep sigh slipped from Lisa's lips. "I know. But I still don't like keeping this from him. It feels dishonest."

"You're not lying, Lisa. You're just showing wisdom. After all —and you know I like Jack!—but what do we really know about him? There's nothing wrong with taking your time."

"I suppose you're right."

The conversation turned to other things as Lisa shared the

last of the carrot cake Martha had sent home with her. Soon Phyllis said her goodbyes, and Lisa readied herself for Jack's promised visit. As nice as it was to spend time with her friend, she couldn't shake the uneasy feeling that keeping this from Jack was the wrong thing to do.

~

Jack clutched the bouquet of bright yellow sunflowers, bought from a street vendor, behind his back as he knocked on Lisa's door. She opened it and stepped onto the porch wearing a brown-and-gold dress that brought out the yellow flecks in her eyes. Would she always leave him this breathless?

"For you," he said, holding out his gift.

"Jack! You spoil me. They're beautiful!"

"*You're* beautiful."

She turned toward the kitchen, the flowers only partially hiding the flush blooming in her neck and face. "Let me put these in water. Are we taking a stroll, or would you rather sit on the porch and talk? I have lemonade."

"Let's just sit, if that's all right with you. I want to tell you about my talk with Carson."

"Good. I've been waiting all day to hear."

He sat in one of the porch rockers and waited for her to return.

She set two glasses on the small table, then poured from a pitcher before taking the other seat. "So?"

After a long swig of the tangy drink, he looked at her and smiled. "It's promising. He wants to discuss the idea with his partner, but he seemed open—even excited—about the rodeo."

"That's wonderful news, Jack! I'm so happy for you."

"I'm trying not to get too excited until I hear back from the partner. I wish I could meet the guy. It feels weird working for someone I've never met." He laughed. "What if it's some old millionaire recluse who lives in a dark, dilapidated mansion and scares little children by staring at them through the window when they walk by?"

"You have quite an imagination." She picked at a loose thread on her skirt. "It's probably just a normal person who wants to remain in the shadows."

"Maybe."

"It might even be a woman."

Jack nearly spit out his lemonade. "Now that would be something."

She shifted in her chair to look directly at him. "Why is that so funny?"

Uh-oh. He'd offended her. "I'm not saying a woman couldn't...I mean...It's possible. Just highly unlikely."

Lisa stiffened ever so slightly. "Why is that?"

"I don't know. It just is."

"Would it bother you if you learned it was a woman?" Her voice was tight.

He leaned back, rocked. This conversation had taken an unexpected turn. "I don't think so. I guess you're right. There's no reason a woman couldn't own a livery. What if it's that old lady who boards Daisy, the brown mare? The white-haired lady?"

She seemed to relax a little. "Perhaps..."

"I hope it's not her."

"Why?"

"She likes me a little too much." Jack grinned at her over his lemonade glass.

"What do you mean?" She took a sip of her drink.

"She winks at me whenever she comes in."

Now it was Lisa's turn to nearly lose her lemonade. "Jack, I do believe you're full of yourself. That woman has vision problems. She's probably just struggling to see you."

"Oh. You may be right." He smirked.

"I know I'm right."

They shared a moment of quiet before both breaking into a reel of laughter.

She peeked at him from behind her glass. "Was this our first spat?"

"I'm not sure I'd call this a spat. If this is the worst communication mishap we have, I'd say we're in pretty good shape."

"You're probably right."

He winked at her, then lifted his voice to a high falsetto. *"I know I'm right."*

~

Two weeks later, Jack could barely contain his excitement about the St. Joseph's Benefit Rodeo. He stopped swinging his hammer and studied the paddock. It was being expanded into a larger ring—an arena, really—with raised benches for spectators. A date was set for mid-November for a short preview rodeo. It would be free to the public and only last about fifteen minutes. But it gave the children a goal date. Jack could teach them some simple, impressive-looking stunts, and he himself would perform a couple of show-stoppers to get people talking. The full rodeo would take place next March, with another free mini-rodeo in January, weather permitting.

"There you are!" Lisa's voice made him smile all over. He turned, and she walked toward him, holding out a piece of paper. She still wore her nursing uniform—she'd come straight from work. "I wanted to show you this."

Jack took the page in his free hand, but he had a hard time pulling his eyes from her. When he did, he saw it was a flyer.

St. Joseph's Orphanage Benefit Rodeo
Coming March, 1899
Free previews:
November 17, 1898
January 24, 1899
Carson's Livery
Featuring the Children of St. Joseph's
and
Trick Rider and Director, Jack

He shook his head, impressed. "That looks great. Do your talents never end?"

"I'm not sure this took a lot of talent, but thank you."

He stared at the flyer. "It looks odd that I don't have a last name."

"Yes, it does. But I wasn't sure what to put."

"I've been thinking about that. I want to take a last name. If and when I regain my memory, I can revert to my name of birth. But what would you think about Jack Smith? In honor of the pastor who found you and cared for you when you were an infant."

She looked taken aback for a moment. Her eyes glistened. "Jack," she whispered. "That's the sweetest thing I've ever heard. I think it's a lovely idea."

He wasn't ready to propose. Yet. But the more he thought about it, the more it made sense. That man didn't leave behind any biological children. This way, when Jack did marry Lisa—and he *would* marry her, if she'd have him—they could carry on the family name. "Jack Smith it is. I suppose I need to fill out some paperwork at the courthouse, for an official name change. Except, I'm not sure what I'm changing it from."

"Papa may know something about the legalities of taking on a new name since he handles adoption. We can go talk to him about it now, if you'd like." Her eyes looked hopeful.

"I'll see him about it later. Right now, I have something else I'd like to discuss with you." He grabbed her hand and led her to one of the benches inside the livery, out of the sun. When they were both seated, he set his hammer aside and asked, "Would you consider riding in the rodeo?"

"Me?" Her eyes widened, and one hand flew to her chest. "No. I don't think so. I'm not a trick rider."

"No, but you're beautiful." He winked, and the blush that rose in her cheeks brought him immense pleasure. "You wouldn't have to do anything but ride around the arena and wave. We could get you an Annie Oakley costume and a cowgirl hat. The crowd will love it."

She shook her head, then paused. "I...I don't know. I'll think about it."

"Remember, it's for the children."

She poked him in the ribs. "Don't try to guilt me. I said I'd consider it."

"Well, consider it hard. If not you, I'll have to ask Mrs. Clark. And I'm not sure she'll have the same effect on an audience, considering she doesn't know how to smile." He made his best sour face.

She laughed and popped him on the arm. "Jack Smith. That is ungentlemanly."

The use of his new, full name gave him pause. "Jack Smith. I like it."

"Do you want a middle name too? If so, now's the time to consider it."

"Nah. I think middle names are a waste." He offered a stern look. "They're only used when a person's in trouble."

"True. So just Jack Smith?"

"That's me. Jack Smith. Just a regular guy."

She chuckled, that beautiful alto laugh. "There's nothing *regular* about you, Jack."

"I'm not sure how to take that."

She stretched up and kissed him on the cheek. "Take it however you want. It's the truth."

He gripped the hammer he'd set on the end of the bench to keep from pulling her close for a full kiss, right here where any customer could walk in and witness it. He may have lost his memory. But right now, that didn't feel nearly as significant as the fact that he'd completely lost his heart.

CHAPTER 24

Lisa's schedule took on the same feel it had during the cholera scare. Only this time, her evenings were filled with rodeo practices. She helped with the children where she could, keeping them focused and behaved. She sketched and planned and sewed costumes, with hopes to eventually build a costume closet they could use for years to come. And yes, she agreed to learn some fancy-looking tricks along with the children and ride in the rodeo. Of all the things she'd *never* seen herself doing, this was about as far off target as she could have gotten. But she was having fun.

One pleasant November afternoon, she sat on one of the new arena benches, watching Jack work.

He lifted his cowboy hat and used his bandana to wipe the sweat off his brow, then the back of his neck. The day wasn't hot, but he'd been working hard. "What do you think of the seating? Is it enough?"

"We'll see. If not, they can stand, and we'll build more. These benches are beautiful, Jack. It's amazing the things you know how to do. You haven't had any more dreams or flashbacks?"

He sat next to her and placed his hat beside him. "I do, but when I wake up, it's like it's all just out of reach. Sometimes I'll see or do something and have the feeling that I've done it before. But after all this time, I'm not holding out hope for any miracles. I'm just glad I'm not incapacitated, and can start a new life here." He looked at her a minute, and she thought he might add "with you" to his statement, but he didn't.

Still, she was pretty sure he was thinking it, and she was okay with that.

He crossed one foot over the other knee. His boots were covered in dust from the arena. "I spoke to Father Hidalgo about changing my name. He said I just need to start going by Jack Smith. Since I'm not inheriting anything—as I don't know who my parents are—I can just sign my name as Jack Smith from here on out."

"Wow. That's pretty easy." She offered what she hoped was an encouraging smile.

"Yes. And I'm glad for it." He steepled his fingers together and gazed forward. "I've been fine with being paid in cash, but I ought to open a bank account soon. I need a last name to do that." He shifted his eyes to hers.

"I guess, to be proper, I should start calling you Mr. Smith." Lisa jabbed him with her elbow.

"And I'll call you Miss Garcia."

They stared at each other a moment.

"I prefer Jack," Lisa said.

"Good, because I actually prefer Lisa." His voice lowered to a whisper. "Or *Ivelisse*. I don't know why you don't go by your given name."

Why did the moment suddenly feel intimate? She swallowed. "Lisa's just easier for most people, and it's what I've always been called."

He locked his eyes with hers, his voice still low. "So you don't mind if I call you Ivelisse?"

Her lips were dry. "I don't mind. Maybe when it's just the two of us, though."

"What if you use Ivelisse as your stage name and Lisa as your everyday name?" Jack's dimples peeped through as he spoke.

"Stage name?"

"Yes! Your rodeo name." The intimate feeling turned to a teasing one.

She laughed. "Do I need a rodeo name?"

"Only if you want one." He reached out, twirled one of her loose curls around his finger, and it did strange things to her insides. "Several times a year, you could be the lovely, the talented Miss Ivelisse Garcia."

She tried to ignore the chills his touch sent through her. Swallowed again. "And what about the rest of the time?"

"You could be Nurse Lisa...Smith."

Her eyes widened. She was pretty sure her heart stopped beating for a time, then made up for the missed beats by pounding extra hard. Was he saying what she thought he was saying?

He winked, then stood. "Are you ready to practice your trick?"

No! She wanted to yell. How could he drop something like that on her, then act as if nothing had happened? But if he wanted to play coy, she could too. She took a deep breath to calm her pounding heart. Practice her trick. It was time to practice. *Focus, Lisa.*

"I'm ready. I'm surprised at how hard it looks when the children do it and how easy it actually is." She climbed into Dusty's saddle, stroked her mane, and clicked the signal for the horse to move to a trot.

Jack had modified this saddle, as well as the ones the children used, to have two small handles on either side at the front, as well as small foot loops in the back. He called them training loops. They were the same color as the rest of the saddle and not noticeable from a distance. They enabled the rider to hold on securely in various positions.

Once they were moving at a steady pace around the arena, Lisa carefully stood in the stirrups. She wouldn't move to a full saddle stand like Jack, but this was fun. She lifted her arms to the side and felt the wind in her hair. Then she practiced waving to the empty benches.

"Excellent!" Jack called from his place near the fence. "Now, try resting one knee in the saddle, then the other, like I showed you."

This was where the split riding skirt came in handy. She did as Jack instructed. Dusty was the perfect horse for this kind of riding. Her calm, even temperament made it easy to try new things without fear. Carefully, Lisa moved to a kneeling position on the saddle, holding onto the hidden handles and placing her left foot through the rear loop.

"Good! Now for the grand finale. Hold one leg out straight behind you."

Gripping the front handles, Lisa lifted one leg behind her and pointed her toe. The costume she'd wear for the rodeo was also a split skirt. But it was full and flowing, with loops inside that attached to her ankles for modesty. She could envision it billowing behind her as she rode. Did she look ridiculous?

Maybe.

But she felt beautiful and free. And the pride in Jack's voice as he cheered her on filled her spirit. Was there anything she wouldn't do for this man?

Right now, she didn't think so.

The preview rodeo was in one week, and Father Hidalgo temporarily suspended the children's afternoon classes so they could prepare. Jack spent every moment he could at the new arena. He wasn't ready to quit his job at Joske and Sons. It paid better than the livery. But each morning, he woke up early and went to the livery for a couple of hours, doing his regular chores so he could focus on the rodeo in the afternoons. Then he'd head home for a quick cleanup before going to his morning job. His duties there had expanded to the furniture department, now that he was physically able to help move heavy objects. Which was fine with him, since it meant he could avoid Mrs. Clark.

Last week, she saw him hang one of the flyers in the store window, with Mr. Joske's permission. "Hmmmm. Jack Smith. Is that you?"

"It is."

"You're teaching these children...trick riding?"

"That's correct."

The woman looked indignant. "How absurd. These are orphans. How can doing stunts in a rodeo prepare them for a stable future?"

"In many ways. In addition to learning equestrian skills, it's building their confidence. They're gaining experience in front of a crowd, which helps them have poise and grace under pressure. Besides that, they're having fun. It's important for people to have fond memories of their childhoods, don't you think?"

"I think, Mr. *Smith*"—she stressed the name as if to emphasize the fact that it wasn't his real name—"that you're setting them up to be beggars and paupers. And I think that's a crime."

"I'm sorry you feel that way. Would you like to reserve your tickets now or later?"

"Hmmph!" The woman did an about face and marched back to the ladies' lingerie department, probably because she knew he wouldn't follow her there. Little did she know, Jack had no desire to follow that woman anywhere. He nearly lost his lunch every time he saw her interact with a wealthy customer—all syrup and honey. But anyone who appeared to be of the working class, she treated with vinegar. Which was the height of hypocrisy, since she herself was a working class woman.

Fortunately, Mr. Joske asked him to reserve two rows for himself and his family. He also donated a generous amount to help them prepare. "This is specifically for the rodeo, to help make it a success. I'll donate more in March. But since the preview show is free, I thought you might find these funds useful now."

Which meant they were able to purchase banners and flags, extra fringe for costumes, and even a retired rodeo horse from one of Buffalo Bill's shows. The dealer said this scaled-down, calmer rodeo was a perfect fit, and from what Jack could see, the man was right.

The second Wednesday of November was the first dress rehearsal. They'd try everything out in full costume, banners and flags and all. That way, if anything went wrong, they still had a few days to fix it. When Jack arrived at the livery, Father Hidalgo and the nuns already had the sixteen children there, lined up on benches, fully costumed in red, white, and blue attire, each with a Western-style hat. Most had a hard time sitting still, and they reminded him of a basket of puppies wiggling to get out.

"Can I go first, Jack?"

"No, silly. We gotta go in order."

"Where's Miss Lisa? She's gotta be here. Her part comes first."

Jack held up a hand, and the noise quieted. "Miss Lisa is working. We'll skip her number for now. But first, I have to say how fabulous you look! I've never seen a finer-looking group of rodeo performers."

Lydia raised her hand. "Mr. Jack, even if you had seen a finer group, how would you know, since you can't 'member nothin'?"

One of the nuns shushed her.

"It's all right, sister. That's a valid point, Lydia. Maybe I should have said I can't remember seeing a finer group. But even if I could, I'm pretty sure you all would be the winners."

She smiled, revealing a large gap in her front teeth.

Father Hidalgo handed him a megaphone. "You'll need this."

Jack held it to his mouth. "Father Hidalgo and I will take turns introducing you. When it's your turn, remember the most important thing is..."

"Smile!" the children chorused.

"That's right. No one in the audience will know if you make a mistake unless you tell them with your face. Whatever happens, keep smiling!"

Lydia raised her hand, then spoke before being called on. "What if I die? Do I have to smile then?"

Jack worked to keep a straight face. He cleared his throat, buying some time to think of a response. "Try very hard not to die, Lydia. If you die, then no. You don't have to smile. But short of death, try to keep smiling."

One by one, the children performed their short tricks. It was amateur. Hats flew off. Shoes came untied. One costume got ripped, resulting in tears. Two of the children forgot what they were supposed to do, so they just rode around the circle before dismounting. But all in all, it was entertaining. After all, there were a bunch of small children in outlandish, colorful rodeo gear. Who wouldn't be entertained by that? Besides, they still had a few months before they'd charge for the show.

Once they were all back on their benches, staring at him

wide-eyed, waiting for his praise or condemnation, Jack felt such a sense of accomplishment and relief and purpose...as though this crazy thing was what he was born to do. "Excellent job, all of you. I love the smiles! Are there any questions?"

A sudden swell of murmurs told him he'd lost them. They were paying attention to something else. Several pointed to someone behind him, and he turned.

There was Lisa. No, *Ivelisse,* looking every bit a queen. She wore a long, flowing white gown trimmed with red fringe, with a matching white hat and red band. Up the front were red and blue alternating buttons, and the waist cinched in to create a striking silhouette. Around her neck was the horse necklace he gave her for her birthday. For a moment, he had second thoughts about putting her on display—she was too beautiful.

But then she smiled, and the sun looked pale in comparison. "Sorry I'm late!"

The children buzzed behind him. "Can we stay and watch Miss Lisa?"

Jack ignored them, moved forward until he stood right in front of her, facing her. "Wow. There are no words."

She laughed. "I feel silly."

"You look amazing. But you need to tuck your necklace in. You don't want anything flying around your face while you're riding."

"Oh, I hadn't thought of that." She adjusted the necklace so it was inside her collar.

He placed one hand on her arm and gave it an encouraging squeeze. "Your fans await. Are you ready?"

"I suppose."

Without further ado, he held up his megaphone as Lisa mounted Dusty in the waiting pen. "Ladies and gentlemen, it's the moment you've all been waiting for." His speech was interrupted by children's giggles at being called ladies and gentlemen. "Brace yourselves for the lovely, the talented, the exquisite Miss Ivelisse Garcia!"

She rode through the gate and urged Dusty into a trot. Then she stood, a picture of grace and poise. The children clapped and squealed. With a flourish, she lifted one arm, then the other and waved to the audience.

She was a natural!

With that same grace, she moved to her kneeling position on the horse. Finally, with the slow beauty of a ballerina, she lifted her right leg to the back, toe pointed, skirt and fringe billowing in the wind. She was perfect.

The children went wild. Jack pulled his eyes away from Lisa for just a moment to watch her admirers. They stood, jumped up and down, and called her name as though she was a celebrity. Even Father Hidalgo beamed with pride.

He looked back just in time to see her return to her normal riding position. She waved some more, like royalty waving to her subjects, before returning Dusty to her stall. Jack lifted the megaphone again. "There you have it, ladies and gentlemen. The belle of every ball, the queen of every heart...Miss Ivelisse Garcia."

The applause went on for several minutes as she dismounted, and even after she joined the children. She held up her hands. "Stop! You're embarrassing me."

Indeed, her face was flushed. But Jack was pretty sure she was enjoying every minute. And he could get used to doing this with her by his side.

CHAPTER 25

The train ride from Lampasas to San Antonio left at seven-thirty a.m. and took just over four hours. After the first half hour, Riley gave up trying to make small talk with his brother and sister-in-law. Both had disappeared into their grief months ago, and though he and Emma hoped this excursion would help them out of it, even a little, that was yet to be seen.

When they pulled into the SA & AP station, Riley and Colt retrieved their bags and escorted their wives onto the platform near the historic Alamo.

Emma pulled a folded map out of her reticule. "I don't know about you all, but I'm famished. What do you say we find something to eat before heading to the hotel? It looks like Wenzel Friedrich's furniture store is located just a few blocks from there. We can settle in, rest up, and maybe walk over there around three-thirty before they close for the day. I must say, I'm curious to see those horn chairs!"

They all agreed with that plan. Fortunately, there was a diner next door to the depot where the day's special was chicken and dumplings with fresh, buttered rolls. Other than ordering their meals, Colt and Allison remained withdrawn.

Riley and Emma kept the conversation light. But inside, Riley ached for his brother. He'd never seen Colt this way. Riley prayed daily for God to restore some kind of life, a little bit of joy to Colt and Allison, but so far, there was no evidence of that. But Riley had long ago accepted that God was God, and He didn't have to let Riley in on how He was working. Riley just had to trust that even when there was no evidence, God was busy.

Please, God. I can't imagine their pain at losing their only child. Show them You still love them.

As if in acknowledgement of Riley's silent prayer, Colt set his spoon down. "After the new year, Allison and I want to take a trip to Cuba. Just to look around. See what we can find out. Maybe it will..." Colt paused. Swallowed. "Maybe it will help us understand what happened."

Beneath the table, Emma grabbed Riley's hand and squeezed. This was progress.

"That's sure to be a hard trip," Riley said. "But I think you're right. It might help." He wanted to say more, but he forced himself to stop talking. Sometimes the less said, the better.

Allison sniffed. Took another small bite of her meal. It was good to see her eat—even just a little. "This is good," she said. "It reminds me of yours, Emma. In all these years, we've never had a cook that came close to your skill."

Now Riley squeezed Emma's hand. That time in Emma's life—working for Allison—wasn't a fond memory. But any compliment from Allison was rare.

"I can give you any recipes you want," Emma said.

Allison and Colt lifted eyebrows in unison, and it was the first hint of a smile he'd seen either of them offer in months.

Colt took a big bite of dumpling, as if he knew better than to comment on his wife's skill in the kitchen.

Allison, on the other hand, offered a low chuckle. "That would be wonderful. I'll be sure to pass them along to our next cook."

They finished their meal, paid the tab, and exited the diner. "Shall we board a street car?" Riley asked, watching one of the modern, electric vehicles pass by on its tracks.

"That sounds fun!" Emma's face lit up. "I've never ridden one. Have you, Allison?"

The woman shook her head. Soon, they boarded a streetcar for the short ride to the Menger Hotel. Riley had telegraphed for reservations the week before.

When they arrived, Colt stared at the large sign. "This is where Roosevelt recruited for the Rough Riders. Jackson would have come here, first."

"I...I'm so sorry. I didn't realize. We can get another hotel if you'd like." Riley's gut clenched. How could he have made such a blunder?

"No! No. I...this is good. This is—" Colt's voice broke. "This is good."

Riley looked around. He could understand how Colt and Allison must feel. Even Riley got a little choked up knowing this was the last place they could trace Jackson's presence.

~

Friday evening

"Hold still!" Lisa spoke around straight pins in her mouth. Trying to adjust costumes for wiggly children was about like trying to harness a herd of hyenas. Not that she'd ever harnessed a hyena—or even seen one—but she could imagine. Lucy was the last one... all the others had gone to bed. "I'm almost done. But if you don't stop moving, I may poke you, and you won't be very happy with me."

"The rodeo's tomorrow, Miss Lisa!" Lucy's voice was higher-pitched than normal. She opened and closed her fists in a display of nervous energy.

"I know, and you're going to be fabulous."

"What if I fall off my horse?"

"Have you fallen off before?" Lisa asked.

"No. But it could happen."

"I suppose it could. But Mr. Jack selected each of the horses for the rodeo especially for their calm spirits. You won't be riding very fast. If you fall off, you may get a bump and a bruise, but that will probably be the worst of it." She paused, then moved to look Lucy in the eye. "But Lucy, you don't have to ride if you're afraid. This is supposed to be fun. It's entirely up to you."

Lucy let out a breath. "I want to ride. I just don't want to mess things up for everyone else."

Lisa wrapped the child in a tight hug. "That's not possible. You are amazing, and it has nothing to do with your performance at the rodeo tomorrow. Your sweet spirit and your beautiful smile will bring joy to so many people."

Lucy hugged her back. "Thanks. I hope so."

"I know so."

A long shadow fell over them from the parlor doorway. "There's two of the prettiest ladies in San Antonio."

"Jack!" Lucy squealed, but Lisa held her back from running to him.

"Careful! Remember your pins. One more second...there! I'm done. Go change into your night clothes and bring the dress back to me. Be very careful stepping out of it so you don't get scratched."

Lucy nodded, gave Jack a careful side hug on her way out, and disappeared.

"I'm so grateful for all you're doing." Jack moved into the

room. "I know you have to work tomorrow morning. You must be exhausted."

"Oh, my nerves will keep me going until this preview is over. At least I was able to get a substitute for tomorrow afternoon. Things have gone much smoother since we started to train some of the nursing students." She gestured to the sofa. "Sit down. You look like you may fall asleep at any moment."

He sat. Patted the place beside him. "Like you, I'm running on excitement. I can't believe this is really happening."

She plopped down, exhaling in exhaustion. "You're doing a great thing, Jack. In so many ways."

He looked deep into her eyes, and the soft, evening lamplight cast a romantic glow. She was pretty sure he was about to kiss her, but Lucy chose that moment to return with the dress. "Here you go, Miss Lisa."

"Thank you, Lucy. Now give me a hug."

She wrapped her little arms in a tight squeeze around Lisa's neck, then repeated the action with Jack. "See you tomorrow!" Then she skipped away, down the hall.

They both laughed.

"It looks like we're not the only ones who are excited." Lisa grinned at Jack. "I don't know if any of the children will sleep tonight."

He stood. "How long will it take you to fix that?" He pointed to the costume.

"Not long."

"Let me escort you home. We both need to at least attempt a few hours' rest."

They said little during the short walk. When they arrived, he leaned against a porch post. "I feel as though this is something I've always wanted to do. It's so strange that I can't remember details, but I can remember feelings."

"I'm still holding out hope that your memory will return, Jack. It may be in bits, or it may be all at once. But whatever comes, know this. The person you are, with or without specific memories of your past, is amazing. And I'm so glad I get to walk this journey with you."

He leaned forward as if to kiss her. Rested a hand on her cheek. But he stopped about two inches from her lips. Held her gaze, as if searching for something beneath her eyes. They stood there, locked in the moment, for probably a whole minute, but it felt like longer. After a time, he kissed her, a slow, gentle kiss, then pulled away. "Good night, Ivelisse."

"Good night, Jack." She watched him disappear down the street, wondering what he'd been thinking. What did he almost say?

~

Emma stirred. Stretched. How long had she been asleep? The clock beside the bed red 7:15 p.m. The bed next to her was empty. She turned over and found Riley sitting in the stuffed chair in the corner, feet propped on the ottoman, reading a newspaper.

"Ahh. Sleeping Beauty awakens."

"Why did you let me sleep so long? We were going to visit Wenzel Friedrich's this afternoon."

"You needed your rest. And I suspect Colt and Allison needed some time. I can't believe I booked the same hotel where Jackson…I feel terrible."

Emma sat up. "This is the nicest hotel in San Antonio, and you wanted it to be a pleasant trip. You couldn't have known. Besides, it may help bring closure."

"I hope so. I haven't heard a peep from the room next door. Should I go check on them, see if they're ready to find dinner?"

"Yes, I suppose. I'll get up and fix my hair."

Riley laughed. "I think you should go just as you are."

Emma caught her reflection in the mirror across the room.

Her hair stuck out every which way, and her face was creased from the pillow. "Yes. Wouldn't that be something?"

Riley dropped a kiss on her cheek and exited the room. She pushed herself to a seated position, stretched her arms overhead, and yawned. She must have really needed that nap. She heard him tap lightly on Colt and Allison's door, the room next to theirs.

No response. He tapped a little louder.

Emma moved to the stool at the dressing table and dug through her bag to find a hairbrush.

She heard him knock a third time. Maybe he should let them sleep.

A moment later, he reappeared. "I don't think they're in there."

"Oh. Perhaps they're downstairs. I'll be ready soon."

A few minutes later, they stood in the lobby. The manager had recommended the Menger Restaurant. They had to walk through the bar to get to it.

The dimly lit bar offered sound effects of low murmurs and glasses clinking. They were nearly to the restaurant when Emma just happened to focus on the bar, with high stools along the front. There were Colt and Allison, sitting on the far two stools, almost hidden by the shadows. Emma tugged Riley's elbow and nodded that way.

Riley heaved a great sigh, as if in anticipation of more of Colt's drama. Whenever he drank, the results weren't good. He led Emma to the stool next to Allison, then moved around to sit next to his brother.

Colt clung to a half-empty glass filled with amber liquid. Allison, too, nursed a stemmed goblet of deep-burgundy something. Emma wasn't like so many in her church group who thought alcohol was the unpardonable sin. But she did know it didn't hold the answers—or the comfort—so many sought. And everyone she knew who turned to alcohol in difficult times ended up compounding their problems.

"I'm sorry I overslept," Emma told Allison.

Allison nodded but didn't say anything.

"Are you ready to eat? The manager said the restaurant here is the best in San Antonio."

Still no reply.

Emma rested her hand on Allison's back. Sometimes, words couldn't fix things. A meal couldn't even fix things. Instead, she did the only thing she knew that could. She prayed.

CHAPTER 26

Saturday dawned bright, the perfect day for a rodeo. The air was crisp but not too cold, and the sun highlighted bright autumn leaves that still clung to their branches or drifted like confetti to rest on sidewalks and park benches. As Lisa took her morning walk to work, she turned her face up and soaked in the sunshine.

Today was the day. She'd either be a sensation, or she'd be humiliated. She giggled. Probably both. But most importantly, the children would have a chance to do something unique and fun, and Jack would see the fruits of his labor. She prayed the day would bring success on every front.

When Lisa arrived, Phyllis stood in the hallway outside the office studying her clipboard. "There's the rodeo star," she quipped. "I found someone to cover for me for a little while so I can come. I'll be in uniform, but I'll be there."

"Really?" Lisa grinned at her friend. "That means so much. Though to be honest, I feel a little ridiculous in the costume."

"I'm going to announce to everyone around me that we are best of friends, and that I taught you everything you know. I know it's a stretch, but you're my claim to fame, and I plan on taking advantage."

Lisa laughed and waved as Phyllis made her way back to her duties.

Inside the office, Nurse Jacobs set aside a file and offered an encouraging smile. "Are you ready for the big event?"

"I don't know. As ready as I will be, I suppose." She struggled to maintain her professional composure. She wanted to giggle like a schoolgirl. "Thank you again for giving me time off to do this."

"Of course. You've worked harder than anyone I know." Her smile was warm. "You deserve time to do something for yourself...though I'm not sure this qualifies. You're actually doing this for the orphanage. I hope you've had fun in the process."

"I have."

"I'm not going to lose you, am I?" Her smile shifted to a teasing smirk. "You're not going to run away and join Buffalo Bill's Wild West Show, are you?"

"Hardly! Although if they do another European tour, I'll be tempted."

Nurse Jacobs chuckled. "If they do another European tour, I may join you. In the meantime, we have a new patient in the children's ward. A young man borrowed his father's bicycle and decided to race downhill. He lost control and crashed into a tree."

"Oh, no! Will he be all right?"

"He has a broken arm, some scratches, and a nasty bump on the head. Dr. Williamson wants to observe him for a couple of days, just to be sure. But from what I can see, he'll be fine."

"That's good. I'm headed that way now."

"Before you go..." A grin Lisa couldn't quite identify spread across Nurse Jacobs's face. "I was wondering if you might stop by, either before or after the show, wearing your costume. I think it might cheer up the patients to see a real live rodeo star."

A blush seeped upward from Lisa's chest, through her neck and cheeks, and set her ears on fire. "You're joking, right?"

"No...but only if you're comfortable with that. Laughter and joy go such a long way toward healing, and I just thought...well, that it might be fun for them."

Lisa laughed. Shook her head. "This rodeo business is taking on a life of its own. I'll be happy to do that. I can't promise what time, but I will definitely stop by in my costume."

"You're a doll, Lisa. Thank you for all you do."

Lisa exited and headed to the children's ward. Four more hours, and she'd step out of these doors to do one of the craziest—and most exciting—things she'd ever done.

~

Emma stood in the middle of Wenzel Friederick's furniture store, slack jawed, and tried to keep her face from showing her true thoughts. She stole a look at Allison, who widened her eyes in an ever-so-subtle show of agreement with Emma's feelings. Their two husbands followed the manager around the store, exclaiming over the brilliance of the obviously male-inspired furniture, crafted almost entirely from cattle horns.

"This is stunning craftsmanship." Riley said. "I've never seen anything like it."

Even Colt looked impressed. He gestured to a piece against the wall. "I think we need this bench for our front porch, Allison."

"Thanks, Emma." Allison's low whisper, laced with wry humor, brought Emma a new perspective. As awful as the furniture was, it seemed to provide a momentary distraction from Allison and Colt's grief. And that made it all worth it.

Riley stopped in front of an oversized dining table and chairs and looked at Emma. "I think this would look great in the inn."

She wanted to say, "Absolutely not!" But with the manager right there, she controlled her tongue. "Perhaps. We have other stops to make today, though. We should look at all our options before making a decision."

Riley looked back at the table with such longing, he might have been a seven-year-old who'd just been told no to a request for a new puppy. "All right."

The foursome walked through the warehouse, observing all the different pieces. The craftmanship was exquisite. It just wasn't exactly what Emma had imagined. When they'd seen everything, Emma pulled out her map. "Next stop, Joske and Sons. I've heard their products are of high quality, and they'll deliver via the railroad."

After a short ride on the streetcar, they entered the department store and were greeted by a woman in her late fifties. "Good morning! I'm Mrs. Clark. How may I help you?"

The other three looked to Emma as their spokesperson. She introduced Riley, Allison, and Colt before saying, "Riley and I own an inn in Lampasas, and I'm thinking of redecorating. I'd like to look at furniture, accessories, wallpaper samples, and anything else we may need in that process."

The woman's eyebrows lifted, and her eyes took on a glint that suggested she stopped seeing customers and only saw dollar signs. "Of course, Mrs. Stratton. Follow me." She led them to a showroom at the back of the store. Around the large room, groupings of furniture resembled small rooms without walls. "Where would you like to start? We have bedroom furniture to the left, parlors to the right, and dining room furniture is all the way to the back wall."

"Let's start here." Emma approached a lovely sofa grouped

with end tables, stuffed chairs, a plush rug, and expensive-looking lamps.

"Excellent choice," the woman said. "As you can see, this piece is displayed in a burgundy damask. But if you look on the tea table, you'll find a book with other upholstery options, including brocades, chintz, jacquard, velvet, and others. Anything you see can be bought as-is and shipped by train. Or you can order a custom piece which will be created at our main warehouse and shipped directly to you on completion."

Something about Mrs. Clark's tone grated on Emma's nerves. She didn't know why. The woman was perfectly polite. Still, Emma wanted time to look without having the woman comment. "Thank you. You've been very helpful. If you don't mind, we'll look around and let you know if we need anything."

Something dimmed in the woman's eyes. Oh, dear. Had Emma dismissed her too soon? Had she hurt her feelings?

"Of course, Mrs. Stratton." She nodded to her left. "I'll be just over there if you need me."

The four of them toured the furniture area, but it didn't take long for Riley and Colt to lose interest.

Riley rested his arm around Emma's shoulders. "You ladies take all the time you need. I think I'll head to the men's department. I saw some pocket knives on display. Maybe I'll get one for Cordell."

Colt wasted no time. "I'll join you."

For the next twenty minutes, Emma and Allison made their way through the mock rooms, gathering ideas and exclaiming over new décor trends. For Emma, the day was already a success. For the first time in months, Allison and Colt seemed distracted from their grief. A temporary distraction…but maybe it was enough to help them breathe a little.

They waved at Mrs. Clark as they left the furniture area to find their husbands. "Thank you," Emma said. "We may be back on Monday."

The woman waved and returned to whatever she was doing.

Colt and Riley waited on a bench by the entrance. Riley held a small box. "Cordell will love this. And I think I've found our entertainment for this afternoon. Look!" He pointed to a flyer attached to the store window.

"A children's rodeo! How fun. It starts at three-thirty. Let's get some lunch and head back to the hotel for a short nap. But don't you dare let me sleep as long as I did yesterday!" Emma looked at her sister-in-law. "Does that sound good to you?"

Allison's face was quickly returning to the grief-stricken expression she'd worn for the past few months. "Yes."

Oh, well. Small steps. For lunch, they took a streetcar to Market Square and were overcome with the variety of options. There was Mexican, Chinese, German, and a number of other immigrant-owned stalls. The four of them walked around and studied the various street vendors and their offerings. In the end, they each got a different type of cuisine, and each sampled the others'.

With full bellies, they returned to the hotel. As Emma stretched out once again on her bed, she lifted up a silent prayer for her hurting family.

~

Jack had done all he knew to make everything perfect for this afternoon. Now he couldn't stop fidgeting.

"Calm down." Carson rested a hand on Jack's shoulder. "You're making *me* nervous, and I'm not even in this rodeo."

"I just want it to be a success. If it fails, no one will want to buy tickets in March."

"I disagree. Lots of people will come to watch a trick rider perform." Carson's voice was upbeat. He dropped his hand and moved toward his work table. "And who won't enjoy a bunch of little kids in Western costumes? You're worried you won't succeed. From where I stand, it looks like you can't fail."

"I hope you're right." Jack watched Carson polish an old leather saddle.

"Why don't you go home?" Carson gestured toward the door. "Eat some lunch. Take a nap. Do something. Like I said, you're making me nervous."

Jack laughed. "I brought my lunch and my clothes to change here."

"In that case," Carson replied, "go lie down on the cot in my office and try to calm down."

"All right. I'll try."

Jack closed the door behind him in the small office and pulled out his packed lunch on the scarred wooden desk. Martha had gone all out with golden friend chicken, fluffy mashed potatoes that were almost as good room temperature as they were hot, flaky biscuits, and a big, shiny red apple, but he didn't have much of an appetite. Still, he needed to eat something. He grabbed the biscuit, tore it in half, and took a bite. Washed it down with some cool sweet tea from his metal flask.

Holding the remainder of the biscuit in one hand, he propped his legs onto the cot and leaned against the wall. *I feel as if today is a turning point, Lord. Like something big is happening... like you're opening the door to my dreams.*

I gotta admit, I'm not sure why things have happened this way. But as much as I've tried, I can't make my memories come back. I don't understand...and I don't really like not knowing about my past. But right here, right now, I'm going to say it.

He spoke aloud to the empty room. "I'll say it out loud, Lord. I'm gonna trust You. I feel like I'm jumping off a cliff, reaching for Your hand, hoping You'll catch me. But I guess that's what faith is supposed to look like. If I knew how things would turn out, it wouldn't be faith."

He took another bite of biscuit and contemplated what he'd just said. *I don't know what You're doing. But I hear Your voice. I've felt Your presence these past months. And I trust You.*

~

Lisa would have to wait until after the show to visit the hospital. Right now, her costume hung on a peg in the orphanage library. She was still in her nurse's uniform, helping the nuns get a roomful of girls in costume. The boys were easier. Most of them were dressed and ready, playing cowboy in the backyard as Papa tried his best to keep them from getting dirty.

But the girls—they all needed braids and bows and curls dangling in front of each ear. And unlike the boys, little girls' clothes had a lot more layers. Even with the split skirts, they needed stockings. Their boots needed to be laced. It was a lot.

When each young lady was sufficiently satisfied with her appearance, Martha—who'd left her kitchen duties to help—took Lisa aside. "There's a plate for you on the stove. We'll take the children on over to the livery and give you time to eat, dress, and settle yourself before the show."

"Thank you, Martha. I'm not sure I can eat anything, but I'll try." She stood at the door as the children lined up and waved goodbye, telling them she'd see them soon. Once they'd disappeared from view, she got her plate from the stove and settled at the small kitchen table. As she nibbled at a green bean, she thought about what lay ahead. She was too tired to even form complex sentences in her mind. *Bless this rodeo, Lord.*

After a few more bites, she set her plate in the sink, washed her hands, and headed for the library to change. It was almost showtime.

CHAPTER 27

At three o'clock, Colt descended the stairs alone and joined Riley and Emma in the hotel foyer. Riley checked his watch, then the stairs to see if Allison followed.

"Allison has a headache. She wants to stay here and rest," Colt told them.

"I'm sorry to hear that." Riley looked at his wife. "Do you want to check on her before we leave?"

"She'll be fine," Colt said. "She's got the lights out and a cool, damp cloth on her head. That usually works pretty well for her."

"All right. If you're sure. I guess we should get going so we can get a good seat."

Outside, Riley hailed a street car. These vehicles would never go over in Lampasas—the small town was too resistant to change. But they sure were handy in the big city.

A few stops later, the streetcar driver let them off in front of a livery. A Catholic priest stood out front wearing a sandwich board sign that read, *St. Joseph's Orphanage Rodeo Preview Today.*

"Good afternoon, Father." Riley held out his hand for a

handshake. "I guess we're at the right place. Where should we seat ourselves?"

After shaking his hand, the man handed him a flyer and pointed through the livery doors. "Go through there and exit the door to your left. That will lead you to the arena."

After thanking him, they walked through the livery, where Emma took the flyer, folded it, and placed it in her reticule. Colt stopped in front of one of the stalls to study a gray spotted Appaloosa.

Riley stepped up beside him. "That's a nice horse." But the color had drained from Colt's face.

"This...this is Jackson's horse."

"Are you sure? I thought all the horses got left in Florida, because there wasn't room on the ship for them."

Colt stared at the horse. "You're probably right. But this sure looks like Fury."

Emma stood on the other side of Colt. "How common is this gray coloring?"

"I guess it's not that uncommon. Probably just wishful thinking on my part."

They stood there a few more moments, giving Colt time to process. After a time, Riley gently nudged his brother. "Come on. We don't want to miss the show."

As they exited, a tall man in a cowboy hat entered the livery from a back room. Sunlight through the window cast a shadow on his face. "Afternoon, folks. Thank you for coming." He tipped his hat before turning to take a saddle from its peg on the wall.

"We're glad to be here," Riley replied.

Colt watched the man, turning his head as they passed, then shook his head as they exited the door that lead them to the simple arena. To one side, a group of children in rodeo attire waited.

"Look!" Emma cried. "They're adorable. I wish Allison were here."

The benches around the arena were already filling up. Riley led them to a bench as close to the center as he could find that had room for the three of them. Just in front of them to the left was a tall, thin woman in a nurse's uniform.

"I hope they don't have need of your services today, ma'am," Colt told her as they sat down.

The woman turned and offered a big smile. "Oh, I'm not here in an official capacity. My good friend is in the show. She's a nurse, too—most of the time. But she agreed to ride today. She grew up at St. Joseph's, so this benefit is important to her."

"I would imagine so." Emma studied the arena. "How fun. A rodeo-riding nurse. It's nice to know the backstory of people in the show."

"The children have worked so hard, as has their director. He and my friend actually met when he was a patient at the hospital."

To their right, a nun directed the children to stand and move to an area out of view. The crowd hushed in anticipation. The priest they'd seen earlier entered the arena holding a metal megaphone. Lifting it, he said, "Thank you all for coming. I am Father Carlos Hidalgo, director of the St. Joseph's Orphanage. We'd like to welcome you to our preview show." His words held the accent of a native Spanish speaker, but his English was clear and precise. "Our first full-length rodeo will be in March of next year, and we hope you'll all come back and bring your friends! I won't bore you with a long speech. I believe the talent we have lined up will speak for itself. Sit back, relax, and enjoy the rodeo stars of St. Joseph's!"

He moved to the side of the arena and handed the megaphone to the man in the cowboy hat who'd greeted them inside the livery. The man sat on a stool against the fence, his back to the audience, and introduced the first act.

"Ladies and gentlemen, this first lady is a shining example of the fine quality people brought up at St. Joseph's. Not only is she lovely to look at, but she's a skillful equestrian, as well. Please give a round of applause for the beautiful, talented Miss Ivelisse Garcia!"

The nurse in front of them turned around. "That's my friend!"

They all applauded as a young woman entered the arena on a brown dappled mare. Her white dress had some kind of chiffon overlay that flowed behind her as she rode. The red fringe and cowboy hat added a fun Western touch.

"Her costume is amazing," Emma whispered.

"She made it herself," the nurse told them, as if bragging on her own child.

The horse went from a trot to a canter. When the woman stood in the stirrups, lifted her arms, and then waved to the crowd, light applause sounded. She moved one knee, then the other to kneel on horseback, and the applause increased. Finally, she straightened both legs, still bending and grasping the saddle, and lifted one leg behind her. Her skirt billowed in the wind. The audience collectively gasped, then erupted in cheers and applause.

With steady control, the woman lowered her back leg, then slid back to a normal position in the saddle before circling the arena and waving to the excited crowd.

The nurse stood to her feet. "Go, Lisa! Bravo!"

When the general hullaballoo died down, Emma leaned forward and tapped the woman on the shoulder. "You were right. Your friend was amazing."

"I knew she would be. I could never do anything like that, though."

"I couldn't, either," Emma replied.

The show continued with the children, two and three at a time, performing little tricks for the crowd. The man in the cowboy hat introduced each one by name and explained a little about what they'd be doing.

Colt leaned toward Riley. "I think I'm going crazy. That guy sounds like Jackson to me."

Riley perked up. "You're right. He does sound a little like him." He leaned toward Emma. "Do you have that flyer?"

She nodded, retrieved the flyer, and handed it to her husband.

"Director, Jack Smith."

"Do you know him?" Emma asked.

Riley stared at the flyer, then squinted his eyes toward the speaker. "Riley thinks it sounds like Jackson. I agree."

From that point, none of the three paid any attention to the children or the stunts. Their eyes remained locked on the young man with the megaphone.

It couldn't be.

It was impossible. Wasn't it?

Surely, Jackson wouldn't have lied. It wasn't like him to put his parents—to put all of them—through something like this.

Surely, they were imagining things. Because they wanted it to be true.

Riley's heart had slowed to a standstill as he held his breath, waiting for some sign that they were wrong. That the young man in the hat was indeed Jack Smith and not Jackson Stratton.

The priest took the megaphone and turned to the crowd. "That was our rodeo director, Jack Smith. Jack came to San Antonio a few months ago to join the Rough Riders. An unfortunate accident prevented him from doing that, but his misfortune became our blessing. Ladies and gentlemen, may I present to you one of the most talented riders I've ever seen...Mr. Jack Smith!"

While Father Hidalgo spoke, the young man had entered one of the stalls and mounted the gray horse Colt had commented on. Upon introduction, *Jack* exited the stall and almost immediately moved to a standing position on top of the saddle. He removed his hat, and his blond hair and deep dimples were unmistakable.

Jackson.

Everyone around them stood and applauded. Riley, Emma, and Colt stood too. None of them said a word. Emma held her reticule to her chest, clenching and unclenching it. Riley's heart momentarily stopped pumping, and he could almost feel the blood drain from his face.

And Colt—Colt just watched. Riley stole a look at him, and he couldn't read his brother's expression. No telling what was going through his mind.

Dear God. Don't let Colt kill him.

Riley dragged his gaze back to the arena, back to his nephew, and watched as he hung from one side of the saddle, then the other, doing flips and tricks and all kinds of shenanigans, each one bringing a greater reaction from the crowd. Finally, he finished with a wave and exited the arena.

As the audience began to disperse, Riley, Emma, and Colt just stood there.

The nurse turned and said, "Well? What did you think?"

Colt clutched his chest and dropped to the bench. "I—can't—breathe."

The nurse was over the back of her bench in a flash. "Does your chest hurt?"

Colt's eyes were huge, scared. He gave the slightest shake of his head, then, as if changing his mind, nodded.

The woman barked orders. "Get him some water. We'll need to get him to the hospital—it's just up the street." She spoke directly to Emma. "Go find the woman who performed first. Her name is Lisa, and she'll be able to help."

Emma disappeared and returned a few minutes later with Lisa. Just behind her was Jackson.

Riley wanted to deck him. How dare he put his parents

through this? How could he just disappear and change his name? But now wasn't the time. Right now, they had to take care of Colt.

Colt's eyes, still wide and scared, rested on Jackson. But it was Jackson's reaction that confused Riley.

"Stay calm, sir. San Antonio has an excellent hospital. They'll get you fixed right up." He looked at Riley. "Do you have transportation? If not, the livery has a wagon out back we can use. It's not far."

It was as if Jackson had no idea who they were. There was no inkling of recognition whatsoever.

Emma placed a hand on Jackson's arm. "Jackson," she whispered. "Why are you doing this?"

His face showed confusion. "I beg your pardon?"

Lisa and the other nurse fussed over Colt, taking his pulse and offering him sips of water. "Jack, go ahead and pull the wagon around."

Jackson nodded and disappeared.

This whole scene was quickly turning into a nightmare. A bizarre, science-fiction nightmare that didn't make any sense at all.

CHAPTER 28

Jack hitched two sturdy mares to the wagon, fumbling as he worked as fast as he could. The preview had gone better than he'd hoped—every seat was taken, and a few spectators stood at the back. Lisa was fabulous, and the kids did their parts without a hitch. When he'd finally taken the floor, it felt as natural as breathing to him.

He hated that things had taken a sour turn, with the gentleman struggling with—Jack wouldn't even guess. Was it a heart attack? Stroke? Hopefully, he just had a minor condition that would straighten itself out once he got proper treatment.

The woman, though. That was strange. She'd touched his arm. In a soft voice, she said, *Jackson, why are you doing this?*

What did she mean?

Did she confuse him with someone else?

Then it hit him. The possibility. Did she recognize him?

The thought was more than he could handle right now. Not if he was going to help that man. He drove the buggy around to the side, pulling up as close to the arena as he could. Father Hidalgo and the other man supported the ailing one on either side.

"Lay him in the back," Lisa said, and Phyllis hopped back there to spread some horse blankets out. At least they were clean.

Lisa and Phyllis stayed in the back, while the lady and gentleman climbed onto the bench next to Jackson. "I'll meet you there after I get the children settled back at home," Father Hidalgo told him.

Soon they pulled up at the hospital, and Phyllis jumped down and ran inside. They'd just gotten the man seated on the edge of the buggy when she returned with Dr. Williams and Nurse Jacobs.

Jack tried to stay out of the way. He studied the two men and the woman who'd spoken to him. The couple—the two who were with the patient—kept looking at Jack as though they knew him, and it made him uncomfortable. His head was starting to hurt. He wanted to leave, but he couldn't.

If he was going to have some kind of memory breakthrough, he'd prefer it happen in private. Not in front of these strangers.

But were they strangers?

It was too much. Finally, they got the man into a wheelchair and rolled him up the ramp to the entrance. At the door, the woman spoke to her husband and waited while they went inside. Then she turned, rested her eyes on Jack, and descended the front stairs to where he was.

Everyone else was gone.

"You don't know who I am, do you?"

"No ma'am. I'm afraid I don't." His gut clenched into a thousand knots. "Should I?"

She stared at him, as if trying to gauge if he was telling the truth. "I'm sorry to be so personal, but the priest mentioned that you'd had an accident. Can you tell me about it?"

Jack laughed and removed his hat, even though there was nothing funny about this situation. "They tell me my horse spooked at some gunfire during a training exercise. She threw me, and I hit my head really hard. Now I can't remember anything from before the accident. At least, I can't remember who I am or where I'm from."

The woman's eyes held his, moisture glistening them. "I'm...very sorry to hear that. That must be very hard for you."

Jack twisted his hat around and around by its rim. He'd surely ruin the shape. "You didn't answer my question, ma'am. Should I know you?"

The woman touched his arm. "I'm your Aunt Emma. My husband is your Uncle Riley."

For a moment, he couldn't breathe. Couldn't form words. After swallowing, he found his tongue, though the rest of him remained frozen. "And...the other man?"

She appeared to be holding her breath. Then, in a low whisper, she said, "He's your father."

Jack needed to sit down.

As if in anticipation of his response, the woman grabbed his arm and moved to his side. "Are you all right?"

"I...I'm not sure." He studied her face. "I mean, you're telling me these things. But you're a stranger to me."

"Maybe we should go inside. You said this is the hospital where you were treated. Is Dr. Williamson your doctor?"

"He is." He was still having trouble speaking.

"All right. Let's wait for them to finish with...Colt, and then we'll talk to your doctor."

"That's his name?" Jackson's jaw felt pinched. "The man you say is my father—his name is Colt?"

"Yes. Colt Stratton." Her eyes were gentle, compassionate.

"So my name is...Jack...Stratton?"

She touched his arm. "Jackson Stratton."

"Oh. Wow."

Emma led him up the stairs, into the foyer, and to the

nearest bench. "Can I get you some water? I'm sure I can find some."

"I'm okay. Thanks."

She sat next to him. Neither said anything. Just sat there in silence, waiting. After about ten minutes, footsteps echoed from a far hallway, and Lisa came into view, still in costume. She seemed out of place in this setting.

"I think he'll be okay. It seems he's had a shock. He keeps saying he saw his son. That his son was dead, but he saw him, and he's not dead. He's rather confused, I think. But physically, he should be all right."

Jackson felt nauseous. He wanted to say something, but all his words seemed to have disappeared.

Emma stood. Offered her hand. "I'm Emma Stratton. We enjoyed your performance very much."

"Thank you," Lisa said.

"As for your patient's muddled thinking..." Emma stopped, glanced at Jack, then back at Lisa. "I'd like to speak to the doctor when he's available."

Mild confusion registered on Lisa's face. "Of course. I'll get him now."

A moment later, Lisa and Dr. Williamson returned. "Hello, I'm Dr. Williamson. Your brother-in-law seems to be in a state of confusion, but we've gotten him stabilized, and his breathing has leveled out. Nurse Garcia said you wanted to speak with me?"

Emma cleared her throat. "Is there someplace private we can go?"

He led them into his office, to the left of Nurse Jacobs's. The room contained a large desk with a leather chair on one side and two smaller chairs on the other. He watched Jack for a moment, a question in his eyes. "Please, have a seat." He shut the door behind them.

"Doctor..." Emma hesitated, as if she were weighing her

words. "I believe this is my nephew, Jackson Stratton. In fact, I'm sure of it. Colt isn't confused. He's as certain as Riley and I are. Jackson is Colt's son."

Dr. Williamson let out a breath. He held Emma's gaze for a moment, then looked at Jack. "Do you recognize this woman, Jack?"

"No. I want to, but I don't."

The doctor leaned back in his chair for a moment and steepled his fingers together. "Mrs. Stratton, do you have any proof that Jack is your nephew? A picture, maybe?"

Emma sat up. "Not with me. But I know someone who does." She stood. "I'll be back." With that, she scooted past Jack and opened the door. She stopped, turned, and studied Jack as if memorizing his features, then shut the door behind her.

"How does this make you feel?" Dr. Williamson's voice was low, and his eyes held concern.

"To be honest, I'm not quite sure." Jack rubbed his temples. "It feels strange to have someone I don't know say they know me. I mean, why would they lie?"

"I don't know. Let's see what kind of proof they can produce before we move forward. For now, I think it best you avoid seeing the man who thinks he's your father." He paused. "This must come as quite a shock. Do you need to lie down? I can find you a private room."

Jack started to say no. But his head was pounding, and his stomach churned. "Yeah. That might not be a bad idea."

The doctor stood, and Jack followed him into the hall where Lisa waited.

"Are you okay?" She faced him, resting both her hands on his elbows, like an open hug. What's happening?"

Dr. Williamson spoke before Jack could answer. "Nurse, please prepare Room 6 for Jack."

Her eyes locked with Jack's for a moment. Then she replied,

"Yes, Doctor." They followed her down the hallway, and Jack waited while she turned back the sheets and fluffed the pillow.

"You get settled here. I'll return in a few minutes." Dr. Williamson left them and headed back toward his office.

Jack sat on the side of the bed and started to remove his boots, but she stepped in and did it for him. "Lie back," she said. "Do you feel nauseous?"

He nodded.

"I'll get you some peppermint tea. I'll be right back."

She left him alone, though he wasn't sure he wanted to be alone with his thoughts. *God, what is happening? I told You I wanted to know about my past. But now I just feel...terrified.*

Lisa returned with the tea, helped him take a sip, then set it on the side table and took a seat in the corner chair. "Do you want to tell me what's going on?"

He gave her a half smile. "You look so beautiful."

She shrugged off his comment. "Does that mean no, you don't want to talk about it?"

Jack let out a sigh from deep in his belly. "That woman—Emma. She says she's my aunt. And the sick man is my father."

Lisa allowed the silence to fill the space between them. Thank goodness she didn't grill him with any more questions, because right then, he just wanted to close his eyes.

He heard her get up. She placed a gentle kiss on his forehead. The door opened, then closed. It didn't take him long to fall asleep, but he was pulled almost immediately into a dream where that same man—the one whose face was blocked—yelled at him. "A trick rider? That's the stupidest thing I've ever heard. You're a Stratton, boy. Act like one!"

Jack sucked in air and jerked awake. *You're a Stratton, boy!*

He sat up in bed, found the garbage pail under the side table, and promptly emptied the contents of his stomach.

~

Lisa paced in front of Dr. Williamson's office. She clenched her hands in front of her. Fidgeted with her dress. This silly dress! She should go home and change. But she wanted to be here, in case...

Then she remembered her promise to Nurse Jacobs to visit the patients. She could at least stop in at the children's ward. That would help her pass the time.

She spent a few minutes visiting with the children and answering their questions. Her presence in costume seemed to cheer them. Good thing she hadn't forgotten. When she returned to Dr. Williamson's office, his door was still closed.

Would the doctor think her impertinent if she asked him to fill her in? That was one thing she'd learned in nursing school —anticipate a doctor's needs, but never question him unless you need clarification. Well, she needed clarification, didn't she?

She was about to knock on his door when the entrance door banged open. A woman she'd never seen burst in with Emma, the woman from before, trailing behind her. The new woman was frantic, wild-eyed. "Where is he? Where is my son? Take me to him now!"

Soon, drawn by the commotion, the doctor, Nurse Jacobs, Phyllis, and several interns were in the hallway.

"Go back to your stations, everyone," Nurse Jacobs said, and they obeyed. All except Lisa. Technically, she wasn't even on duty right now. The lead nurse focused on the new arrival. "Ma'am, why don't you come into my office so we can talk about this calmly?" Nurse Jacobs knew how to keep her head in a crisis. Her voice was a blend of gentle lullaby and drill sergeant.

"Calmly? I can't talk about this calmly. You have my son here, and I want to see him. His name is Jackson Stratton. Here is his portrait!" She held out a wooden oval frame with a young man's portrait.

Lisa couldn't yet see the photo, but Nurse Jacobs's face told her all she needed to know. She studied it, pressed her lips together, and lifted her brows. Looked at Lisa, then handed the portrait to Dr. Williamson.

When he took it, Lisa peeked over his shoulder. Her palm shot to her mouth to keep from vocalizing her shock. The woman was telling the truth. That was definitely Jack.

Dr. Williamson held onto the frame. "We'll let you see your son as soon as possible, ma'am. But there a few things you should know, first. It might be best if I talk to you and your husband at the same time. Follow me."

Emma, who had her arm around Jack's mother's waist, led her down the hallway behind Dr. Williamson.

Lisa looked to Nurse Jacobs. Should she go? What was her place? To her relief, her boss put her hand on Lisa's back as if to say, "Come along." They followed the others to the room where Jack's father was.

The woman went straight to her husband. "Colt! Emma said you found Jackson? He's alive? What are you doing in this bed?"

The other man sat next to Colt, but he stood and offered the chair to Jack's mother.

Dr. Williamson took command of the situation. Addressing Jack's father, he said, "I believe we have whatever was ailing you under control, so I'm going to release you at this time. However, it's important, given the circumstances, that you remain calm, or you may end up back here again." The man nodded, and the doctor continued. "Mr. and Mrs. Stratton, we've had your son here for several months. He was training with the Rough Riders when his horse spooked and he suffered a severe blow to his head. When he awoke, he couldn't even remember his name. Fortunately, Nurse Garcia here had a brief meeting with him before the accident and remembered he'd introduced himself as Jack."

Four sets of eyes moved to Lisa, then back at the doctor.

"Jack can remember skills. He can read and write—quite well, I might add. And he remembers how to ride horses. He is perfectly functional in every way. But, although the hospital staff and I have worked with him to try and help him regain his memory, he hasn't been able to recall details about his past. He's suffering from a brain trauma. He has amnesia, which means a partial or total loss of memory. It's thought that different parts of the brain have different functions. I believe he injured the part of his brain that stored that information. Unfortunately, we don't know a lot about this type of injury, but we've been doing all we can for him."

Mr. Stratton sat up in his bed. "You're telling me he doesn't remember us? He doesn't know who he is?"

"Being around you may trigger some memories. But given what he's been through, we'll need to take it slowly. It's unlikely he'll just blend right back into your family as though nothing happened. It will take him some time."

Jack's mother stood up. "I don't care. It doesn't matter to me if he's changed. I just want to see him. *Please.* Take me to my son!"

Dr. Williamson looked again at the portrait, then at Lisa before addressing Jack's parents. "Nurse Garcia here has become...close with your son. She and I will go talk to him now and try to prepare him for meeting you."

Jack's mother looked at Lisa as if seeing her for the first time. "This woman's a nurse? She isn't dressed like a nurse..."

Jack's father took his wife's hand. "She performed in Jackson's rodeo, Allison."

"Jackson's rodeo?"

"Let the doctor and the young lady talk to him. Riley, Emma, and I will fill you in."

Lisa took a few steps to follow the doctor out of the room. Then she stopped and returned to the foursome, who examined her as though she was some kind of zoo exhibit. "I...it's very nice to meet you, Mr. and Mrs. Stratton." Then she left them there.

What a way to be introduced to Jack's family! What must they think of her? And what must they have been through these last months? She pushed them to the back of her thoughts. Right now, her first priority was Jack.

~

Jack laid back in the bed and tried to empty his mind of the last few hours. He didn't want to think. As much as he'd wanted to recall his past, right now, thinking made his head hurt. Made him sick. If these people were his family, if the man in his dreams was, indeed, his father...Jack wasn't sure he wanted to know more.

He closed his eyes. But though he tried to still the chaos in his brain, he couldn't.

After a while, the door opened, and Dr. Williamson and Lisa entered. Lisa sat on the end of his bed and rested a hand on his leg. Her eyes held concern. Compassion.

The doctor sat in the chair. "How are you feeling, Jack?"

"Not great."

"That's understandable. But I need to talk to you about something."

Jack shifted so he could see the man better.

"As you know, the patient we admitted earlier claims to be your father. The woman you spoke with earlier—Emma Stratton—says she's your aunt. A little while ago, she returned with a woman who says she's your mother. She has a portrait as proof. Would you like to see it?"

Jack nodded. Sat up in bed. Lisa got up and adjusted the pillow behind him.

Dr. Williamson handed him the picture.

Wow.

An eerie feeling flooded through Jack's veins, a coldness. "That's either me or someone who looks exactly like me."

Dr. Williamson and Lisa remained quiet.

"It feels strange, looking at a picture I have no recollection of ever posing for."

Still no response.

"So what happens now?"

The doctor moved in his chair, stretching his legs out in the small room. "As you can imagine, they're anxious to see you."

Jack didn't respond.

"I told them what you've been through, and that you may not remember them. I emphasized that they'll need to take things slowly."

For a minute, nobody said anything.

The doctor continued. "I do think it's a good idea for you to talk to them. Maybe it will stir some recollections for you. But if you need more time, we can schedule that for another day."

"I think they're right," Jack said. "I had a dream, and the name *Stratton* sounds right."

"Would you like me to schedule a formal meeting with them on Monday?" Dr. Williamson's voice was low, his eyes gentle.

Jack's gaze landed on Lisa. She reached over, grabbed his hand, and squeezed.

"No. I'll talk to them today. But is there a better place? I'd rather not be in bed when I meet them." As soon as he said it, he realized that for him, it was a first meeting. But for them, it was a resurrection of sorts.

Lisa spoke up. "Would you like to come to my place? I know it's small, but it will offer a more private setting."

Jack looked at the doctor, who shrugged and said, "That sounds fine to me. I think I should be present, as well."

With a nod, Jack offered Lisa a half smile, then swung his legs off the bed. "I'd like to already be there when they arrive. I really don't want to get caught walking down the street with them at the same time."

Lisa dug in her reticule and handed him her key. "Why don't the two of you go on? I'll wait a few minutes, then bring your family."

Jack took the key, placed it in his pocket. His actions felt liquid, as if he were underwater. Everything felt hazy. Nothing felt real. Most of the dreams he'd had that he'd thought might be from his past were dreams he didn't want to be reality. Yet he wanted to know the truth. Something told him he might be on the brink of opening a Pandora's box. Was it better to live in ignorance?

Regardless, that box was about to be opened. He'd asked God for some connection to his past. For better or worse, it looked as though He may have provided it.

CHAPTER 29

Emma sat next to Allison in the chair a nurse had brought from another room. The four of them spoke in low tones so as not to disturb the other patient.

"I still can't believe it," Allison said. "I'm not sure I will believe it until I set my eyes on him."

Colt shook his head. "I'm not sure I believe the whole *amnesia* story. Part of me just thinks he wanted to leave. After all, that's what he did. He ran away and sent us a letter. Maybe he just—" Colt paused. Cleared his throat. "Maybe he just didn't want to come home."

Emma looked to Riley, waiting for him to speak. When he said nothing, Emma spoke up. "All of that is true, Colt. But he did write. He did let you know his intentions. The Jackson I know wouldn't purposefully put you and Allison through months of not knowing."

Allison stood up. Walked to the door. She opened it and surveyed the hallway before returning to her seat. "What's taking them so long?"

Riley opened his mouth to say something, then closed it

again, as if thinking better of it. He leaned over and rested his elbows on his knees, his head in his hands.

He was praying. That's what she should be doing too. But right now, she had trouble forming coherent thought. What should she even say to God?

Thank You?

Help?

Fix this?

After what seemed like hours, the nurse in the rodeo attire —Lisa?—entered with the head nurse behind her.

The older woman spoke. "Jack has agreed to see you all."

Allison, Emma, and Riley all stood. Colt sat up in his bed, and Riley moved to help him.

The nurse waited for their attention. "He didn't want to meet here, in the hospital. It felt too clinical. Nurse Garcia, here, lives just a short distance away. She has graciously invited you all to spend time with Jack in her home."

"Let's go!" Allison grabbed her reticule.

The woman held up her hand. "Dr. Williamson will be there, as well. He asked me to remind you of the trauma Jack has experienced. Please keep the interaction calm and short. It may take time for Jack's brain to heal, and trying to force things could possibly cause more delay."

Emma seized Riley's hand and squeezed hard. He squeezed back.

Nurse Garcia smiled at them, her expression a combination of warmth and...fear? "Follow me."

As promised, the small home was only a short walk from the hospital. When they arrived, the nurse invited them in and told them to make themselves comfortable. "I'll make some tea," she said.

There, in the small parlor, was Jackson. He stood when they walked in. Poor thing looked terrified. He held out his hand, as though he was meeting them all for the first time. "Hello. I'm Jack."

Dr. Williamson stood, too, as if to offer support and protection for his patient. This all felt so strange. Emma couldn't imagine the deep layers of emotion coursing through Colt and Allison at the moment.

Allison stepped forward and took Jackson's hand. Then she moved both her hands to his cheeks, embracing his face. Tears fell freely, dotting her jacket. "My boy. My beautiful, beautiful boy." She wrapped her arms around his neck, and Jackson awkwardly rested his hands on her back, enduring, but clearly not enjoying, the hug.

Colt hung back. When Allison finally moved away, he offered his hand to Jackson. "I'm your father. This is my brother, your Uncle Riley, and his wife Emma. We've been worried about you, son."

Jackson nodded. "I...I understand. I'm...I'm sorry, I don't—"

"You don't have anything to be sorry for," Riley said. "We're just glad you're alive. All these months, we thought you were in Cuba. And when they couldn't find you, well...we assumed the worst."

During this interaction, the nurse had carried some dining chairs from the kitchen and placed them around the parlor. "Please, have a seat. The tea's almost ready."

Emma had no idea how to act in this situation, but she could at least offer to help. "Nurse Garcia, is there anything I can do?"

The young woman smiled. "Lisa, please. If you'd like, you can arrange some cookies on a tray for me."

Relieved to have a job, Emma followed her into the kitchen, a quaint space with a nice blend of tight efficiency and coziness. Lisa handed her a blue tin of butter cookies and a tray.

"What a lovely tray. Is it an antique?" Emma began unloading the cookies and arranging them in an attractive way.

"Yes. I inherited it."

That statement brought red flags to Emma's mind. Hadn't they said at the rodeo that the woman was raised in the orphanage? If she was an orphan, who would she have inherited from? But that was a silly thought. She could have been adopted. There were plenty of explanations. Emma just felt protective of Jackson. After all, they didn't know anything about these people who had cared for him all these months.

"We're so grateful for all you've done for my nephew. As you can imagine, this has all come as quite a shock. A good shock, but...it will take a while for us to absorb all that's happened."

Lisa flashed a nervous smile. "I can only imagine. I've wondered about you all over the past months. Knowing he probably had a family somewhere, worried about him... I've prayed for you many times. I don't know how all this will play out, but I'm so grateful God brought you here today."

And with that, all of Emma's misgivings about the woman washed away.

~

Jack was usually pretty good with words. But right now, he didn't have a clue what to say to these people. The woman—his mother—she seemed to genuinely love him. But Colt—his father—kept eying him with something like suspicion, as though he didn't believe Jack really had amnesia. And that made Jack feel like a treed squirrel, and his father was the hungry hound.

Where was Lisa?

Soon, she and the aunt—was it Emma? He was having a hard time with names—came back from the kitchen. Lisa carried a large tray with a teapot and several mismatched teacups, and Emma set a tray of cookies on the table before taking a seat.

Once Lisa had served everyone, she started back toward the kitchen, but Jack held out an arm in invitation for her to sit next to him on the sofa.

"I'll be right back," she told him in a low voice. "Just let me set this down."

Soon she returned, and he rested his arm around her, on the back of the sofa. Somehow, he didn't want to feel alone with these people. That show of affection felt like an armor. It let everyone know he had a partner.

If only somebody would say something. Maybe he should ask a question... "So...what brought you all to San Antonio?" What a stupid question when they should be discussing his life and his memories, but how was he supposed to open such a conversation with strangers?

Tension hovered in the air as the Strattons shifted their gazes from one to another, as if waiting for someone else to answer the question. Finally, the uncle spoke. Ricky? No...Riley.

"Aunt Emma and I own an inn in Lampasas, where you're from. Emma and your mother wanted to look at some furniture stores to get ideas for redecorating." He leaned forward in the wooden dining chair. "You worked for us for a couple of summers, giving riding lessons. You're an excellent instructor, and you have a way with people."

Lisa reached one hand across her chest, took hold of his hand on her shoulder, and squeezed as if to agree with Riley's statement. "That makes sense," she said softly.

His father—Colt?—spoke up. "So...Jackson. I don't understand how you can remember all those crazy horse riding tricks, but you can't remember your name or address."

Dr. Williamson cleared his throat, as if to issue a warning.

Jack met Colt's eyes. "I don't understand it either, sir. It's been frustrating, to say the least." They stared at each other. Colt was the first to break eye contact.

His mother—Allison—hadn't taken her eyes from him. Softly, almost reverently, she said, "I remember the day you were born...the first time I held you in my arms. You were perfect. There wasn't a single day of your life I wasn't grateful to have you as my son. When I thought I'd lost you, I...I didn't—" A sob broke into her words, and she dabbed at her eyes with her lace handkerchief. "It's as though you've risen from the dead."

For a time, the only sound in the room was the clock ticking. Finally, Dr. Williamson stood, a signal that it was time for everyone to leave. The four visitors rose with him. Lisa and Jack said goodbye to his family, and they promised to meet again tomorrow. When the door shut, and it was just Jack and Lisa, he practically fell onto the sofa. "That was horrible."

Lisa sat next to him. "I didn't think it was so bad."

"That man—my father—he thinks I'm lying."

"I'm sure it's a shock. Amnesia isn't a common diagnosis. Give him time. Give yourself time."

Jack nodded. Covered his face with his hand. Leaned into Lisa's arm which lay around him on the back of the sofa. At least he had one person in this world he knew he could trust.

~

Riley rested his hand on his wife's back as they stood on the sidewalk and listened as Dr. Williamson spoke—mainly to Colt and Allison. "From the research I've read, it may be a good sign that your son's memory isn't all coming back at once. After this amount of time, a sudden onslaught could be quite traumatic. As I've said, give it time. Be patient."

Allison hung on the doctor's words. She seemed stronger than Riley expected. Colt, on the other hand—Riley was worried about his brother. His coloring still didn't look good. As if to confirm Riley's concerns, Colt's hand shot to his chest again.

"Are you all right?" Riley tried to think of how to help his brother. "There's a bench just ahead. Do you need to sit down?"

Colt made it to the bench and sat. Dr. Williamson checked Colt's pulse, then said, "Understandably, this has been a shock. I may have been premature in releasing you. I'd like you to come back to the hospital with me for overnight observation."

"No." Stubbornness flared in Colt's eyes, echoed in his voice. "I'm fine. I'll be fine."

Allison sat next to him. "Yes, you will be fine. But it won't hurt for you to stay overnight at the hospital. I can't handle anymore tragedies. Please. Do this for me."

Colt held his wife's eyes for a moment. "All right. But it's not necessary."

They walked the rest of the short way back to the hospital slowly. Once there, the doctor got Colt into the same private room.

"I'll run back to the hotel and get some of your things, to make you more comfortable," Riley offered.

"Good idea." Emma moved from where she'd stood next to Allison. "I'll go with you. Colt, is there anything specific you'd like us to bring?"

Colt shook his head. Riley and Emma left him with Allison fussing over his pillow.

When they returned less than an hour later, they knocked softly on the door.

"Come in," Allison called.

They squeezed into the room and handed Allison Colt's small travel bag with toiletries and a change of underclothes.

"Thank you," she said, before checking to make sure the door was shut completely. "We were discussing that woman—that so-called nurse in the crazy dress."

Riley held his tongue. Her dress was perfectly fine considering she'd just been in a benefit rodeo. And she seemed genuine to him. But there was no point in arguing with Colt right now.

"She seems like a lovely person," Emma commented.

"I don't trust her." Colt's face reddened. "I think she's the problem. Jackson knows we wouldn't approve of him cavorting with some orphan. Did you see her house? She clearly hasn't got more than two pennies to rub together. She's figured out who Jackson is, and she's trying to get him to marry her before he comes home to us. Who knows? She may even be trying to get pregnant."

"Colt!" Allison scolded him. "We don't know that."

Emma spoke up. "I don't get that impression at all. I think we should trust that Dr. Williamson knows what he's doing. He wouldn't have diagnosed amnesia for no reason."

"You saw him!" Colt raised his voice. "He remembers perfectly fine. He's still doing those crazy horse tricks that nobody in their right mind can do. It's that woman, I tell you! She's a con artist if I ever saw one."

The door pushed open and the nurse—the one that had sat in front of them at the rodeo—brought a pitcher and a glass with water. "Here you go, Mr. Stratton." Her voice was tight. Pinched. It was pretty obvious she'd heard the conversation, or at least part of it. In fact, half the hospital had probably heard it.

Riley struggled to find a way to redeem this situation. They'd just found Jackson. If Colt didn't calm down, he could lose his son for good this time.

~

Lisa scoured her brain for some way to relieve Jack's tension, apparent in his posture and the way he paced back and forth, his steps clipped and echoing in her small parlor. "Let's push all this with your family to the side, for just a moment. The rodeo was a great success! I'm so proud of you. And you should be proud of yourself."

He smiled, but it didn't go all the way to his eyes.

"Why don't we go over to Market Square and find something to eat? You must be famished."

He nodded, then patted his pocket. "I left my wallet at the hospital. Can we stop by there first?"

"Of course. Why don't you wait on the porch while I change out of this costume?"

A short time later, they were on their way. Inside the hospital, Phyllis stood with a tray at the far end of the hallway, her back to them, outside the room Jack's father had occupied. As they approached, Colt Stratton's voice boomed through the closed door.

"I don't trust her. I think she's the problem. Jackson knows we wouldn't approve of him cavorting with some orphan. Did you see her house? She clearly hasn't got more than two pennies to rub together. She's figured out who Jackson is, and she's trying to get him to marry her before he comes home to us. Who knows? She may even be trying to get pregnant."

Jack went stiff as a penicillin shot. He moved toward the room, but Lisa held him back. More talking came through the closed door, but the voices weren't as loud.

About that time, Phyllis entered. "Here you go, Mr. Stratton."

Lisa waited for her to exit, but she didn't. Instead, Phyllis's voice carried down the hall, tight, clipped. "I do apologize for intruding, but I couldn't help overhear your conversation. I'd like to clear some things up. Lisa Garcia is one of the purest, kindest, most generous people I've ever known. She's certainly not the conniving harlot you think she is. And for your information, she's not a pauper. She's an heiress and a business owner. She owns half of the livery where the rodeo took place!

So your conception that she's trying to take advantage of Jack is entirely unfounded. Lisa has her own money. She doesn't need yours."

With that, she exited the room, her hands clenched. When she saw Lisa and Jack, the red drained from her face. "Oh... Lisa...I'm so sorry..." Her voice quivered, and her eyes filled with tears. She rushed past them and out of view.

A cog seemed to have gotten stuck in Lisa's head. She couldn't move forward—her muscles felt corpse-like. She couldn't process what she'd just heard. Jack's father saw her as a gold digger? A floozy? She'd been called *orphan* enough—the word whispered behind open palms or splayed fans—that the term didn't faze her anymore. But the other things...

And now Jack knew she was the silent livery partner. Feeling Jack's eyes on her, she met his gaze, and what she saw there terrified her.

Betrayal. Distrust.

"Lisa?" The word was a question. "Is that true?"

"Yes," she whispered.

"Why...why didn't you tell me? Why would you lie to me?"

"I didn't lie." Even as she said it, she felt like a liar. "I just didn't tell you everything."

He stared at her, his face revealing pain and disbelief. "That's the same thing."

"Jack, I—"

"I need some time alone." He entered the room he'd occupied earlier, retrieved his wallet, then hurried past, away from her and out the front doors, leaving her standing alone in the cold, tiled hospital hallway.

CHAPTER 30

As soon as the hospital doors shut behind Jack, he began to run. He had no idea where he was going, but right now, he just had to get away. Away from this place and these people. For the first time since his accident, he felt truly, completely alone.

He felt *forsaken.*

He ran until he was out of breath, and then he slowed to a walk but didn't stop moving. The San Antonio sky took on dusky pink and purple hues as the sun disappeared over the horizon. If only *he* could disappear.

Actually, he felt as though he *had* disappeared.

He ended up in an area of the city he didn't recognize. Could he ever find his way back? Then again, did it matter? He was nobody. A man without a past. Expendable. Even with these strangers who claimed to be his family...what was the point, if he had no memory of them?

After a time, he came to a park and sat on one of the wrought-iron benches. Pulled out his pocket watch and checked the time. A quarter to eight. His attitude wasn't helping anything. He'd give himself fifteen minutes to sit here and wallow in self-pity, as he'd done since he left Lisa at the hospital. Then he'd come up with a plan.

He saw the irony in his own self-pity when Lisa's pity made him furious. It wasn't just her lack of honesty. It was the idea that he'd been working so hard to prove himself worthy of her, and all along, she'd been paying his salary! How could he face her again?

Right now, he was hurt and humiliated and confused. Part of him wanted to get Fury from the livery and ride off into the sunset, never to be heard from again.

But he couldn't do that. Because as uncomfortable as those Stratton people made him, he also believed them. And if they had truly worried all these months, if they had truly mourned his death—well, he couldn't disappear again. He wouldn't do that to them. He was better than that. Or at least, he wanted to be.

Who am I, God?

Who are these Stratton people?

Why did you let me trust Lisa, only to have her lie to me?

Nothing makes sense. I don't know what to do.

He sat there a long time, until the sky was black and the stars were bright and the crickets sang their lullaby. And though he didn't hear God talking to him, he did come up with a plan. A tentative plan, anyway.

Tomorrow, he'd say goodbye to Father Hidalgo and the children. Pack his few things, then go tell the Strattons that he'd like to return with them to wherever was called home. Lampasas, he thought they'd said.

Maybe where he grew up, his memories would become clearer. But even if they didn't, he had to leave. Because right now, the only person he'd trusted with his whole heart had betrayed him, and he wanted to be as far from this place as he could get.

~

Lisa didn't see Jack again that night. After he left the hospital, she returned home, hoping he'd end up there so they could talk. But he never did. It was after midnight when she finally blew out the kerosene lanterns and went to bed. Not that she slept much. She mostly cried.

Sunday morning, there was little she could do to mask her puffy face. But she dressed and went to church, anyway, in hopes Jack would be there. He wasn't. She retained little of the sermon and barely mumbled through the hymns as she tried to keep from crying. She should have been all cried out by this point, but the tears just kept spilling.

After church, against her better judgment, she stopped by the orphanage. He clearly wanted to be left alone, but she had to see him. Had to try and explain. When she arrived, the place was empty. Maybe Jack had attended mass with Papa and the children. If so, they'd be home soon enough.

But when they arrived, Jack wasn't with them. And Papa looked at her with such pity, she knew immediately something was wrong. She stood from her seat on the parlor sofa. Endured the onslaught of hugs from the children.

When they'd all disappeared to change out of their Sunday best, Papa pulled an envelope out of his coat pocket. "Jack asked me to give you this."

Her heart stopped. She held her breath as she tore into the letter.

Ivelisse,

Thank you for all your help during my recovery. I don't know what I would have done without your friendship. Right now, I need to sort through some things. I'm going with the Strattons to Lampasas, to my childhood home, in hopes I'll recover some of my past.

Again, thank you for everything.
Jack

She dropped to the sofa. This couldn't be real.

He was leaving? Just like that?

She understood his need to explore his past and fight for his memory. But the letter...it sounded so formal, so final, like a goodbye note to an acquaintance. Was that how he saw her?

Maybe he believed those things his father said about her. After all, he already thought she was a liar.

Papa held out his arm in invitation. "Come. Let's talk."

"No, thank you. I need to be alone now." She stood again, gave him a quick side-hug, and rushed out. If she lingered too long, with Papa's gentle ways, she'd be blubbering all over the place. Which is what she wanted to do...but she didn't want an audience.

She tried—not very successfully—to dam the tears until she got home. But when she turned the corner to her house, there, tied to the porch railing, was Fury. And on the porch, sitting in one of the white rockers, was Jack.

The tears wouldn't stay back any longer. She rushed up the steps. He stood, and she threw herself into his arms. They stood there like that for a long time, her sobbing, soaking his shirt with tears, and him not saying a word, just holding her in a stiff, awkward embrace.

After a long time, her tears abated. "I'm so sorry, Jack. I really didn't want to keep anything from you. But I didn't know about the livery until after you and I were already courting. And Papa advised me against telling anyone. He said that since I'm a young woman, it would be easy for someone to take advantage of me. And apparently even Pastor Smith wanted it kept a secret, because...well, it doesn't even matter now. I wanted to tell you. I should have told you. I was *going* to tell you. I really was...I just..."

Jack didn't say anything. Just gestured for her to sit. They stayed there, quiet, for several minutes.

Finally, he spoke. "I'm confused about a lot of things right now. I don't know who I am or what to believe. It was probably a bad idea for us to start courting when I had amnesia."

Lisa felt as though a serpent had wrapped itself around her heart and was squeezing the life out of it. Did he really feel that way? That they were a bad idea?

"I understand Father Hidalgo wanting to protect you. I'd have probably advised the same thing. You don't know anything about me. I don't even know anything about myself. I need to go home with my family, see what I can figure out." All the life was missing from his voice. He sounded mechanical.

She pulled out the letter. "I stopped by the orphanage. Papa gave me this."

"After I left it with him, I realized I didn't want to say goodbye that way. That's why I'm here. To...to say goodbye."

"Goodbye?" Her voice broke over the single word. "Forever?"

He fidgeted with his hat in his hand. Shrugged. "I just need to go home and try to figure stuff out."

More silence. She was too stunned to speak. What could she say?

Fury whinnied. Jack stood.

This was it.

"When do you leave?"

"Tomorrow afternoon. I'm supposed to meet them for lunch now. I'm already late. And I know you work tomorrow, so..."

He looked as sad as Lisa felt. She rose from her chair. Wrapped her arms around him again. *Don't cry, don't cry, don't cry.*

He hugged her back, a stiff, formal hug. Then he stepped away, popped his hat on his head, and exited the porch, grabbing Fury by the reins and walking down the sidewalk toward downtown. He didn't look back.

She watched until he was out of view. Then she entered her home, shut the door behind her, and sank to the floor. She'd cried so much, her head hurt, but that didn't keep her from crying some more until at some point, she fell asleep on the cold, hard wood.

~

Sunday night, Jack stayed at the Menger Hotel in a room down the hall from his family. They'd offered, and he figured he might as well go ahead and cut ties with the people he'd met here.

The swanky room was a far cry from the orphanage. But he felt out of place. He'd gotten used to the simple furnishings and décor and the sounds of children playing outside his window or giggling past bedtime in the room next door.

The next morning, he joined his new—old?—family on a few errands, one of which included a trip to Joske and Sons. That worked out well, since he wanted to speak to Mr. Joske personally about his abrupt departure. The man had been so kind, and he hated to leave him in the lurch. But this was something he needed to do.

When they arrived, he left the Strattons and headed for Mr. Joske's office. After Jack explained what had happened, Mr. Joske was gracious.

"This must be quite a shock, son. But I'm glad for you. I hope you find the peace and healing you are looking for." The man pushed a notepad across his desk. "We still owe you for the hours you've worked. Leave your forwarding address so we can send it."

"I'll have Father Hidalgo get that to you. I don't know it offhand." Jack shook the man's hand, thanked him, and went to find his family. They'd said they'd be in the furniture department. There they were, deep in conversation with Mrs. Clark. They were placing an order, and she looked like cat who'd found his way into the fishbowl. This order would probably bring her a promotion.

When she saw him, her face took on haughty irritation. "Mr. Smith. How *kind* of you to join us. Please go back to the warehouse, fetch two of these lamps, and make sure they're delivered to the train station by two p.m." She handed him a slip of paper with the information on it. "We will address your tardiness later. I know you're aware that lateness is not acceptable."

Jack took the slip, looked at his family, and shrugged before heading to the warehouse. As he walked away, he heard Colt say, "Pardon me, ma'am. But that's my son, and I don't appreciate the way you just spoke to him." His voice held the authority of a king—a Texas cattle king who would brook no disrespect.

Jack grinned but kept walking. So far, he wasn't quite sure of his feelings for his father. But for right now, he was happy to leave him in charge of Mrs. Clark. That he somehow knew, without being told, that his father was a cattleman was something to ponder on the long train ride to Lampasas.

~

Lisa was living a nightmare. Her actions were wooden as she went through the motions of caring for patients, overseeing interns, and checking supplies. By the time she left work today, Jack would be on a train, well on his way to another life.

Her automated motions didn't keep the thoughts from slipping into the empty spaces. The ward Jack had been in, when he was first injured, was especially hard. She made a note to change assignments with Phyllis.

The bench in the hallway, outside her office, where Jack first kissed her...every time she walked past it, she felt his presence, and now his absence, keenly.

Would she ever see him again?

Would he even write?

The knowledge that his opinion of her had been so far reduced left her with little hope.

She couldn't be angry with him. It would be easier if she could. If he were a cad, she could call him all kinds of unspeakable, insulting names in her mind. She could invite Phyllis over for a scathing gossip session that would, no doubt, leave her feeling avenged. But the fact that he was a good, kind person... the fact that he struggled with trying to heal...the fact that she'd withheld the truth from him despite her gut feeling that she needed to be honest...all of that made it impossible to play the role of the spurned lover.

No. He had more of a right to feel spurned than she did.

It didn't change the way she felt, though. Her heart was broken.

She looked at her watch. He'd be boarding the train now. For two more hours, she needed to hold herself together. Two more hours, and she could go home, crawl beneath her covers, and sleep until morning, when she'd have to wake up and do it all again.

She'd avoided Phyllis all morning. It had been easy, since they'd admitted six new patients today. But when they passed in the hall, Phyllis stopped her. "Lisa, I'm so sorry. I had no right, and now I've blown it. Can you ever forgive me for my big mouth?"

"Of course. You were defending me."

Phyllis stood there, awkwardly, as though she wanted to say more. To make the situation okay. After several seconds, she took a deep breath. "You were amazing at the rodeo. And I know it didn't end up like you wanted, but it's great news, I guess—Jack finding his family?"

His family who thought he was too good for her. "Yes. Wonderful." Lisa avoided eye contact and tried to bypass her friend in the ruse that she was too busy to talk. Which she was.

"Wait!" Phyllis made a U-turn and followed Lisa down the hall. "I…I can tell you're upset with me. And I don't blame you. Can we talk about this? Maybe after work today?"

Lisa couldn't talk about it. If she did, she'd turn into a sobbing fool, and now was not the time or place. Besides, she'd already cried herself dry. "I'm not angry. I'm just busy."

Phyllis put a hand on her shoulder. "Look at me."

Slowly, Lisa raised her eyes to meet her friend's.

"What's wrong?"

"Really, Phyllis. I'm not mad. I just have a lot on my mind."

Phyllis dropped her hand. "Meet me out front when our shift is over. Dinner's on me."

Lisa didn't want dinner. She hadn't eaten since…when? She couldn't remember. Saturday, maybe? She'd had some tea this morning. That was all her stomach could handle. But she didn't have the energy to explain or argue. She gave the slightest nod and continued down the hall. For now, she needed to push Jack from her mind. There was little she could do about him, and her patients needed her.

CHAPTER 31

Phyllis waited on the front steps when Lisa exited the hospital. She linked arms with Lisa and asked, "What are you hungry for?"

Lisa held her breath. She'd held in her emotions all day, and now, if she spoke even a word, the floodgates might well break open.

Seeming to understand, Phyllis led them toward downtown, where several restaurants offered a variety of cuisine. "We could visit that new German restaurant if you want. Or what about that sidewalk café that sells meat pies?" She turned for Lisa's response—and gasped at the silent tears, flowing freely down Lisa's cheeks, dripping onto her neck, staining her blue nurse's uniform. "Lisa! Oh, my goodness. Talk to me."

Lisa shook her head but said nothing. Couldn't have, if she'd wanted to. There were no words to describe the depth of her sorrow or her self-loathing. That Jack had lost faith in her was her own fault.

Phyllis changed direction, leading them back to Lisa's home. On her porch, Phyllis took Lisa's key and unlocked the door. Led her inside and seated her on the sofa. Went to the kitchen, where she rummaged around for a few minutes.

She returned with a cup of tea and some hard, crusty bread slathered with butter. "I'll be back. I'm going to get us something more substantial to eat."

After the door shut behind Phyllis, Lisa stared at the tea and bread on the tea table but couldn't find the desire to partake. Instead, she pulled her knees to her chest, buried her face in her knees, and sobbed.

A half hour later, her sinuses were blocked and she could only breathe through her mouth. The door creaked open, and a moment later, Phyllis entered carrying a paper-wrapped bundle. She deposited the package on the side table, next to the lamp, and soon was next to Lisa on the sofa, arms around her. "Oh, honey. Can you tell me what you're feeling? It helps to talk about these things." She offered Lisa an embroidered handkerchief, and Lisa promptly blew her nose. Then she laughed, and Phyllis laughed, and Lisa's head pounded at the action. "I'll wash this before returning it."

Phyllis sat there with her for a while before Lisa finally spoke. And when she did, everything tumbled out, about the letter and how distant Jack seemed and how he needed to go find himself, and how Lisa didn't know if she'd ever see him again, and she didn't know how to feel. How she should have listened to her gut and told Jack the truth. How she should have known no respectable man would want to be with an orphan. How, even though the things Jack's father said weren't true, she could understand why he thought that. Most upstanding people thought those things about those who didn't have parents.

And how she thought she'd never feel happy again.

All this time, Phyllis didn't say much, other than to indicate she was listening and that she understood.

After Lisa's words finally dried up, they sat there in the

dusky light, for neither had bothered with the lamps. Finally, when it seemed the storm had passed—at least for the time being—Phyllis ignited the lamp on the side table and reached for the paper bundle on the table. "Meat pies. I've heard they're amazing. Can you try just a few bites?"

Lisa nodded. Took a bite. It was good, but she still wasn't hungry. After one more bite, she set the package back on the table.

Phyllis took both Lisa's hands in hers. "Look at me."

Lisa tried to but had a hard time holding eye contact.

"I said, look at me."

Lisa obeyed.

"I know you're devastated. But much of what you just said is foolishness. You're an amazing woman, and any man would be fortunate to have you. As for the Strattons, I have no idea who they are or how much money they have. But if Jack gives you up, he'll be forfeiting the treasure of a lifetime."

Lisa sniffed. As much as she wanted to absorb her friend's words, they bounced off her skin and fell flat.

"What you need is a distraction." Phyllis gathered up the leftovers and returned them to the paper wrapping. "And I have an idea. Since Thanksgiving is next week, let's plan a feast for our patients. The children at St. Joseph's can help deliver the meals. Maybe they can even sing some Thanksgiving songs. What do you think?"

Lisa didn't want Thanksgiving without Jack. It was hard to celebrate with a shattered spirit. But Phyllis was right. She needed to keep busy. With a slight nod, she leaned her head on her friend's shoulder and tried to push away the ache in her head, her gut, and her heart.

~

Jack leaned his head against the train window and concentrated on the gentle rocking motion. That was easier than thinking about Lisa. Or about these people who called themselves his family.

His four traveling partners were at least sensitive enough to give him space. They didn't grill him with questions or conversation. Only offered him food and drink. His mother rolled up her coat and placed it against his window, to cushion his head.

And then something strange began to happen around the third hour of his journey. He didn't know if it was the passing landscape, changing to the familiar scenes of home, or if it was spending time with his parents and aunt and uncle, or something else, but his memories began to stir. He'd thought, if and when it happened, it would be dramatic. And though the past weekend had certainly been the stuff of dime novels, his memory now returned like gentle snow, like the stretch and yawn of a morning when he'd overslept.

No fireworks.

No explosions.

More like he remembered things he hadn't thought about in a while. There was no question, no wondering if the memories were authentic—they were. They'd just been locked away for a while, and now they were back, some more blurry than others. But they were real.

Like how he used to swing from a rope tied to the towering oak tree and let loose over the deepest part of the pond, and how he'd come home smelling like algae. And how he'd hidden a frog in his pocket to entertain himself during church, and it accidentally got loose and caused Mrs. Wheatley to scream, and soon the whole congregation was trying to catch the small creature. Jackson had never admitted to anyone that he was the culprit.

He remembered Mom trying to smooth things over when

he and Dad had a fight, which was pretty often, especially once he was a teenager. He remembered the disappointment in Dad's eyes, and his nostrils flaring every time Jackson tried to talk to him about trick riding, until finally, Jackson avoided talking to him about anything.

He remembered spending time with Uncle Riley and Aunt Emma, and his cousins Skye, Cordell, and Anita at The Big Skye Inn, and the feeling of safety and warmth he experienced in their presence, and lying in bed at night imagining what it would have been like to grow up in their home instead of his own.

He looked at his mother in the seat facing him, her eyes closed, her head resting on his father's shoulder. She'd lost so much weight. He knew he was to blame.

Even his father, whose head was back against the seat, mouth open, sound asleep, looked years older.

From across the aisle, Jack caught Aunt Emma watching him. Uncle Riley, next to her, focused on the passing landscape out the opposite window.

"Can I get you anything?" Her voice was soft so as not to awaken Jack's parents.

Uncle Riley turned his head and offered an encouraging smile.

"No, thank you. How much longer until we arrive?"

Uncle Riley pulled out his pocket watch and said, "An hour. Maybe less."

Jack looked out his window. He wasn't ready to reveal his memory was back. How would they take that? Would they think he'd been lying this whole time?

He'd wait until they were home. Right now, he had less than an hour to consider his course of action. And to consider all that had taken place in the last months. He'd prayed for his memories to return, and God had answered. But in the course of that happening, had he lost Lisa?

Because he wasn't sure he could leave his parents again after what he'd put them through. And now, with his father's apparent health issues...

Plus, knowing his father's history, his father's attitude about marrying within one's class, and hearing the things he said about Lisa...there was no chance of bringing her to Lampasas. Why would he put her through that? Colt Stratton would make all their lives miserable. The only way Jack could envision a future with Lisa was to leave home, as he'd done. And look where that had gotten him. Would he have been better off never remembering, never seeing them again?

~

When they disembarked the train, Jack might as well have been stepping out of a long dream and into reality. Except, he wasn't sure how he felt about this particular reality. He'd left this all behind for a reason. He'd hoped to escape. Now here he was, right back where he started.

Around the depot, several people gasped and pointed at him. He recognized them from around town. Uncle Riley, apparently sensing Jack wouldn't want to interact, was quick to guide him to their covered carriage—a sleek black horse-drawn brougham. His cousins Cordell and Anita sat up top, but both jumped down as Jack approached. Despite the turmoil in his gut, seeing them made him smile.

Anita nearly knocked him over with a hug. "When Mom and Dad sent the telegram on Saturday, I couldn't believe it. We've been worried! I'm so glad you're home."

Cordell offered his hand to Jack, along with a delighted smile. "Welcome home."

Jack nodded, then looked at Uncle Riley. "What about Fury?"

Uncle Riley waved. "You all go on ahead. I'll get her from

the horse car and ride her back to your place. Unless, of course, you'd rather do it."

He would. But the people whispering and pointing changed his mind. "Thank you, no. You go ahead." He slipped inside the brougham, followed by his parents and Aunt Emma, and was grateful when the door shut behind them.

His father was the first to speak. "Your return will cause quite a stir, Jackson. The community felt your loss keenly. When you're ready, I'm sure they'll want to have some kind of welcome-home celebration."

What was he supposed to say to that? "That's...nice." An odd question popped into his mind. "Did you...I mean, was there... Did I have a funeral?"

His mother sobbed once, then held her handkerchief to her mouth, as if trying to push down her emotions.

His father shook his head. "You were missing, so we didn't know if you were truly gone. We were pretty sure, but we couldn't bring ourselves to have a funeral until—" His voice broke. "Your mother and I planned to go to Cuba after Christmas. We'd hoped to...to bring you home. Or at least learn more about what might have happened to you. After that, we were going to...you know..."

Having a hard time meeting their eyes, Jack looked out the side window. Yes, he'd wanted to escape. If he had gone to Cuba, this story might have had a different ending. Running away as he had, though it had felt right at the time, now seemed cowardly and immature. He should have faced his father like a man, rather than sneaking off.

Maybe God was giving him a second chance to stand up to his father. To be a man of character. But right now, Jack had no idea what that would look like in the days to come.

They said little else on the ride home. When the brougham pulled up in front of his house, his eyes burned with moisture. It was as though he saw it with new eyes...familiar, yet new, all at once. He got out and just stood there for a moment in the circle drive, taking it all in—the house that was far too large for just the three of them... the wide front porch where he'd played with his miniature soldiers, the stables to the left where he'd spent so many hours, the open fields for cattle grazing, the tangy smell of manure. His brain felt like it was waking up from a long sleep. Everything was hazy, but he didn't question its authenticity.

Cordell and Jack's father unloaded their luggage and took it inside. Jack and his mother followed, with Anita and Aunt Emma behind. His aunt and cousins waited for Uncle Riley so they could all ride home together. After Jack joined them, they all sat in the parlor for about half an hour making pointless small talk. As soon as Uncle Riley arrived, they said their good-byes and left Jack there, alone with his parents and his house and his hazy, watercolor recollections. He didn't want them to leave, but he didn't ask them to stay. They'd be anxious to get home too.

Jack's mother stood next to him, touching his back lightly.

His father cleared his throat and gestured around the room. "Stir up any memories?"

Jack met his eyes for a moment and gave a slight nod. Nothing was stirred, so to speak. It was just as if everything had been put back into place, the same as it was before. Except that everything was so, so different. And right now, Jack didn't know what to do with that. "I'm tired. If it's okay with y'all, I'd like to get some rest. Can we talk in the morning?"

Fortunately, his parents didn't push him. Just showed him to his room, and he didn't tell them he didn't need to be shown.

His mother hugged him again. "Would you like to come down for dinner? Or I can bring you something, if you'd like."

For the first time since they'd shown up in San Antonio on Saturday, a little smile quirked up his cheek. Where were the servants? No one had greeted them. Was his mother really offering to *cook*? He was hungry, but he wasn't sure he was *that* hungry. "I'll come down in a little while and fix a sandwich. I think I'd like to lie down for a while, first."

"All right. I...it's so good to have you home, son." His mother's voice cracked again.

Jack covered the short distance between them and wrapped his arms around her.

When he released her, he turned to his father and reached out his hand, and the man shook it. Then he did something Jack couldn't recall happening before. He pulled Jack into a tight embrace and held him there for several seconds. It was both awkward and comforting at once. "Get some rest, son. I'm glad you're back."

With that, they closed his door and left him to his room, his bed, and his memories. As much as it made his head hurt, it was time to sort through them, separate the good from the bad, and decide whether he wanted to stay here and work things out with his father. And somewhere in there, he also had to decide how Lisa might fit into all this.

CHAPTER 32

The next morning, Jack woke up with a clear head—as if his amnesia never happened. He could remember everything about his life vividly, and with a clarity and purpose he'd never experienced before the accident. Everything seemed brighter and stronger. Almost as though his head trauma had given him a sixth sense. Or maybe it was just God, giving him wisdom he'd never possessed before.

He opened his wardrobe doors and selected his attire, pausing to feel the expensive fabric of his shirts and admire the excellent tailoring in his trousers. He'd forgotten what it felt like to have so many options, and it almost made him feel guilty, but he didn't know why.

He found his parents in the library.

They stood when he entered.

"Good morning," his mother said. "I made coffee—I know you prefer coffee in the mornings. I'm afraid it's a little... strong." Somehow, she managed a grin and a grimace at the same time.

Jack smiled at her. "I'm sure it will be fine."

"I let the cook and the maid go a few months back, but I'll go to town today and see if they'd like to return."

"No hurry. We can make do. I actually learned to cook a few things while I was in San Antonio. I helped in the kitchen at the orphanage where I stayed."

His parents sat, hanging on his words.

He took a seat across from them. "I don't know how to start. I don't want you to think I'm making any of this up, because I'm not. But seeing you both again, being back here... I don't think I have amnesia any more. But I did. I really didn't remember anything, other than a few dreams I had. But they were fuzzy, and not enough to go on."

His palms were sweaty, and he kept grabbing his pant legs, crinkling the excess fabric at his knees, then letting go. What if they didn't believe him?

His father leaned forward. "You're saying you all of a sudden have your memories back?"

Jack met his father's eyes. "Yes. It sounds farfetched, even to me. But it's the truth. I never would have let you think I was dead. I know we didn't always see things the same way, Dad, but I wouldn't have done that."

Tears streaked his mother's face, but this time, they were accompanied by a smile. His father, on the other hand, quirked his brow and flattened his mouth.

Jack sat tall. Held his father's gaze and refused to look away.

Finally, the older man leaned back and crossed one foot over the opposite knee. "I believe you, son. I don't know why, but I do. And honestly, I don't even care. I'm just glad you're home."

That was the last response he'd expected from his father. He let out a long, slow breath. Felt a tentative smile creep across his face. "Me, too, Dad. Me too."

His mother stood. Clapped her hands together. "It's a miracle, is what it is. And this Thanksgiving is going to be the best one we've ever had. We'll have all your favorites. And we'll invite Riley and Emma and your cousins, of course. And whatever friends you'd like to invite from school. And church!"

She headed through the double library doors, toward the staircase, talking as she went. "I need to get changed and go to town right away. I have so much to do!"

Jack really had no desire for some big shindig, but he wouldn't deny his mother the joy he saw, reborn on her face, for anything.

His father chuckled. "Might as well accept whatever she wants to dish out, son. Now that you're back, there'll be no stopping her."

The time alone with his father was fortuitous. Jack cleared his throat. "About the night I left..."

Dad held up his hand. "Before you go on, I have something I'd like to say about that."

Jack tensed, readying himself for one of Dad's long, scathing lectures. And this time, he'd stay calm, respond with respect, and gently speak the truth. He may not agree with his father, but after what he'd put his parents through, he wasn't about to start another fight.

"Over the past few months, I spent a lot of time thinking about what I could have done differently." Dad toyed with one of the fancy throw pillows on the sofa. "I'm a stubborn man. I know that. I was wrong about a lot. And you know that's not easy for me to admit."

If Dad had stopped there, Jack would have been thrilled. But after a moment, he continued. "I had plans for you, son. I saw you as an extension of myself, instead of as a unique individual with your own goals. I tried to force my ambitions for this place on you, instead of respecting your desires. I can't say I'll ever understand this interest you have in trick riding. But if that's what you want to do, I'll support it."

Jack felt like a thousand boulders fell off his shoulders. It took him a moment to find his voice. "I…I don't know what to say. Thank you."

"No. Thank *you*, for coming home." He stood up. "Now, what do you say we head out to the stables? I have a hankerin' to buy you a welcome-home gift, in the form of the best trick horse in these parts. But I'll need you to guide me on that purchase because I'm afraid when it comes to rodeos, I'm out of my depth."

Jack and his father walked outside through the kitchen, grabbing a cup of coffee on the way. After the first swig, Jack choked. No way could he swallow the stuff. It was mostly silt.

Dad laughed at him. "Go ahead. Spit it on the ground. After we look at your horses, we'll go to Grace's café and get some breakfast. And pray your mother can find a cook before the day's out."

Jack chuckled. "That sounds good. And if she doesn't, I can always say I want us to spend time with Aunt Emma and Uncle Riley."

Dad slapped him on the back. "You always were a smart young man. You get that from me." He walked ahead, leaving Jack standing just outside the kitchen door.

Jack watched his father retreat, hesitant to move, as if he'd ruin the moment. Dad's last statement almost sounded like… like he was proud of Jack. And Jack couldn't ever remember being a source of pride for his father. It felt…nice.

It didn't erase the past. But maybe…maybe it was a start.

~

Thanksgiving came and went, and Lisa fell into a complacent acceptance. She didn't know if she'd ever love someone again as she loved Jack. She doubted it. But he was gone, and she had to keep moving. Keep putting one foot in front of the other. She had her job. She had the children. There was no time for moping.

But each night, when she was left alone with her thoughts, she felt the depth of the fracture inside. It brought to mind a stanza from a poem she'd studied in school, titled *In Memoriam.*

I hold it true, whate'er befall;
I feel it, when I sorrow most;
'Tis better to have loved and lost
Than never to have loved at all.

While she was pretty sure the poem had been written about someone's grief after a loved one's death, her own grief was keen. Was it better to have loved and lost?

Yes. Even after a few short months, Lisa couldn't imagine her life without Jack in it. Didn't want to imagine it. But she'd rather have this grief than to have never had him in her life. He'd awakened a part of her she'd not known was asleep. He'd encouraged her to do more, be more than she ever thought possible. He showed her she could try new things...that she was worthy of love and joy and respect and that...well, he'd made her think she might be able to have a family of her own one day.

Why, even his injury had offered her a chance to hone her nursing skills and led to her becoming second-in-charge, below Nurse Jacobs. That would never have happened so quickly without Jack.

And it was Jack who convinced her to ride in the rodeo. That experience, to her, was about more than a short time in front of an audience. It was about stepping outside her comfortable spot and doing something she'd never have had the courage to do without him. It was almost as though he'd been telling her, *If you can do this, you can do anything. I believe in you.*

So yes. She was glad for her broken heart, as painful as it was. Because without it, she wouldn't have developed the skills or strength or confidence she now possessed.

Eventually, she gained the courage to visit the places they'd been together. Downtown looked different now, with festive Christmas-themed window displays. She pulled out the gray wool cape with the burgundy lining she'd made for herself the previous Christmas and wished Jack were here to see it.

Staying busy was the best way to keep herself out of the depths of sadness. She helped Papa and Martha hang tinsel and paper swags throughout the orphanage. She sat with the girls and taught them some simple crochet stitches they could use to make stars and hearts. They could hang them on the tree on Christmas Eve. She worked with the children on a short Christmas presentation they could share with those poor souls who were in in the hospital over the holiday. They even made Christmas cards to give them.

But there was always that time at the end of the day when her thoughts turned to Jack. She missed him so much. The loneliness was *so deep.*

If she had his address, she could to him. She could probably address it to *Jack Stratton* in Lampasas, and the letter would surely find its way to him. But she shouldn't interfere with whatever healing process he needed to go through. That his parents found him was a miracle. She'd played her part in his journey, and now he needed to move forward without her.

The question was, could she move forward without him?

One evening, Papa asked her to spend time with him in the parlor after the children went to bed. "I'm concerned about you."

"I'm all right, Papa."

"I don't like the sadness in your eyes. I know what put it there, and I feel responsible. I'm so sorry, mija. I only advised you out of love, out of trying to protect you. But I think maybe I was wrong."

Lisa studied her hands as he spoke. She didn't respond, but she felt grateful for his acknowledgment.

"Your heart will mend, Ivelisse. God has the right person for you, and He will lead you together in His time."

She looked at him. "I don't want anyone else. I want Jack."

He leaned his head to one side, his face filled with compassion. "I know. I did not mean to belittle your feelings. My heart is heavy for my role in your pain. I hope in time you can forgive me."

She studied her hands again. "I forgive you." Her voice was low, and she didn't look at him until after she said it.

"Thank you for that. I know I've let you down, but God never will. He loves you more than He loves His own life. He will never forsake you."

Looking up, she said, "This feels like forsaken to me. Good night, Papa." With that, she left him in the parlor. Made the short walk back to her home, to the safe space within her own four walls, where she could cry without anyone telling her to stop. In all her days, this was the first time Papa had disappointed her. And it made her wonder...would God let her down too?

CHAPTER 33

December 22, 1898

Jack couldn't believe the change in his father. He showed an interest in Jack, in rodeo horses and trick riding. He listened when Jack talked about different horse breeds and the differences in temperament. Dad had always bought expensive horses, but that was simply because he could. It was a way to show off his wealth. But now, he actually seemed to want to learn.

One day, Dad took him to the northeast corner of the property. "What if we create an arena here? We could close in this area and set you up with the best facility in the West. This is already a tourist town. You'd have a built-in audience, new folks every week in the summer. What do you say?"

A year ago, he'd have jumped at the chance. But now, without Lisa by his side, it felt like a hollow victory. He wanted to go back to San Antonio...mainly because he knew he couldn't bring her here. Because as much as his father had changed, Jack couldn't place his hopes in a change *that* big.

Colt Stratton was a still a bigot. Jack could not—would not

—expose Lisa to that. To bring her here would only hurt her and drive a deeper wedge between Jack and his father.

"I…I'll think about it."

"Think about it?" Dad's voice raised a few pitches, as if he couldn't believe Jack wouldn't be elated at the offer. "I don't understand, son. Tell me what's holding you back."

Jack ducked his head. He wasn't ready to get into this. He'd never had this kind of a relationship with his father, and he still didn't trust it would last. He wanted to enjoy it a little while longer. But with each day, he missed Lisa more. He wanted her by his side. And the knowledge that he couldn't have both was tearing him in two. He'd have to make a decision soon…and he knew what that decision would be. He just…wasn't ready.

"It's that girl, isn't it?"

Jack jerked his head up. "What do you mean?"

"That cowgirl—or nurse—or whatever she is. She's got you all tied up in knots, hasn't she?"

Here it was. All good things must come to an end. Something akin to rage welled up in his gut. "*Lisa,* Dad. Her name is Ivelisse, and she goes by Lisa. And I love her."

Dad leaned against the wooden fence. Looked off into the distance.

Jack pounded his fist on the top rail. "I *heard* you that day. In the hospital. Lisa and I were in the hall when you questioned who she was. You called her an orphan and said she was probably trying to take advantage of me. You said some terrible things about her that aren't true at all."

Dad furrowed his brow. Studied his boot as he traced a pattern in the grass. "Perhaps I misspoke. She wasn't trying to take advantage of you. But she is an orphan, isn't she? I wasn't wrong about that."

"So what if she is? What does it matter? Why are you so stuck on believing everyone has to be like you, or they're not worthy? My whole life, you've looked down on people who aren't white, or who don't have as much money as you, or whatever else you decide makes you better than them. You ran Skye off, Dad. *Skye!* Your own niece. Your own flesh and blood, because you couldn't stand that she was part Indian. Why can't you just respect people for who they are?"

The expression on Dad's face was the one Jack remembered...that one that told him Dad was about to blow his fuse. Still, he kept going. Once the words started spilling, there was no way he could stop their flow.

"You may be ashamed of me if I don't marry someone you approve of. But the truth is, *I'm* ashamed of *you.* I'm ashamed to be your son. I don't think I'm better than anybody else. And I'm sorry... I don't want to disappoint you. But I can't stay here and live like this. That's why I left. Not because you didn't want me to be a trick rider. It was because I was tired of trying to prove to everyone in this town I wasn't like *you.* Because I'm not, and I don't want be."

Had he really said all those things out loud? Things he'd wanted to say for years, but never had the courage. And now, when he finally had a chance at a decent relationship, when Dad was finally showing an interest in him, he'd said it. It was a relief to get it off his chest, even if he'd blown any chance at peace. It felt good.

And it felt awful.

"You done?" Dad said after a minute.

"I suppose."

"Feel better?"

Jack didn't answer. He tensed. Readied himself for whatever kind of abuse Dad was about to hand him.

Dad sighed. "You're not wrong."

What? All the heat in Jack's body went cold. Had he heard right?

"As I told you, I did a lot of soul searching while you were gone. And I have a long way to go. I've made plenty of mistakes in my life, and I'll make plenty more. But I've been talking to God. More than I ever have. And believe me, Jackson, I know what a scoundrel I've been. But I promised God that if I could have another chance with you, I'd do things differently. I never thought I'd get that chance. But to the best of my ability, I want to make good on that promise."

Jack gaped at his father. "What are you saying?"

"I'm saying, God gave me another chance with you. Not because I deserved it, but apparently, because He loves me in spite of myself. I never really understood that kind of love until I thought I'd lost you. And I realized, God gave His Son willingly. As much as I failed you as a father, I never would have given you up for anyone. But God did that for me. And then... well, He helped me find you. And I'm going to try not to make the same mistakes again. I hope you'll give your scalawag of a father another chance...a chance to make things right."

Tears stung the back of Jack's eyes. How was he supposed to respond to that? Could he trust what Dad was saying?

After a pause, Dad continued. "You think about it, son. Let me know what you decide. But about that nurse..."

Jackson clenched his fists. If Dad said anything derogatory about Lisa, he'd—

"If you love her, go get her. Bring her back here. Marry her. Have a whole passel of rodeo babies. I'll be the best father-in-law and grandpa I know how to be. I can't promise I won't ever make you angry again. I can only promise to try and be better. With God's help. All I care about is that you're happy."

All the air left Jack's lungs. Was he hallucinating? He reached over and pinched his father.

"Ow!" Dad jumped back and rubbed his arm. "What are you doing, boy?"

"Just checking to see if you're for real."

"Check again, and I'll whoop you. Keep your cotton-pickin' hands to yourself!"

Jack laughed. Could he believe this version of his father? He wanted to.

Dad chuckled, but his laughter gave way to a serious expression. "Son, I'm not proud of who I've been. But I'm proud of who you are. And I'd like you to help me be a better man. I hope you'll forgive me."

Jack let silence sit between them for a thick minute. Finally, he brushed the pesky tears away with the back of his hand and made eye contact with his father. "I forgive you."

Was that moisture in Dad's eyes too? Had he ever seen his father cry?

Dad rested a hand on Jack's back. "Let's head back to the house. Your mother will wonder where we are."

Jack matched his father's steps. "If I bring Lisa back here, are you going to keep calling her an orphan? Do you even know how condescending that sounds?"

His father looked truly baffled. "What do you want me to call her?"

"*Lisa*. You can call her Lisa."

Dad nodded. "I prefer that other name—Ivelisse. It's a pretty name for a pretty girl."

"She's the most beautiful girl I've ever seen."

"Well, in that case, what are you waiting for?" He gave Jack a playful shove. "You'd better go saddle your horse."

"Thanks. But I think I'll take the train this time."

~

It was Christmas Eve, and Lisa had agreed to spend the night in her old room at the orphanage. Jack's room. On the one hand, it would be hard. But in a way, it made her feel close to him.

She and Martha had just finished hanging the handmade stockings over the mantel and on the wall on either side. Each child would get a new scarf and gloves. Mr. Joske had donated small dolls for each of the girls, balls for the boys, and a little toy horse for each of them. In addition, they each had a peppermint stick and an orange. She couldn't wait to see their reactions in the morning. Despite the blanket of sadness that had cloaked her spirit since Jack left, she did enjoy seeing the children smile.

"Their program was wonderful, Lisa. Thank you for putting that together." Martha added the last of the candy to the stockings.

"They were good, weren't they? And it really cheered the patients. I was happy to do it." She tried to add more joy to her voice than she felt. She didn't want her grim mood to spoil everyone else's holiday.

Papa entered, wearing a festive red scarf. He swept his arms out, taking in the room. "It looks wonderful in here! But I think you might want to look out the window."

Lisa and Martha crossed the room to peek into the night.

"It's snowing?" Lisa cried. "It hasn't snowed here since I was twelve. Maybe we should wake the children."

"No, let them sleep. It's cold enough that the snow won't melt by the morning. It will make their Christmas even more special."

Lisa nodded. If they woke them now, they'd see their stockings, and the adults would never get them back to bed.

A knock sounded at the door. Who could that be? It was already late. The three of them looked at one another, as if to ask if any of them had invited a guest.

"I'll get it," Papa said.

Lisa and Martha followed close behind him, partly from curiosity and partly from a desire to protect the older man, in case it was a ruffian. Not that they could provide much protection, but there was safety in numbers.

Papa opened the door a crack. "May I help you?" In an

instant, his face lit up like the candles on the Christmas tree. He swung the door open. "Oh, my! This is a good Christmas, indeed. Come in, my boy!"

A man stepped in, bundled in an expensive-looking coat, gloves, and scarf. He wore Western boots and a cowboy hat. Lisa took in his attire before landing her gaze on his face. When she did, her heart did a somersault.

"Jack." It came out in a whisper.

He grinned at her, those deep dimples piercing his cheeks, those eyes even greener than she remembered. He removed his hat, and snow scattered on the floor. "Merry Christmas!"

In an instant, she was in his arms, nearly knocking him over. "I never thought I'd see you again." Her voice caught, the floodgates opened, and there was no way she could hold back the tears.

Papa said something, and his and Martha's footsteps retreated.

"I'm sorry to barge in like this on Christmas Eve," Jack whispered. His voice was husky, and it sent a thrill up her spine. "But I have a question to ask you." He pulled back, put a finger under her chin, and tipped her face up. Held her gaze for a long minute. "Gosh, you're beautiful."

She wanted to tell him he was the beautiful one, that he was the most beautiful thing she'd ever seen. But her throat was closed up, and she couldn't find the words.

He let go of her but didn't move away. Instead, he knelt on one knee, there in the foyer of her childhood home, and held out a little black box. "Ivelisse Garcia, will you do me the honor of becoming my wife?"

She laughed and cried all at the same time. "Yes! A thousand times, yes. Oh, Jack! You've made me the happiest woman alive."

"Don't you want to see the ring?"

She laughed again and nodded. He opened the box, and

inside was a gold ring with three stones—a ruby in the center and a diamond on either side. "Oh, Jack. It's beautiful!"

"It doesn't hold a candle to you." He removed it. Slid it onto her finger.

She only had a moment to admire it before he pulled her into his arms and lowered his mouth to hers. His lips were still cold from the weather, but she didn't care. The kiss was long and tender, and it wasn't long before warmth took over her senses. She could have kissed him all night, but they were interrupted by giggles on the stairway behind them.

She pulled away, and they both turned to find many eyes watching them, some of the children pointing and laughing, others making gagging sounds. Lucy called, "Hey! It's Mr. Jack!"

In a stampede, they rumbled down the stairs and surrounded Jack and Lisa, nearly causing them to lose their balance.

He lifted Lydia into his arms, and she kissed his cheek. "We heard a knock at the door, and we thought it was Santa. We didn't know it was you!"

Jack set her down. "It's funny you say that, because I passed Santa on the street. He was running behind on his deliveries, and he asked me to bring you this." He opened the front door and pulled a large snow-covered sack from the porch. Wrapped presents overflowed the bag, each with a different child's name. The room filled with cheers, many of the children jumping up and down in excitement. Even Papa and Martha had reappeared because of all the noise.

Jack held up a hand to quiet the kids. "But he said you're not supposed to open them until morning. So you'd better get back to bed. The sooner you go to sleep, the sooner morning will come."

Their grumbles and moans were laced with laughter, and after a good amount of urging and herding, they returned to their rooms.

Papa clasped Lisa's hand and studied her ring. "Didn't I tell you that time has a way of working things out? And that God would not forsake you? Maybe next time you'll learn to trust your papa."

Martha invited them into the kitchen, and the four of them shared a plate of cookies and drank mugs of hot chocolate for the better part of an hour. Then Papa yawned and said, "I'm ready for bed. Martha, I'm sure you are too."

Taking the hint, Martha agreed. "Morning will come early." She and Papa shuffled out of the room, their heavy steps showing their weariness.

And with that, Lisa was alone with Jack. Her betrothed.

"I love you," he said.

"I love you too."

He stood and pulled her to her feet, then led her to the foyer. They shared a few more kisses, and Lisa admired her ring in the low lamplight. After a time, she said, "I'll go get your room ready."

"I have a room at the hotel, but I'll be back first thing in the morning."

"You're not staying here?"

"I figured you'd be spending the night, and I wasn't sure Father Hidalgo would approve." He winked, and her cheeks flushed.

After one more long, lingering kiss, a kiss that left Lisa weak in the knees, he shut the door, and she moved to the window to watch him disappear into the darkness.

Two hours ago, this was the loneliest Christmas ever. In a moment, it had turned into the best. She went to bed with praise on her lips, a song in her heart, and a yearning for the day she'd never have to say goodbye to Jack Stratton again.

~

Lisa had planned to get up early and be ready for the children, but their footsteps on the stairs roused her from a deep sleep the next morning. Normally, she would've pulled her hair back in a bow and joined them in her dressing robe, but one look at her ring reminded her she needed to don her Christmas best. Jack would be here soon!

Good thing she'd become adept at dressing quickly and pinning her hair in an elaborate-looking style that was actually quick and easy. A few minutes later, she opened her door to the twins, who were getting ready to knock.

"Hurry, Miss Lisa! Father Hidalgo won't let us open presents without you."

"I'm ready. Sorry to keep you waiting." Hopefully, Jack would be here to watch the Christmas morning chaos, but either way, she couldn't make the children wait any longer.

When she entered the parlor, there was Jack, looking so handsome, he stole her breath. He smiled and she smiled. And she joined him on the sofa, where he'd saved her a seat.

Father Hidalgo looked delightfully silly in his priest's collar and red Santa-style nightcap. He passed out stockings and gifts amidst children's squeals. He'd made them all promise not to open their gifts or stockings until everyone had theirs, and just when Lisa thought he was finished, he handed her a beautifully wrapped gift that had surely come from Jack's sack.

"For me?" she whispered. "But you're my Christmas gift. And this ring. Jack, you've done too much."

"It's not from me. Read the card."

On Papa's count, the children tore into their gifts. Meanwhile, Lisa lifted the flap on the envelope and pulled out the beautifully illustrated card depicting the baby Jesus with two angels hovering over him. A folded piece of paper fell out, and Jack picked it up. The printed message on the card said, *For unto us a child is born*. On the left side of the card was a handwritten note.

> *Dear Ivelisse,*
> *We are thrilled to welcome you into our family, and we can't wait to spend more time with you. Merry Christmas,*
> *Mom and Dad Stratton*

Mom and Dad. Her eyes burned. Could she take any more joy? She'd had her Papa, though she always knew he wasn't her Papa. And though Pastor James Smith had loved her, she couldn't remember him. Could it be that now, as a grown woman, she'd finally get the family she'd always yearned for?

Yet the echo of what Jack's father had said in the hospital tightened her stomach. If that's what he really thought of her, would he ever truly accept her?

Jack handed her the slip of paper, and she opened it. This one, in a different handwriting, said, *Ivelisse, I owe you an apology. I hope you'll come home with Jack so I can say it in person. -Dad*

She looked at Jack, her heart full.

"Aren't you going to open the gift?" His excitement gave him a childlike expression.

"Oh. I almost forgot." She untied the ribbon and set it aside. Unfolded the paper, careful not to tear it. She wanted to savor every part of this memory. She lifted the lid to find a wooden box with an exquisitely carved horse on the lid. "Oh, Jack. It's beautiful!"

"Open the box."

She lifted the hinged lid, and a soft, tinny song filled the air. The children hushed their squeals to listen. "It's a music box," she whispered. The tune became clear, and she could hear the words in her mind.

Amazing grace,

How sweet the sound,
That saved a wretch like me.
I once was lost, but now I'm found,
Was blind but now I see.

Amazing grace, indeed. On this day, she had more of it than she could contain. Her cup runneth over.

EPILOGUE

January 30, 1899
La Villita Church
San Antonio, Texas

The tiny chapel was just the right size for Lisa's family—Papa, Martha, the nuns, the children—and Jack's family—his parents, aunt and uncle, and cousins. There was also room for Phyllis, Nurse Jacobs, and Dr. Williamson. Even Mr. Joske and his wife were present.

The church organist played a soft melody as Lisa and Papa waited on the front steps. When the music changed to Richard Wagner's bridal chorus, Papa looked at her, his lips wobbly. "Are you ready, mija?"

"I'm ready."

She wore an ivory satin gown with long sleeves, a criss-crossed bodice with floral embellishment at the waist, and a long train that would button into a bustle after the ceremony. The fabric had been a gift from Jack's mother, and Lisa had spent every spare moment putting it together. She carried a bouquet of snapdragons, pansies, and sweet alyssum.

Papa opened the heavy wooden door, and the music grew louder. They entered the small sanctuary where Jack waited at the altar. She held Papa's arm all the way down the aisle. Though she felt everyone's eyes on her, she only had eyes for Jack. He took her breath away in his dark suit, starched white shirt, and tie.

At the front, Jack took Lisa by the arm, and Papa moved in front of them to face the audience and perform the ceremony. As Papa began speaking the words he'd spoken at so many weddings before, Lisa had a hard time concentrating. All she could think of was the beautiful future in store for her as Mrs. Jack Stratton.

They'd stay in San Antonio through the end of March to finish out the planned rodeo. Then she'd move with him to Lampasas to help him build a brand of rodeo that would attract tourists for years to come. She and Jack would be married, but they'd also be business partners.

After discussion, they had decided to keep the small San Antonio home so they could visit as often as they wanted with their own place to stay. Lisa had also decided to gift her share of the livery to the orphanage, to provide a steady income for them.

"Do you, Jackson, take Ivelisse to be your wife, to love and cherish, for better or worse, in sickness and in health, until death parts you?"

Jack's smile lit up his face, and his dimples, along with his green-gold eyes, caused a tickle in Lisa's belly. "I do," he said, his voice deep and husky.

"Do you, Ivelisse, take Jackson to be your husband, to love and cherish, for better or worse, in sickness and in health, until death parts you?"

Lisa couldn't stop the smile that covered her face and filled her soul as she looked at Jack. "I do."

"In the presence of these witnesses, I now pronounce you husband and wife. You may kiss your bride."

And Jack did—or did she kiss him? She couldn't be sure. All she knew was she felt that kiss, that promise of love, all the way down to her toes. Giggles sounded from the audience, but she didn't care—just wrapped her arms around Jack's neck, bouquet and all, and pulled him closer, tighter. They'd never have another first kiss as man and wife, and she planned to make it last.

The kiss ended, the applause began, and Lisa's feet lifted off the floor as Jack picked her up and planted one more kiss on her. He set her down, and she beamed at the people in the room. God had proven to be the God of hope. He'd given her a place to belong. These were her people. This was her family. She was an orphan no longer.

AUTHOR'S NOTE

Most of us are familiar with the term PTSD, which deals with the symptoms one experiences after a single traumatic event, such as witnessing a violent crime or living through a natural disaster. But there's another diagnosis on the horizon—one that's soon to be included in the Diagnostic and Statistical Manual of Mental Disorders (DSM). It's called Complex PTSD, or C-PTSD, and refers to symptoms resulting from ongoing, repetitive trauma such as child abuse or long-term domestic abuse. Whether mental, physical, or emotional, this kind of trauma causes deep wounds in the spirit, and the child often grows up with ongoing mental health issues like depression and anxiety because of it.

This book tells Jackson's story of trying to escape his father's abuse...and hopefully offers hope to those who struggle with this kind of trauma. Even when your trauma goes so deep and runs so far back you think there's no possible way to unravel it or move past it, all things are possible with God. Healing may not be quick or easy. It's more likely to be a long process involving much hard work. But whatever your traumas, God has never left you alone. He will hold your hand as you face your memories head on. And He will help you forgive, for with forgiveness comes healing—even more for you than for your abuser.

If Jackson and Colt weren't fictional characters, they'd have a long road ahead of them. In 1898, doctors were just starting to suspect the effects of various types of trauma, but it would be nearly a century before they had clear evidence. If Jackson lived in current times, he'd hopefully seek help from someone trained in assisting those with mental health struggles. Every step on the healing journey—with God as our guide—leads us deeper into hope, peace, and joy.

Hang in there. The God of hope loves you, just as He loves people like Jackson and Ivelisse and Colt. He thinks you're amazing. And He's on your side.

--Renae

Tribulation brings about perseverance; and perseverance, proven character; and proven character, hope; and hope does not disappoint, because the love of God has been poured out within our hearts through the Holy Spirit who was given to us. - Romans 5:3-5

***As a way to protect my own mental health, I'm not extremely active on social media. I do have a website, www.RenaeBrumbaugh.com, and a Facebook page, Renae Brumbaugh, author (RenaeBrumbaughWrites). You can also reach me at RenaeBrumbaugh@gmail.com. I'd love to hear from you!

Did you enjoy this book? We hope so!

Would you take a quick minute to leave a review where you purchased the book?

It doesn't have to be long. Just a sentence or two telling what you liked about the story!

BOOKS IN THE

STRATTON LEGACY SERIES

Legacy of Honor (The Stratton Legacy Series, book 1)

Legacy of Love (The Stratton Legacy Series, book 2)

Legacy of Hope (The Stratton Legacy Series, book 3)

ABOUT THE AUTHOR

This is the place where **Renae Brumbaugh Green** is supposed to provide impressive things for you to read. But since the most impressive thing about her is the fact that she almost won a car in one of those little fast-food scratch-off games one time, years ago, but she didn't actually scratch off the car until she found the card in her desk drawer, long after the deadline had passed, there's not much to say.

But if you really want to know about her writing stuff—she's the author of many books, made the ECPA Bestseller list twice, and has contributed to many more books. She's written hundreds of articles for national publications and has won awards for her humor.

She's married to a real hunk, and she's a mom to some amazing young-adult kids. She's a college English instructor, writes music, sings, and likes to perform on stage.

To learn more about Renae, sign up for her newsletter or visit her website at www.RenaeBrumbaugh.com.

ALSO BY RENAE BRUMBAUGH GREEN

Lone Star Ranger (Texas Ranger Series, book 1)

Ranger to the Rescue (Texas Ranger Series, book 2)

Lassoed by the Lawman (Texas Ranger Series, book 3)

Want more?

If you love historical romance, check out the other Wild Heart books!

Lone Star Ranger by Renae Brumbaugh Green

Elizabeth Covington will get her man.

And she has just a week to prove her brother isn't the murderer Texas Ranger Rett Smith accuses him of being. She'll show the good-looking lawman he's wrong, even if it means setting out on a risky race across Texas to catch the real killer.

Rett doesn't want to convict an innocent man. But he can't let the Boston beauty sway his senses to set a guilty man free. When Elizabeth follows him on a dangerous trek, the Ranger vows to keep her safe. But who will protect him from the woman whose conviction and courage leave him doubting everything—even his heart?

~

A Heart's Gift by Lena Nelson Dooley

Is a marriage of convenience the answer?

Franklin Vine has worked hard to build the ranch he inherited into one of the most successful in the majestic Colorado mountains. If only he had an heir to one day inherit the legacy he's building. But he was burned once in the worst way, and he doesn't plan to open his heart to another woman. Even if that means he'll eventually have to divide up his spread among the most loyal of his hired hands.

When Lorinda Sullivan is finally out from under the control of men who made all the decisions in her life, she promises herself she'll never allow a man to make choices for her again. But without a home in the midst of a hard Rocky Mountain winter, she has to do something to provide for her infant son.

A marriage of convenience seems like the perfect arrangement, yet the stakes quickly become much higher than either of them ever planned. When hearts become entangled, the increasing danger may change their lives forever.

~

Katherine's Arrangement by Blossom Turner

Marrying him is her only choice to save her family, but Josiah Richardson isn't at all the man she expected.

Katherine Williams's family was left destitute when their home was burned to the ground by Yankee soldiers, so the ready solution presented by the prominent Mr. Josiah Richardson seems almost too good to believe. He'll provide a home, work for her pa, and a new beginning for her family...if only Katherine will accept his proposal. A marriage of convenience is the last thing she wants, but there doesn't seem to be a better option for her family or herself. Setting aside her dreams of love, Katherine agrees to the arrangement.

The gentleman in Josiah Richardson can no more force his frightened bride into his bed, than he can force her into loving him, so he sets out to gently woo her. He works hard to befriend her, to earn her trust and win her love.

Katherine is pleasantly surprised to find herself drawn to the man she thought she would never love, until an unexpected friendship tears apart all they've worked for. Where once the promise of love had budded between Josiah and Katherine, now they wonder what to do with their so-called marriage. Is love strong enough to weave its healing power through two broken hearts?

Printed in the USA
CPSIA information can be obtained
at www.ICGtesting.com
CBHW062019040824
12637CB00016B/201

9 781963 212129